don't miss . . .

downtown beirut . . .  rowdy crowd, $2 foreign beers and a rollicking jukebox, in the Village—who could ask for anything more!

lesbian and gay big apple corps . . . invites amateur musicians to perform symphonic, marching band, jazz, Dixieland and rock music in Midtown; being in the high school band was never this great!

danal . . . a great place for an afternoon tea of sandwiches, scones, dessert and tea. Enjoy yourself in the garden when the weather permits.

colonial house inn . . . a European-style bed-and-breakfast in a beautiful Chelsea brownstone.

lesbian avengers . . . a militant direct-action group with manifestos and videos that meets in the West Village.

the kitchen center for video, music, dance, performance, film and literature . . . a Chelsea building packed with theaters, video viewing rooms, exhibition spaces, and a 200-seat "black box" for one-person shows. If you watch what the Kitchen does, you will be ahead of the trends.

monster . . . a disco, a piano bar, a cruise bar, a floor wax . . . this unique bastion of New York late-nightlife in the West Village is not to be missed.

mixed company . . . introduces lesbians and gay men to people of the opposite sex for purposes of marriage, having children, social or business escorts, particularly to serve the needs of men and women in the closet. Truly unique!

richard laermer has appeared on numerous TV shows as a New York City "expert," and is the author of both *Native's Guide to New York* and *Bargain Hunting in Greater New York*. He has written articles for numerous New York publications, including the *New York Times* and *New York* magazine, and articles on Laermer have appeared in such periodicals as the *New York Post* and the *Daily News*. He is the director of Richard Laermer Media Relations.

other books by richard laermer

native's guide to new york: 750 ways to have the time of your life in the city

bargain hunting in greater new york

richard laermer

the gay and lesbian handbook to new york city

A PLUME BOOK

PLUME

Published by the Penguin Group
Penguin Books USA Inc., 375 Hudson Street, New York, New York 10014, U.S.A.
Penguin Books Ltd, 27 Wrights Lane, London W8 5TZ, England
Penguin Books Australia Ltd, Ringwood, Victoria, Australia
Penguin Books Canada Ltd, 10 Alcorn Avenue, Toronto, Ontario, Canada M4V 3B2
Penguin Books (N.Z.) Ltd, 182–190 Wairau Road, Auckland 10, New Zealand

Penguin Books Ltd, Registered Offices:
Harmondsworth, Middlesex, England

First published by Plume, an imprint of Dutton Signet,
a division of Penguin Books USA Inc.

First Printing, May, 1994

10 9 8 7 6 5 4 3 2 1

Copyright © Richard Laermer, 1994
All rights reserved

Ⓟ REGISTERED TRADEMARK—MARCA REGISTRADA

LIBRARY OF CONGRESS CATALOGING IN PUBLICATION DATA
Laermer, Richard, 1960–
    The gay and lesbian handbook to New York City / Richard Laermer.
    p. cm.
    ISBN 0-452-27022-7
1. Gay communities—New York (N.Y.)—Guidebooks. 2. Gays—Travel—
New York (N.Y.)—Guidebooks. 3. New York (N.Y.)—Guidebooks.
    I. Title.
    HQ76.3U5L34 1994
    917.47104'43'0240664—dc20   93-41786
                                                                    CIP

Printed in the United States of America
Set in Gill Sans and Goudy

Designed by Steven N. Stathakis

Without limiting the rights under copyright reserved above, no part of this publication may be reproduced, stored in or introduced into a retrieval system, or transmitted, in any form, or by any means (electronic, mechanical, photocopying, recording, or otherwise), without the prior written permission of both the copyright owner and the above publisher of this book.

BOOKS ARE AVAILABLE AT QUANTITY DISCOUNTS WHEN USED TO PROMOTE PRODUCTS OR SERVICES. FOR INFORMATION PLEASE WRITE TO PREMIUM MARKETING DIVISION, PENGUIN BOOKS USA INC., 375 HUDSON STREET, NEW YORK, NEW YORK 10014.

I have always felt that New Yorkers are inherently lucky. I dedicate this book to the gay and lesbian New Yorkers who are in many ways luckier.

contents

introduction: **the spirit of community** 1

■ section one **orientation** 9

one **essential resources** 11
two **lodging and how to get out—and stay here!** 21
three **a look at gay neighborhoods from the most to the least** 25
four **oh please—info lines** 29
five **special events calendar** 35

■ section two **entertain, baby** 41

six **restaurants we can't live without no matter what!** 43
seven **bars all around town** 51
eight **dance and sweat (clubgoing)** 73
nine **quiet places for romance** 85
ten **shopping and things to buy** 89
eleven **freebies in new york city** 93
twelve **gyms for your body** 99
thirteen **jazz clubs, cabarets; sit and watch the music** 103

contents

fourteen **eighty-eight keys (piano bars)** 111
fifteen **where to go when everyone's asleep (or, where to sleep when everyone's going)** 115

■ section three **anything arty** 127

sixteen **theater and dance, gay and otherwise** 129
seventeen **galleries and museums for the gay at heart** 141
eighteen **literary new york** 151
nineteen **film and video (if you like to watch)** 161
twenty **the music chapter: sing this list** 165

■ section four **social, medical, and political** 171

twenty-one **mixed events and organizations of note** 173
twenty-two **where the girls are—social happenings for lesbians** 187
twenty-three **where the boys are—social happenings for fun gay males** 191
twenty-four **political orgs, professional orgs and business orgs** 195
twenty-five **things spiritual and anything remotely religious** 203
twenty-six **educate thyself!** 207
twenty-seven **lean on them—support groups** 211
twenty-eight **aids pages** 215
twenty-nine **volunteerism** 231

■ section five **oddities and a completely subjective list of things i like** 241

thirty **odd places, odd people and, of course, odd things** 243
thirty-one **a few personal favorites that i get to put in because i'm the author (nyah, nyah, nyah)** 247
glossary: **endearing terms and otherwise** 249

acknowledgments 257
index 259

introduction

the spirit of community

On Gay Pride Day 1993, I sat down and tried to make some sense of the last years of writing a gay and lesbian guidebook. I had spent twenty-five months compiling and revising information meant to inform gay men and lesbians about the city of their choosing—New York. During that time I discovered much of the good and the bad about New York City as it relates to this much-maligned and yet relatively liberated subgroup.

I am pleased to report that the gay citizenry thrives in ways that most gay men and lesbians do not realize. Rather than existing as a bunch of isolated sorts who happen to have converged in an identical geographic space, this so-called gay community is a force to be reckoned with, a proud conglomeration of men and women and children who have come to realize just how lucky we are.

When I say lucky, I do not mean the fortunate who are still alive, though believe me, that thought occurs to me too. We are in the midst, still, of a gigantic killing season that none of us ever thought we'd see in this postwar lifetime. AIDS has ravaged our homes, our families; it has seized so much joy. But it has also helped galvanize a common assembly out of all the devastation.

I speak of the fortunate who live in what I call a gay-positive environment. We are the blessed who can, without fear of reprisal,

the spirit of community

walk down the street with our baseball caps perched backward (after all, we did invent the look), wear earrings on our right ear (ditto, see Glossary), have on a T-shirt that says "Eat a Boy for Breakfast" (and be a boy), kiss our girlfriend hello (or goodbye), sashay down the street if we feel like it (but it's *so* showy), and simply act openly gay or lesbian or bisexual. Even if you feel closeted at work or at family meals, there's a place called New York where basically you can act and react as you please.

Here we are, then, with 100-odd establishments to patronize in which we are the majority. Though a recent study says only 2 percent of the country's citizens are homosexual, in New York the increase in the number of gays and lesbians is the single greatest leap in demographics produced by the 1990 census. We are *out*. We're here. We're queer.

But so many of us just don't seem used to it.

On Gay Pride Day, when I had finally completed most of the research for the book, I took a look at how many of the men and women I befriended during this bookmaking activity were not happy with their community. They told me our subgroup was too into shopping, cocktails and cruising—and they hated the fact that so many were out on weekends but in the closet at work.

I have to agree.

Many of the unhappy wanted more activism, more involvement, more pride, less affectation, and a lot less emphasis on the sleeping together thing. "It's not about sex, it's about being part of a society," they told me.

It's difficult to imagine what being part of a society is unless you have a history lesson first. So I pored over the books and guess what? There was life *before* Uncle Charlie's. See Chapter 3, "A Look at Gay Neighborhoods from the Most to the Least."

In the early 1940s, bars opened and closed consecutively, thanks to raids. Eventually that prompted something we now call activism. Activism was big in the forties, fifties, and sixties.

I hear complaints from fellow gays and lesbians about the fact that a lot of us are militant "queers"—it bothers many in our family to see such out-and-out faggotism. I looked and discovered we have been a militant bunch for quite a while.

If you think Queer Nation is radical, imagine the actions of the

the spirit of community

members of the fifties and sixties group Council on Equality for Homosexuals. Or the Homophile Youth Movement (HYMN). Try the Street Transvestites Action Revolutionaries. And the Christopher Street Liberation Day Committee.

Women's splinter groups included Daughters of Bilitis and the Mattachine group, which, in addition to men's causes, pushed lesbian-feminist causes to the forefront with a fervor in the sixties. If you want to learn more about the Stonewall Riots, read a really good book by historian Martin Duberman titled *Stonewall*—appropriately enough. (This is a blatant plug that my publisher is forcing me to add—no, really, it's a good book.)

Of course, the biggest noisemakers were the Gay Activists Alliance (GAA), probably at the forefront of Stonewall, and the Gay Liberation Front (GLF), whose members used civil rights activists' working committees to bust out of the closet in the sixties.

I wanted to point out the radicalness of the sixties as a means to say that activism did not begin with the onset of the AIDS movement—and to show how far we've come.

In many chapters in the *Handbook* you will find comparisons to the old ways of gay New York.

Whether you think our community in 1994 is good or bad, keep in mind that it makes an enormous impact on New York. There's all the news we've made lately. Besides the twenty-fifth anniversary of Stonewall, there's Gay Games '94 in the city, the hoopla over military, political and corporate officials coming out or getting outed, the gay TV news explosion, gays making headway in AIDS education, the gay fashion angle, lesbian chic, and the little characters on TV who have gotten America to realize that being gay is okay after all.

Gay *is* okay after all. Politics made that a fact. In 1993, hundreds of thousands of gay men, lesbians, bisexuals and the likeminded converged on the Mall in the capital . . . to cheer on Bill Clinton and remind him that we're serious. It was thrilling to be involved and it drove home a message that I wish to emphasize to readers of this book, a labor of real love for two-plus years: *Do not go backward. Keep united and keep striving for more than being accepted.* As Martina said in Washington in 1993, "We are just as boring as the straights." The more we speak up, the better it is for us.

That's what books like this do: make you aware of the hundreds

the spirit of community

of activities, groups and establishments that are there for the taking
... if you are gay, lesbian or plain sympathetic.

Back to history: Our community has been made strong by history. We started as activists and became a very important force. Everything that has occurred has come about through struggle. (The Lesbian and Gay Community Services Center had to fight the city to be *allowed* to purchase the building it is housed in—and that was in 1984!)

It may seem trivial, but in a marketing sense the community cannot be ignored. In the fashion consciousness of so-called straights, in the fact that anyone who knows anything about hip only goes to gay nights at clubs, in our ability to work together as a group: We exist in huge numbers and we make a strong showing.

Take the consumer issue. Local shop owners and magazine advertisers learned a painful lesson: Do not take the gay dollar for granted. We spend in gay-friendly places. We are the centerpiece of many marketing campaigns—in New York do heteros shop? There's a "gay D'Agostino's" in the Village, where gay men and lesbians are the only shoppers I see!

After listening to the complaints, I think the people who bitch that we are not active enough make an important point. Since the onset of AIDS, people have had to fight for their lives more than their rights. And while gay rights are gaining prominence again—witness the Pride Agenda and the fight to see that gay rights are included in the Civil Rights Bill of New York State—AIDS has made it so that gay people feel they need to be heard constantly.

If the obvious ones hadn't made such a scene in 1969, we'd probably have been pushed back in the closet even further. Our freedom is due to efforts as a community that culminated in that historic riot twenty-five years ago. And we should be proud the stand was taken.

It all started in New York—in the West Village, which is no longer the main stage of gay and lesbian life in New York (Chelsea and the East Village are settings for most events today). It was the site of the scuffle in the raucous spring of 1969.

At the corner of what is now Stonewall Place, the cops were told to shove it after they began arresting young men for being blatantly gay. The *Daily News* headlines that day spoke of "fags" fighting arrests. Read Chapter 7, "Bars All Around Town," and see how the strong men and women fought cops vehemently.

the spirit of community

"Cops Raid Homo Nest/Queen Bees Stinging Mad," went the nasty headline. *The New York Times*, which today covers more gay stories than ever before in its daily pages, ran an editorial proclaiming the riots a danger to quiet family life. It would, they said, ruin the moral fabric of our fair city. What a laugh—this is the same town where the "Tenderloin" porn district survived and thrived on a daily . . . or hourly . . . basis.

Today our neighborhoods are alive with homo culture; yesterday they were merely decorative closets for our brothers and sisters. That was 1969. Twenty-five years is nothing in historical terms.

So, what's in this book besides the radical chic? I believe it's the first complete compilation of facts about gay and lesbian New York. It's not a Gayellowpages or a cruising guide like *Bob Damron's Address Book*, but there are sections that cover what those tomes cover. This is not a bar and activities guide like *Metro Source*, though that stuff is certainly strewn throughout, and it's not in the same format as a talky weekly like *Homo Xtra*, a resource many of us have come to rely on. The word "Handbook" in the title says it all: This book is inclusive of many of the social, political and sexual aspects of a group that I report on as a participant.

The community I have written about is not as common as you think. Sure, there's the baseball-cap-backward, ripped-jeans, earring-in-the-right-ear crowd that cruises and dishes and plans trips to Fire Island, etc. They are everywhere. (I'm one of them.) I would not denigrate this mass by trying to define them. Instead I'll call us The Proud. Proud to have what we have, where we have it. Proud to Be Here. If your friends bitch, "I hate gay bars," smack them and say: "Do you know how many men and women in small-town America would die to have fifty gay bars to choose from? Find one you like and call it your own!"

I have incorporated in this book a list of what's happening in the city. There are those fifty bars, the clubs, the sex places, the oddities, the music happenings, the AIDS help groups, the activist collectives like the ones started by our forefathers and -mothers, the clubs for those who like bowling and dating chubby people, the secret organizations and the ideas whose time have come.

And there are activities that are not gay but are thrown in because gay men and lesbians might want to know about them. The *Handbook*

the spirit of community

presents a smattering of activities discovered in my work as a mainstream reporter who likes to have a good time all the time—basic enjoyment material that involves "mixed company."

Chapter 28, "AIDS Pages," is an overall look at AIDS groups throughout the city. I have included information about what's known as the "AIDS culture": the groups that make living with AIDS and caring for people with AIDS (PWAs) easier.

In Chapter 30, I've added a group of oddities—unusual places and ideas—that I couldn't find another spot for. Some are fun, some mysterious.

The glossary in the back is a reminder to gay visitors and the New York set that we speak a different language most of the time.

Throughout, I tried to keep in mind that this is a book on *lesbian* and gay New York. Not being a lesbian, this was not the easiest task for me. But many groups and helpful people who either were lesbian or knew about female same-sex activities arrived to rescue me each time I was stumped. I am thankful to all the lesbian sources who came out to help. And I am glad that our community has become so "mixed" of late: I mean, how long did it take for the late-June Gay Pride Parade to be renamed the Lesbian & Gay & Bisexual Pride Parade?

Girls, be happy. As for the boys, not one single complaint!

Chapter 29, "Volunteerism," gives ideas of how to get and stay involved in the community. I've included a form you can tear out (neatly) and send to the Lesbian and Gay Community Services Center, to help get you into volunteer mode.

The last thing I discovered while fact-checking is that involvement is the best way to get in on what's happening. During a quiet moment in a conversation with Richard Burns, director of the Lesbian and Gay Community Services Center, I figured out that the most ingenious scheme for finding a spouse or a sex partner is to wander into a gay place and find an activity in which to busy yourself. Someone with a similar interest (even sex) will eventually wander your way. Since men and women hate bars—yeah, right—and always want to know if they can do something else to meet men and women in this dark and scary town, I point to "Volunteerism" as bait. Besides the dozens I mention, there are other organizations listed through the center at 620-7310.

Who knows? If we all lend a hand, maybe the above mentioned

the spirit of community

grievances will at last vanish. By making New York the best place possible for this gay and lesbian community, we'll not only be Proud, we'll be seamlessly *fab*ulous.

Every effort has been made to ensure that all establishments and events listed in this book contain accurate, up-to-date information at press time. We know that many places and much information has been changed, closed, reopened, been dyed purple, etc. But the seasons have changed so drastically of late that we could not get everything taken care of. *Mea Culpa*, you know.

All addresses are in Manhattan, unless otherwise stated. Please note that all phone numbers in this book are in area code 212 unless otherwise noted, except for beepers and mobile phones, where the area code is 917.

section one

orientation

Here is an opportunity to learn everything you can about gay culture and gay life—and you don't even have to open this book past page fifty! (You bought it, now leave it on your coffee table.)

The following are a few chapters devoted to the process of discovering your city, New York. I have come to the conclusion that in order to fully comprehend the goings and comings of this town, everyone, including this guidebook author, has to become better educated about the basics.

Herein lies five areas in which you will need to become best equipped: First, resources to read, watch and listen to in order to educate yourself. Second, places to stay and how to get out of town when the shopping, er, going gets tough. Then, a few peeks at neighborhoods—east side, west side, Queens, etc.—followed by invaluable information lines from the people who care (both volunteers and the places to call with employees who get *paid* to listen to you, none of them phone-sex lines, though; that comes later). Finally, it's an introductory passage on *Special Events*, a calendar for the person—be he gay or she lesbian—who wants a quick fix on a particular day or night of the year.

After you get past these pages, the rest is a piece of cake. Because after all, the remaining information is just dessert!

chapter one

essential resources

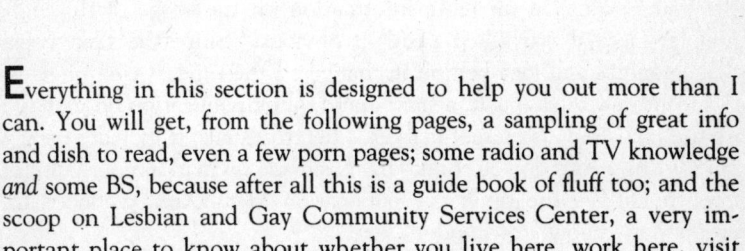

Everything in this section is designed to help you out more than I can. You will get, from the following pages, a sampling of great info and dish to read, even a few porn pages; some radio and TV knowledge and some BS, because after all this is a guide book of fluff too; and the scoop on Lesbian and Gay Community Services Center, a very important place to know about whether you live here, work here, visit here, or just happen upon this book in someone's living room.

■ magazines and newspapers to help

the advocate
liberation publications, p.o. box 4371, los angeles, ca 90099

This glossy, widely read national gay and lesbian news magazine has undergone several makeovers in the past couple of years—all for the better. The *Time* of our community, *The Advocate* offers national and international news coverage that's quite well thought out; the political coverage has become the mainstay of the magazine. *The Advocate* is all over New York—its cultural coverage is mostly concerned with the city, and it's available at most newsstands and bookstores that sell

orientation

magazines. Subscription prices vary, depending on the offer you read in the magazine that week.

homo xtra

A weekly guide to clubs, bars, theater, cultural events and other goings-on for gay men in New York. A few listings for lesbians but mostly men stuff. Lots of news about sex clubs, lots of "dish." Continuing sagas, inside news, and its own soap opera. I must say the bar information is incredibly up to date, and as one bar owner told me, "During the weeks I advertise in *Homo Xtra* I can tell just how much my business goes up!" Around since 1991. Available for free at bars and clubs and for sale at gay bookstores for $1 (may be going up to $1.50).

When I called for more information on the scope of this now popular piece, I was asked, "Isn't it obvious?" Since the size, scope, demographics and idea behind it change all the time, it isn't obvious. A recent new release is *It*, a similar and duller publication on club life by the H/X crew. *It*'s target market is heterosexuals; *It* includes no sex club listings. And do you think H/X has made no mark on our culture? You should see the ripoff gay publication *Metro Xtra*, produced in, around, and about . . . London!

the list

This magazine of the Gay and Lesbian Visitors Center of New York, a membership organization for businesses that was founded in mid-1993, offers free advice and discount coupons redeemable at participating restaurants, stores, and other venues (theaters, cabarets, etc.). A twenty-page guide to recent and upcoming events, *The List* gives a perspective unlike *Homo Xtra* and even this guide. Rather than seeking to enlighten or amuse—or both, as I am diligently attempting—this monthly periodical has basic knowledge for the person in town only for a day or two, and no longer than a week.

The GLVC's opportunities for members (the membership list grows all the time) include ads in their magazine and a way to com-

essential resources

municate with other gay-friendly and gay- and lesbian-owned businesses in New York. For information, call 463-9030.

The magazine's May 1994 issue is devoted to travel; June to the Gay Games and Gay Pride; July to summer in New York; August to theater; and September to restaurants. The magazine is to be found displayed in gay businesses all over the city.

new york native

The *Native* is a weekly gay and lesbian news magazine. This was the first publication to write about the AIDS epidemic, and it continues to explore the etiology of AIDS. The *Native*'s extensive coverage of AIDS and chronic fatigue has been highly controversial. The *Native* publishes art reviews, listings, travel articles, and interviews. $2 in NYC, $3 outside.

While not exactly a favorite of the gay community, thanks to its putting the acronym "AIDS" in quotes and making other notorious moves seemingly to garner press coverage, *NY Native* is available at newsstands and bookstores around NYC and at gay and independent bookstores across the country.

next

Well, it had to happen. Someone saw what a great advertiser market you are (*I* did) and put out another weekly listings guide, with a beautiful glossy cover and some great columns and improvements to the above format: Next Scoop (pretty funny gossip); a real muscle section on bodybuilding (our favorite sport); Sun Spots (good ideas for people who leave town); Ask GMHC (knowledge we can't live without); Next Choice, a look at their advertiser market and specific areas known to be important to gay men (not lesbians); Star Gays (not worth it, we have Joyce at the *News*!); Dallas's Next's Bests (great finds, he says); and for us couch potatoes, Next Channel, a comprehensive viewer's guide to gay TV, which is covered in this chapter but you can always find more to watch. You *like* to watch, huh?

orientation

on the wilde side

A monthly entertainment and news magazine for lesbians and gay men in the tristate area. General interest, news articles. Lots of listings, with emphasis on the Long Island scene. Free, available at bars, restaurants, gay-friendly businesses, nightclubs, etc.

project x

The self-proclaimed "Inside guide to N.Y.C.'s Trendiest Scene!" Good source for the dirt on clubs, and where to buy fur-lined pumps. Lots of fashion spreads and club-life gossip. Published occasionally and available at gay and lesbian bookstores, some independent bookstores and some gay-friendly businesses. *Project X* produced by people who refuse to offer their phone number, so none of my information about it can be proved accurate. (Read the periodical for fun, not for details!)

sappho's isle

Sappho's Isle is the source for news and listings for lesbians in the New York area. A monthly lesbian newspaper, it covers the tristate region, though info is predominantly about NYC and Long Island. *Sappho's Isle* provides news stories, columns, articles on health and sports, a calendar of events, reviews, comics and listings.

Sappho's Isle is available for free at women's bars, community centers, restaurants, women-owned bookstores and other businesses, and therapists' offices. About a thousand copies are also distributed for sale at NYC newsstands for $1.50. *Sappho's Isle* has been in business since 1987.

spunk
studio iguana, 501 first street, room 419, san francisco, ca 94107

A gross publication dedicated to sex and sleaze. Not that there's anything wrong with either, but *Spunk* makes them seem so *dirty*. Listings

essential resources

for bars' back rooms, boothstores, cinemas, dark rooms, baths and places to get off—all over New York City and San Francisco. Not for women.

The insider's guide is called "Jizbiz." Whatever. Write to the above address for a five-for-$6 subscription. If you're all hot and bothered hearing this, check out Chapter 15, "Where to Go When Everyone's Asleep."

stonewall news

A free weekly magazine published by the people who publish *Christopher Street* and *New York Native*. *Stonewall News* is a more user-friendly, insightful rag than the *Native*, as it has extensive theater listings, movie reviews and listings of events and activities of interest to gay men and lesbians. Has been coming out since 1991. Available free at bars, restaurants and other gay-friendly businesses. Also sold at the Oscar Wilde Memorial Bookstore and at various newsstands for $1.

■ radio and tv

gay entertainment network (gen)

A new gay cable broadcaster, GEN has one show to date and plans to premiere another soon. *Party Talk* is broadcast on Channel 35 on Sunday night from 11 P.M. to midnight, and again Thursday evening from 9 to 10. *Party Talk* is an entertainment show—what's happening in the city, interviews, film clips, etc. The segments have an MTV quality. "Best new show on TV," said a local scribe. Next show is *Party Talk Inside and Out: Documentary*, wherein cameras follow the cohosts through their "regular" gay days, showing the spectrum of gay life.

A third show is on the way, GEN says. GEN plans on going national into several major markets. Find GEN's listings in the above mentioned *Homo Xtra*.

orientation

gay cable network (gcn)

GCN produces four television shows for cable broadcast in New York and one for national cable broadcast. GCN has been producing gay TV for 11 years. *Stonewall Place*, a variety show with host John Burke, a.k.a. Sybil Bruncheon, appears on Channel 35, Sunday from 10 to 11 P.M. *In the Dungeon* keeps people informed about the leather and S&M "lifestyle." This chat show includes news of events around town, at 11 P.M. on Tuesday on Channel 35. *Candied Camera* is a novel entertainment/variety show of no certain format, hosted by a lovely thing named Nora. In this show, they use a studio audience that resembles a big nightclub crowd. You can zoom in on *Candied* Wednesday at 10 P.M. on Channel 35. Then there's *Men & Film*, a half-hour porn review that gets away with more than the Playboy Channel in terms of what it will show. Porn stars come for interviews, with sexy clips from new video releases. That airs Thursday at midnight (it's well watched) on Channel 35. Last, there's *Gay USA*, a one-hour national distribution feast shown in twenty-two cities. It's a TV magazine featuring community news and goings-on, hosted by activist Andy Humm, who once beat up Morton Downey, Jr. *Gay USA* can be found on Thursday at 11 P.M. on Channel 35.

GCN shows are broadcast on Time Warner Cable and, with the exception of Gay USA on Thursday nights, are not broadcast on Paragon Cable, which has somehow decided the shows aren't right for *their* viewers.

For up-to-date listings and last-minute additions, see *Homo Xtra* or *Next*, or call the Gay and Lesbian Switchboard of New York, 777-1800. (For more on the Switchboard, see Chapter 4, "Oh Please—Info Lines.")

out in the nineties and other homo-broadcasting at wbai/99.5 fm   279-0707

WBAI is an independent public radio station with a roster of gay and lesbian programming. Shows include *This Way Out*, Monday at 9 A.M., a syndicated radio news magazine from KPFK/Los Angeles; *OutLooks*, produced by GLIB (Gays & Lesbians in Broadcasting), and *The Gay Show*, produced by Gay People's Radio Collective. These two shows

essential resources

are broadcast alternately on Sunday at 7 P.M. *Alternativa Latina* airs on Friday at 2:30 P.M., addressing a spectrum of issues of interest to the Latino community and including an occasional specific segment on gay and lesbian issues, *"Rompiendo Silencio."*

Particularly notable are WBAI's *AIDS in Focus* and *Positive Connection* on Thursday at 9 A.M. There's lots of gay and lesbian programming during Gay Pride Month. (For more on that, see Glossary.)

For more about WBAI programming, or to subscribe, call.

pbs

PBS is also offering *In The Life*, an insightful though often dull show about gay and lesbian real life, that has had its share of controversies. It's the first gay-oriented TV show on public television, and it arrived after a boycott—heavily manned and womaned by Act Up and other organizations—of the local PBS affiliate (channel 13, WNET). Though *In The Life* has some good shtick, it is still relegated to weekend late nights, and still hasn't done anything ground-breaking. But the jury's still . . . out. The show is produced locally by WNYC.

wusb/stony brook
516/632-6500

A weekly show, *Lavender Women*, is broadcast from SUNY/Stony Brook's WUSB, Thursday evenings from 6 to 7. Live, talk, music, requests. This is the only specifically gay or lesbian show on Long Island.

At press time, some more TV included *Stonewall Place After Dark*, an entertainment program of interviews and fun events; *In The Dungeon*, with some guys doing rough stuff or at least pantomiming; and *Candied Camera*, a variety show with, well, variety. Plus, my *fave* talk show, *The Barry Z Show*, with Mr. Z interviewing just about everyone. Hmm. Lastly, there's *Dyke TV* on Tuesdays at 8 P.M. on Channel 34. Public Access is wonderful to fags. For appearance information for many of the above shows, call 677-8494.

orientation

lesbian and gay community services center
208 west 13th street, 620-7310
♀

This is it. The Community Center is a real center for many political, social, and entertainment-oriented activities. It's home to social service groups and organizations, provides meeting space for more than 250 gay and lesbian registered groups in the city, hosts numerous social events every week, and serves as a clearinghouse for information about what's going on in the community. Six anchor tenants have their offices at the center: the Coalition for Lesbian and Gay Rights, the Community Health Project, the Lesbian Switchboard, the Metropolitan Community Church/NY, the NYC Gay and Lesbian Anti-Violence Project and Senior Action in a Gay Environment (SAGE). The center is also home to the Pat Parker and Vito Russo Center Library.

It's a must-stop-by; the staffers at the front desk are helpful, the bulletin boards are packed with interesting information, and there are always people bopping around. For the new in town, there are tons of flyers announcing upcoming events and group meetings. I learned a lot about the center while compiling the information for this book. According to director Richard Burns, "The Lesbian and Gay Community Services Center exists to facilitate gay and lesbian empowerment."

This lesbian and gay safe hub came into being after some difficult negotiations with the city, which had problems with the idea of selling the former Food and Maritime Trades High School to queers. But the sale went through, for $1.5 million, with the city providing a market-rate mortgage. At the time even leaders in the gay community were skeptical about the deal's being closed, but eventually $200,000 was raised and the center happened. A $10-million capital campaign fund is under way to support a complete reconstruction and expansion.

Some 400 gay, lesbian and AIDS organizations meet here regularly. The center mails a newsletter to more than 25,000 households (get one sent to you by calling the number above). In 1985, the center became the temporary home of the Harvey Milk High School, a program of the Hetrick-Martin Institute for the Protection of Lesbian and Gay Youth. (The high school has since moved to 401 West Street, between West 10th and Charles streets.) The center's prime function is to provide affordable meeting space for gay and lesbian organizations.

essential resources

ACT UP, Queer Nation and GLAAD were born here. Anyone with an idea can reserve a room for a meeting, as long as it's gay, lesbian or bisexual in nature and you collect $2 from everybody who attends. And you clean up.

The center also runs many health-related and cultural programs. They include Project Connect, a substance-abuse prevention and intervention program established in 1988; Youth Enrichment Services (YES), a substance-abuse and HIV/AIDS education and prevention program for lesbian and gay youth; CenterBridge, an AIDS bereavement project; Orientation on the Road, the center's outreach program in the outer boroughs; Center ILGA (International Lesbian and Gay Association), which advocates for gay and lesbian political prisoners around the world; Center Kids, a family project; the Pat Parker and Vito Russo Center Library, a gay and lesbian lending library jointly developed with Publishing Triangle; and the National Museum and Archive of Lesbian and Gay History.

The center's third-floor bathroom features beautiful pornography installed by Keith Haring, a sort of *Remember When?* portrait. The center's annual Garden Party, held the Monday of Lesbian and Gay Pride Week, is the premier fund-raising event, the most popular community celebration, and the launch of Pride Week in New York City.

Whenever you have a birthday party, you might ask friends to donate money to the center rather than buy you another stupid tie. Stonewall 25, a group dedicated to the memorialization of the Stonewall Riots, has all its meetings here.

And last, membership: Find a form on the next page and fill it in, send a minimum of $25 and hopefully more, and help the center build a new building. Your membership dollars also get you discounts at businesses and professional services around town (mostly around Chelsea and the Village).

Drop by and see what's up, and pick up a copy of *Center Voice*, the Lesbian and Gay Community Service Center's monthly newsletter. Or call.

lesbian and gay community services center

volunteer data form

name: _____
address: _____
gender: _____ **date of birth:** _____
phone: day _____ eve _____
occupation: _____

1. Do you currently volunteer at The Center? _____
If yes, on which committee? _____
2. Describe any ideas you have as to <u>how</u> you would like to volunteer.
_____
_____

3. Please list any <u>skills</u> you would like to utilize as a volunteer.
_____
_____

4. Would you like some assistance in finding a volunteer committee placement? _____
5. Are you interested in a volunteer work that is a:
   one-shot deal _____ short-term project _____
   ongoing committee work _____ unsure _____
6. Are you interested in a volunteer committee that is related to: [number, in order of preference, all those that interest you.]

       arts _____   The Center
       fundraising _____   - the building _____
       political _____   - clerical assistance _____
       recreational _____   - community/public relations _____
       social services _____   - newsletter _____
       sports _____   - volunteer management _____
                                - board of trustees _____

7. Please circle when you are available to volunteer:

day	m	tu	w	th	f	sat	sun
eve	m	tu	w	th	f	sat	sun

8. Please specify any limitation/disability and how it would affect your volunteer work _____
9. Do you currently receive Center mailings? _____ Do you want to be on the mailing list? _____
10. Committee selections: _____
_____

please mail or give this form to:
Trish Kerla, Director of Special Projects, The Center, 208 West 13th Street, New York, New York 10011

chapter two

lodging and how to get out— and stay here!

■ **if you need a place to stay**

brooklyn bed & breakfast
128 kent street, greenpoint, 718/383-3026

Housed in a shipbuilder's Civil War–era house, this lovely bed-and-breakfast is on the East River in an arty section of Brooklyn. The house is eclectically decorated with period furniture and has a garden in the back. Rates are reasonable and vary considerably. The establishment does not take credit cards. It's open throughout the year.

chelsea pine inn
317 west 14th street, 929-1023

Seventeen rooms filled mostly with gay men and lesbians. Rooms with private bath and shared bath are available. Two-night minimum stay required on weekends. Rooms have television but no phone. Breakfast is included. Reservations two weeks in advance are often necessary during the summer. Rooms are $55 to $65 with shared bath and $85 with private bath.

orientation

colonial house inn
318 west 22nd street, 243-9669

A European-style bed-and-breakfast in a beautiful brownstone built in the 1850s. The twenty rooms are patronized mostly by gay men, though women are welcome. The building has been completely renovated, a large art collection hangs on the walls, and concierge service is available twenty-four hours a day. Continental breakfast and rooftop sun deck. Rates are $65 to $99, including breakfast. Special weekday rate. Reservations are required several weeks in advance during the summer months.

gay roommate service
133 west 72nd street, 580-7696

Though not recommended as a be-all-and-end-all source for gay men looking for roomies, the Gay Roommate Service is the one service that exclusively caters to the gay and lesbian community. Unorganized—highly inefficient—and used by many clients as a dating service, the business charges $100 to show you apartments (clients with spaces to let are not charged). Your membership is valid for six months. In several cases I have heard about, young gays have found reputable shares through the service. Use, but proceed with caution.

incentra village house
32 eighth avenue between west 12th and jane streets, 206-0007

This building, listed with the National Trust for Historic Places, was built in 1841 and has twelve guest rooms. All have private bath and kitchenette, television and telephone, and some even possess a working fireplace. The rooms and the parlor are decorated in a traditional style. Guests are mostly gay and lesbian. Reservations are required in the summer; rates run between $89 and $99 for rooms and up to $140 for a two-bedroom suite. An additional $10 is charged for a double room. For travel buffs, this place is managed by the same family as Incentra Carriage House in Key West (a family of men, I should add).

lodging and how to get out—and stay here!

■ **if you need a place to go**

battery travel associates
587-9100

Michael Yampolsky provides personal travel arrangements and is sensitive to issues of concern to lesbian and gay travelers, and to special requests. Corporate and personal arrangements.

international gay travel association (igta)
p.o. box 4974, key west, fl 33041, 800/448-8550

This association of gay and lesbian travel professionals assists travel agents in planning vacations for gays and lesbians. The definitive resource for travel agents. The newsletter *IGTA Today* includes lots of points of interest, listings of gay events around the world, tours, etc.

pridetime productions
617/723-5130

Pridetime produces and distributes a series of gay and lesbian travel videos that focus on destinations of interest to gay and lesbian travelers (Key West, Provincetown, Boston). Pridetime has also introduced a series of entertainment videos that feature gay and lesbian performers. The travel series is available for rent at A Different Light Bookstore (see Chapter 18, "Literary New York").

rsvp gay cruises
800/533-1482

They had to be listed somewhere, so: Here's *The Love Boat* for amorous homosexuals. RSVP has dozens of sailings throughout the year, in the Caribbean, along the Atlantic seaboard and in the Pacific. The travel magazine *Out and About* says RSVP is the best of the bunch. Call for information and a fee schedule.

chapter three

a look at gay neighborhoods from the most to the least

■ chelsea

In the seventies, *the* gay neighborhood was the Village, a.k.a. the west side of Greenwich Village. Christopher Street was once a sea of gay men. Now gays seem to flock to Chelsea. This enclave between West 13th and West 25th Streets was founded when Barneys New York, the gay men's paradise, purchased a large chunk of 17th Street and forced many tenants out. After the mom-and-pop shops moved away, the fashionable and questionable boutiques moved in, and gays and lesbians converged on the neighborhood. The rest is our story. But since this has become such a popular area, many stores with a gay flair have opened. This is good, except, as a friend points out, you now are in such a gay-oriented neighborhood it's difficult to walk around looking less than great. Such problems.

West 17th Street between Eighth and Fifth avenues is probably the gayest (not the lesbian-est) area in the city: With Chelsea Gym, Splash, Video Blitz, two Gap stores, and even nearby David Barton Gym on this strip, how can you do anything *but* be gay here?

orientation

■ **east village**

The second most popular gay neighborhood is the East Village, the Lower East Side, or as it's often called, "Loisaida." What makes this nabe so trendy now is not the people who dress in black, it's the number of lesbians you see everywhere. As for the bars, hop in and hop out: You can make a great evening of bargoing among the neighborhood establishments.

■ **west village**

Christopher Street, which runs between the Hudson River and Greenwich Avenue, was once the center of the gay ghetto. Featured on obscure television episodes of *The Odd Couple*, Christopher Street meant swish. (See Glossary for details.) Christopher Street has undergone a complete rethinking from the gay community's point of view. Even the oldest bar, Badlands, on the corner of Christopher and West streets, is now gone. Like every old chestnut, unless it amends to fit the times, it grows extinct. The West Village excels in bars that have gotten stale.

In the fall of 1966 gays started making the corner of Christopher Street and Seventh Avenue South their home. Two bars, two jukeboxes, two dance floors, and a large crowd of young lookers who were all men—the only things that made it obvious this was a gay bar. Completely unlicensed, the Stonewall Inn was a "private club," and anyone with a fiver in his hand could gain entrance. (This was not the Roxy, and nobody looked to see what kind of shoes you were wearing before allowing you entrance.)

The place rocked from sunset to dawn. All seemed happy, until the night the cops arrested the manager and bartenders, collected evidence that liquor was being sold illegally, and started banging heads. The task force arrived and a paddywagon processed the patrons—by this point, men *and* women—at the station house. It was all very dramatic, and the patrons, who were being arrested for not breaking any laws, were terrified to be caught in such notorious circumstances and submitted to the harassment, paid a "nuisance" citation and hoped nobody found out about their perversion.

a look at gay neighborhoods

Men dressed as women could actually be arrested for "lewd and indecent behavior," and all this must have been funny to the cops. Eventually, however, a few nights of this turned ugly. A crowd formed to watch—and eventually dove into the melee. First they threw coins, then bottles. Trash cans were heaved through the windows and cops took refuge inside as the patrons poured outside to join their brothers and sisters in what became a huge riot.

Really, this became a big media story because journalists tended to hang out at the Lion's Head bar just up the street. Across the street from the Stonewall Inn, meanwhile, on what is now called Stonewall Place, is the Gay Liberation Monument, designed by famous sculptor George Segal during Gay Pride Week 1992 and depicting two openly gay couples. (Segal is not gay, and you can imagine the uproar that fact caused in '92.)

The Stonewall stands as a monument to the events of 1969. It was the place where Mayor Dinkins went for a drink after he joined gay and lesbian marchers during the tumultuous and divided St. Patrick's Day Parade in 1992.

■ west side

Midtown West Side and the Upper West Side are not the gayest places. Midtown is a tourist section and uptown is a yuppie haven. But you can get lucky anywhere, and that's advice from someone who spends time in Ohio. As for the Upper West Side as a bar area, I quote a local waiter I know intimately: "Enjoy."

■ east side

I can't recommend the East Side as a barhopping neighborhood or even one that dotes on gay culture. Since it is part of Manhattan, I have included in Chapter 7, "Bars All Around Town," a few fun spots. Be sure you realize you're expected to dress in better than a muscle T when you arrive on the not-crowded scene.

orientation

■ **park slope/brooklyn**

So much is going on in Park Slope for gays and lesbians (being politically correct is a hobby there) that I put together the perfect scenario for living there: You have a nice brownstone here, work in the city, and go hang out in the city. Unless you happen to be lesbian, in which case you have girls-only nights like the ones at several beautiful local church parlors. But alas, no phone—a strange sign—so write to them at Box 369, Brooklyn, NY 11365.

There is The Roost (Seventh Avenue and 8th Street, 718/965-7578), which has gay male activity on Tuesday nights, and there are a variety of small restaurants and even the recycle-oriented Food Co-Op . . . ever so cruisey. All activities are located near or around Seventh and Eighth Avenues, and here's a hint: On Saturday mornings, hit the streets, stare and hold hands, and visit Grand Army Plaza's Farmer's Market. Men, men, men. Women, women, women. (My friends tell me the Slope's Eastern Athletic Club at 17 Eastern Parkway (718/789-4600), replete with pool and good-looking young men, is called "Spa Agog" because it's housed inside a synagogue.

■ **queens**

I was born in Jackson Heights, so I have a soft spot for the Borough of Queens. Since Julio Rivera was killed along the gay strip in Jackson Heights, I feel it's important to applaud the community's sense of camaraderie. Just as in Manhattan, there's a sense of pride and community in the borough. If you want to get involved in what's happening, contact the Julio Rivera Lesbian & Gay Anti-Violence Coalition of Queens at P.O. Box 8223, Jct. Boulevard Station, Flushing, NY 11372 (718/639-4951).

chapter four

oh please—info lines

■ **help lines for information only**

bi-ways new york
459-4784

Monthly social events for the bisexual community.

dial for gay places
900/446-4gay

By calling this telephone number you can get listings of gay and lesbian bars, hotels, bookstores and other "places of interest" in cities in the United States, Canada, Mexico and the Caribbean, twenty-four hours a day. Calls cost $1.95 a minute. Information is taken from the self-published *Places of Interest* guide.

orientation

gay and lesbian switchboard of new york
777-1800

Usually called The Switchboard, and a very important part of gay life in New York and many other American cities. Rap, referral, information: free and confidential and TTY-equipped for hearing-impaired users. Open noon to midnight. They will answer the most bizarre questions ("What do I do if I meet someone and they say, 'Be back here at twelve-thirty,' and I'm not sure if they meant A.M. or P.M.?") and those about serious issues, such as alcoholism, disease and safer sex. Since 1972 the board has been a friendly listener. Everyone who answers is a volunteer, so be nice.

Good to note: When you call the switchboard after hours you will be able to access an information retrieval system. Push 1 for info on volunteering; 2 for making a donation; 3 for AIDS information; 4 for emergency and suicide hotlines you can call; 5 for bars and clubs; 6 for comments and feedback or to suggest ideas or changes for them to make on this line. This is a new service set up during those moments when no volunteers can make it to the GLSWNY.

Also good to note: The Samaritans Suicide emergency phone number is 673-3000. (I got that from accessing the above retrieval system.)

lesbian referral hotline
numbers below

A pay-per-call telephone listing of events of interest to women. The hotline tries to ferret out events that don't get covered in the mainstream press, including underground parties, lesbian nights at clubs and so forth. At least ten listings per category, they promise. Messages last about four minutes, and listings include a contact person. $2 per minute. Listings are for New York and New Jersey and are as follows:
   900/370-3710 extension 217, cultural events and travel
   900/370-3710 extension 218, women of color events
   900/370-3710 extension 675, social events

oh please—info lines

lesbian switchboard
741-2610

Information about what's going on, resources, where to get help and so forth. Monday through Friday 6 to 10 P.M.

park slope activities for lesbians
718/630-9505

A large group of active lesbians in Brooklyn who can help with problems, general support, or just plain introductions to the "right" people.

■ hot lines for real help

act up
496 hudson street, suite g-4, hotline 564-2437

To find out about ACT UP it's best to go to a Monday-night meeting.

aids discrimination project
hotline 800/523-aids, in manhattan 870-8624, ttd 870-8999

The AIDS Discrimination Division of the New York City Human Rights Commission handles complaints from people who have suffered discrimination in housing, employment and public accommodations. Call to file a complaint about discrimination.

alcoholics anonymous and adult children of alcoholics hotline
254-7230

Call for a schedule of Alcoholics Anonymous and related organization meetings throughout the five boroughs. Gay and lesbian meetings are

orientation

listed on the hotline tape, but you have to listen through the whole thing to hear about them.

education in a disabled gay environment (edge)
718/723-6620, tty 718/749-9438

A hotline for the physically disabled lesbian and gay community.

gay men's health crisis hotline
807-6655, ttd 645-7470

For information about safe sex and HIV-related health services, and for one-time, walk-in AIDS counseling services. GMHC's hours are Monday through Friday 10:30 A.M. to 9 P.M. See Chapter 28, "AIDS Pages," for the workings of GMHC.

mayor's office for the lesbian and gay community
788-2706

This is the place to call when you have a serious complaint about a city-sponsored group or politician. This line is getting busier all the time.

neutral zone drop-in center
924-3294

Neutral Zone, a small center for information and real support for gay, lesbian, bisexual and transgender kids, can also be a phone-in place to get some peer support. It's open from 4 P.M. to midnight seven days a week.

oh please—info lines

new york city gay and lesbian anti-violence project rape intervention hotline
807-0197

The Anti-Violence Project is described in detail in Chapter 21, "Mixed Social Events." The services to assist lesbians who have been raped include a twenty-four-hour intervention hotline; in-person counseling; support groups; advocacy with police, legal, medical and social service agencies; court monitoring; assistance with crime victim compensation; and information and referrals.

people with aids coalition
hotline 800/828-3280, office 645-4538, info line 647-1420

The PWA Coalition is a clearinghouse for information useful to people with AIDS. The hotline is staffed entirely by people living with AIDS (PWAs). PWA Coalition helps PWAs with urgent needs: food, clothing, shelter and medicine. The coalition also runs an underground drug-buying program to provide drugs to people who need them.

chapter five

special events calendar

saint-at-large parties
674-8541

For a wild time—once in February, once in March, and on New Year's Eve and Halloween—try the Saint-at-Large parties. *Once*. The outrageous blowouts are dressy affairs that call for you to wear all white (February) or all black (March), and to wear chains, leather hats, chaps or even a harness. They start at midnight and offer live sex acts on stage, more drugs than at any other public place, and dancing until way into the next afternoon! Must recommend that you bring with you something skimpy—not for the reason you think, but because you'll dance and sweat so much you won't want anything heavy clinging to you. Saint-at-Large is not to be confused with The Saint, a club at Second Avenue and East Sixth Street that was *the big weekend event* in the seventies. Same promoters, but the feeling is gone. At Large is held at a different location for each party. (For the definition of The Saint, see the Glossary.)

orientation

international gay ski week—february 25–march 5
800/526-2827

A company called Holidays on Skis arranges this annual ski event in Europe, in which fifty or more gay men participate. Holidays on Skis arranges the air transportation, hotel accommodations and some activities and claims that people from all over the world participate—though mostly Americans. Call for a glossy brochure.

night of a thousand gowns
roosevelt hotel, grand ballroom, east 45th street and madison avenue, 794-8780

You've already witnessed this gala event if you saw the film *Paris Is Burning*. Well, this is a real-life $100-ticket party that occurs in mid-March to benefit the Lesbian and Gay Community Services Center. It's sponsored by the Imperial Court of New York. Hotel rooms are available at good rates.

new festival, a.k.a. new york lesbian and gay film festival
807-1820

The New Festival, held every year in the first two weeks of June, has been going on since 1989. In 1993, some 172 films and videos were shown. The festival shows feature films, short films and videos by and about gay men and lesbians. You can call the info line anytime during the year for schedules, prices and listings of special events that have nothing to do with the actual festival.

special events calendar

queer culture
219-3088

A series of shows by gay performers that is in its second run. Hundreds of shows participate at eighteen theaters. The official name of this early-June montage is "Hot! The Annual New York Celebration of Gay Culture." Cosponsored by the $3 Bill Theater Company, mentioned in Chapter 16, "Theater and Dance, Gay and Otherwise," as something essential. The shows are performed in early June.

gay games 1994—june 18-25, 1994
633-9494

Some thirty-one sporting events and a cultural festival, and gay and lesbian visitors to New York from all over the world! Social activities are being planned by the people at Gay Games and by others in New York, which will make the week lots of fun. The games have been held every four years since 1982 and have been getting bigger and bigger every time.

The games were first held in San Francisco in 1982. They were originally called the Gay Olympics, and then the Gay Olympics were given a court order to cease and desist: In the same way that MGM stopped the Pink Panthers (now Outwatch; see Chapter 21, "Mixed Social Events") from using their name, the Olympics did not want queers jeopardizing the virile image the Olympic Games have tried dutifully to protect. That is, the courts forbade the use of the word "Olympics" in conjunction with homosexuals.

At the San Francisco opening, then Mayor and now Senator Dianne Feinstein, not one to miss a media opportunity, defied the court order and called the games the Gay Olympics. Cheers were heard throughout the land. Call for details on sports being entered this year. Personal Note: this handbook is being released at the inauguration of Gay Games events. Go.

orientation

stonewall 25—june 26-27, 1994
439-1031

To turn our attention to some crucial matters: On the last Sunday in June, 1994, as part of Gay Pride 1994, gays and lesbians around the world will commemorate the Stonewall Riots of 1969 (see Neighborhoods and Bars chapter for more complete history). Gay historians will exhibit documents (letters, diaries, banners and whatever material is deemed appropriate) as part of the Stonewall History Project going on throughout the month. Participants are to include the Brooklyn Historical Society, Museum of the City of New York, the New York Historical Society and the New York Public Library. Working with scholars at the Center for Lesbian and Gay Studies at City University, curators of several exhibits will chronicle gay and lesbian history since Colonial times. Now it's not about being accepted—it's about being made to feel old!

the pride party

Held on the last Sunday in June, this party celebrates the belief that being gay and lesbian is not just okay—it's a reason to rejoice. Gays, bi's, lesbians, transgender types, and people who support and love the above, all show up along Fifth Avenue and in the West Village (namely Christopher Street) for a rambunctious, often touching, reflection of our lives. And they march. Quite a collection, a good media show, and a dance at the parking lot of the pier off Christopher Street. (The dance starts at 4 P.M. and continues until 10 P.M., and usually involves quite a wonderful group of hot men who somehow drop all the bullshit for one night and act awfully friendly. After the "pride dance" all the nightclubs and bars do something special—it's a big night.) See Pride listings in Chapter 29, "Volunteerism," and for more information call Heritage of Pride, 807-7433.

special events calendar

greenwich village jazz festival

Each year, late in August, you can go to dozens of free events for the price of a $15 festival pass. These include a free opening concert, usually at the **village gate** (160 Bleecker Street, 475-5120); a **steamboat jazz cruise** (call 406-3434) aboard the *DeWitt Clinton* off South Street Seaport; and then music at the umpteen best jazz houses in New York: **greenwich house** (27 Barrow Street, 242-4140); **sweet basil jazz club** (88 Seventh Avenue, 242-1785); **arthur's tavern** (57 Grove Street, 675-6879); **bradley's** (70 University Place, 228-6440); **fat tuesday's** (190 Third Avenue, 533-7902); **55 bar** (55 Christopher Street, 929-9883); **village corner** (corner of Bleecker Street and La Guardia Place, 473-9762); **village vanguard** (178 Seventh Avenue South, 255-4037); and **visiones** (125 MacDougal Street, 673-5576).

section two

entertain, baby

How entertaining. Well, since New Yorkers are always so on the go, I decided to get busy and make a list.

After all, I get the feeling most of us would like to possess a key to what's going on at any given moment. What's the best dish? What's the best dish at a restaurant? Where's the best place to go for a date? Where're the best cabarets, concerts, events and the like? (For information on theater, dance, galleries, film, and video—and special music events—see Section 3, "Anything Arty".)

Anyway, now that you have all this information at your fingertips, two things will happen: first, you won't be reading about all this stuff in the *Times* after it happens and going, "Ah, damn, I missed it!" Then, you will find that you're so in the know, you'll soon be telling everyone too many stories about what's hot.

The following ten—count 'em, ten—chapters are meant to get you excited about New York. They include all aspects of a real good time. (Sex too.) Gays and lesbians will, however, note in all this reverie that the places mentioned may not be specifically queer-related. They are, some of them, meant for a mixed crew. The truth of it is that our city is truly a melting pot. We have to be the ones to join in the melt.

Included in this section are fine food we can't live without; a

entertain, baby

listing on bars and clubs that's as up-to-date as possible; several quiet places to romance someone special (or hot); a necessary shopping chapter; a chapter on freebies for the heart and soul; the all-important look at gyms to tone up and trim down (and meet people); jazz clubs, cabarets, the essential piano bars and musical events; and the last bit of good news: sex shops, sex parlors, sex theaters, sex notions, sexual turn-ons, and cruise spots.

Now, read, and cheer this great city for being so full.

chapter six

restaurants we can't live without no matter what!

■ **cheap**

food bar
   149 eighth avenue at west 17th street, 243-2020

The better variation of the upstart Universal Grill, described in "Moderate" below. The food is terrific (entrees $3 to $10) and the wine is served unpretentiously in orange-juice glasses. Of course the servers are cute—or very very nice—but they don't run around acting snobby like the ever-popular Universal thing. However, service here is terrible, so if you're in a rush go to Burger King at Sixth Avenue and 14th Street (243-6626). One other problem: Wouldn't it be nice if the owners removed all those silly tables so we could please dance!

gus' place
   149 waverly place, 645-8511

The tiny restaurant with the "cheap" pasta ($10.50 to $17.50) and no atmosphere whatsoever. Every gay man and lesbian has been here at least once if he or she has lived or worked in the Village. It's so tacky certain, baby

they use it as the reception for *Tony 'n' Tina's Wedding*, a farcical version of a typical Italian wedding that passes for a play. Gus' works —it's typically Italian and almost a farce. Go for the bread—strictly Italian loaves.

manatus
340 bleecker street, 989-7042

The twenty-four-hour bistro for the late-night set, Manatus is an expensive diner with decent food and a terrific-looking crowd. Prices begin at $5 for a salad and can end up around $14.

positively 104 street
2725 broadway at west 104th street, 316-0372

Fine place for lunch: decent, simple food at $5 to $8 and in a great neighborhood—the Morningside Heights that George Carlin once condescendingly called white Harlem. But the area is filled with old record stores, and since this place is a throwback to an old Dylan song, you can reminisce about the sixties here and enjoy a chicken sandwich for lunch. Closes early at ten, so don't consider a late meal here. Dinner? Same menu as lunch, only not as enticingly cheap!

※ **rocking horse mexican cafe**
182 eighth avenue at west 19th street, 463-9511

With an ever-changing chef in tow, Roe's rocking palace is a Chelsea favorite of gays and lesbians, with $10 burrito dishes and special sauces you would never expect from "another Mexican joint." Prices for entrees start at $6 for typical tacos and go to $16 for the steak fajita.

restaurants we can't live without no matter what!

sazerac house bar & grill
533 hudson street at barrow street, 989-0313

A salad and fish place for the weary-eyed local patron, Sazerac is one of those spots that amazes people because it's still in business. Everyone goes there but no one would ever recommend it. Food is $9 to $12, drinks expensive. But the waiter's been the waiter since it opened in the seventies.

time cafe
380 lafayette street, 533-7000

Great magazine rack, fantastic jukebox, good service, decent wine list; the food is just so-so. But lunch prices at this place start at $9 and go to $16, which is when most people in the NoHo (north of SoHo) go to Time Cafe for eats. Dinners are $9 to $16.50 and run to entrees including pizza-pasty and other faddish dishes. But really, why bother eating too much when you can read, look at the people and listen to the music? "Enjoy."

universal harmony
34 downing street, 675-4499

The quiet version of the up-to-date Universal Grill, with food that's harmonious and not as expensive as the Grill's. Entrees begin at $9 for burgers and go to $17.50 for pasta dishes. They're entertaining here like the waiters at the Grill, but they don't go out of their way to push the friendliness and make you think they need your business. They do need it, but Jack the owner is so kindly to those who grace his door that having a few drinks and a nosh here every now and then seems like a charitable thing to do. See Universal Grill in "Moderate" below.

entertain, baby

■ **moderate**

marion's/the kahiki lounge
354 bowery, 475-7621

A fun, loud East Village version of the Universal Grill (see below). It makes for a raucous good time for gays and lesbians who don't mind dining in the din. Prices for entrees are $7 to $14. Many of the items involve German/Hungarian/Polish cooking. That means it's heavy, so bring a huge appetite. Kahiki Lounge occurs midweek and on Friday night, and the drinks are cheaper.

nick and eddie's
203 spring street, 219-9090

Fine bistro—and in SoHo, where the fine ones are limited. Prices for Italian fare start at $7 and end up at $19. And the atmosphere is quite easy to take—nice ventilation, unsolicitous service—which for nighttime diners is rare.

paris commune
411 bleecker street, 929-0509

The oldest gay icon for eaters except for One Potato (see Chapter 7, "Bars All Around Town") and for a reason: seasonally changing foodstuffs for the adventurous, and a few good chicken dishes thrown in for color. Prices for entrees begin at $7 and end at $16, with a few specials priced higher on weekends.

universal grill
44 bedford street, 989-5621

The mother of all gay and lesbian restaurants. I have never seen people wait so long for a piece of chicken. Admittedly, Chris the cook is very cute and his Hungarian/Romanian recipes are scrumptious (priced ever

restaurants we can't live without no matter what!

so ridiculously at $9 to $17). But to make people wait because you feel like it is so eighties, and I would have to say pass on this elitist restaurant. And another thing—they scream and shout and play "She's a Lady" for *every* gay man's birthday. And charge you $8 for the measly slice of cake. Whoops, do I have an ax to grind . . . ? (This is also Jack's place, as is Universal Harmony.)

■ real expensive

black sheep
344 west 11th street, 242-1010

With entree prices starting at $16 and ending at $27, this anything-but-modest Village mainstay has been serving gays and lesbians (and stray heteros) for years. Its specialty is meat; come with a hearty appetite. Exceptional wine list *and* service.

cafe luxembourg
200 west 70th street, 873-7411

A very pricey joint that merits talking up because you can sit at the bar and, for $30 a person, eat a few appetizers and be seen with the merry. Entrees are $16 to $29. Very beautiful place with the best lighting in town. Oh, and there are tables.

entertain, baby

indochine
450 lafayette street, 505-5111

A great French bistro that remains trendy even as the block around it falls apart (Indochine is across from the crumbling Joseph Papp Public Theater). The prices begin at $10 (and end at $20), the food is scrumptious, and Bianca still calls it her home.

44 at the royalton
44 west 44th street, 944-8844

A fine dining experience for anyone who happens to be cruising midtown. Pricey (from $18 to $26 for an entree), this is a perfect place to start an evening, particularly since the small bar beside the entrance is a great spot to get plastered without any of your acquaintances noticing you. This is part of the fancy Royalton Hotel, where the young hosts who greet you are taught to speak with Southern accents (fake).

luma
200 ninth avenue at west 22nd street, 633-8033

For vegetarians only, dear. The food is exceptional: every veggie dish on earth, even yucca. Pricey, from $14 to $25 for an entree, and the service is slo-o-w. Which is odd, considering there are only nine tables. Go to Luma on special occasions and spend a long time there—you'll pay rent at the table. Order the soufflé without asking what's in it and you'll have an adventurous good time.

odeon
145 west broadway at duane street, 233-0507

Standard—one of *the* hip places of 1983. The food at this cafeteria is still good, though, and recommended by all gay and lesbian eaters I know: Entrees start at $11 and end at $21. And by the way, check out the bathrooms.

restaurants we can't live without no matter what!

provence
38 macdougal street, 475-7500

Pricey French cooking the way Mama wanted it: entrees at $14 to $21 ($31 for the "rare" couscous special) and a table by the window with a flower for your loved one. Not a *lot* of ambience, but what it has, it offers well.

roettele a.g.
126 east 7th street, 674-4140

A German-Italian-Swiss restaurant, the best of its kind—the only of its kind. Entrees start at a low $10 and end at $25, and the wine list is exceptional. Go in good weather, bring your favorite person, sit in the makeshift garden and listen to the yodelers or German crooners. Order the cold soup, the liver pâté and a bowl of fruit. Entrees? Sure, why not. How about the duck? Roettele, in the heart of the East Village, is a find—good food, good service, and very nice to all types. The music outside is authentic—and odd!

chapter seven

bars all around town

Bars, more than anything in New York City, are transient entities. They pop up, they go away. First there was The Slide on Bleecker Street in the early 1900s. Paresis Hall, on the Bowery around 1899, was for "fancy gentlemen," I'm told. For many years there was the Corduroy Club somewhere in midtown—a private men's organization and kind of posh. I read about wild weekly dances at SoHo's The Firehouse. Historian Lillian Faderman says lesbians in New York were a strong subculture before places like Network in Chelsea and The Duchess in the Village were opened in the 1970s. During the twenties and thirties, clubs for women and men—gay, straight, bisexual, white, black—were the Drool Inn, Clam House and Hot Feet—all in fashionable Harlem! The 1930s brought about private clubs. Heterodoxy was a middle-class professional organization made up largely of lesbians. Women had special places like Jo's and the famous series of clubs along the heavily populated MacDougal Street Strip in the thirties. Later on the women had respectable gay clubs such as the Flower Pot in the Village and Paul & Joe's nearby on West Ninth Street.

The rest is what you see today—Uncle Charlie's, The Break, Splash and all the bars that opened between 1970 and 1994. The only way to help preserve the watering hole you like today is to continue patronizing the place. Otherwise, even if the people are attractive, a

entertain, baby

place can be overrun by the "wrong crowd," those that may not drink and one that won't translate into money. Pretty soon that space will be out of business, since a bar must have regular customers to stay in business: regular drinking customers.

Here's a list of the places I think won't be going anywhere. (Hanjar Bar at 115 Christopher (627-2044) seemed, at press time, doomed.) They're in order of the gayest neighborhood to the least gay area in the five boroughs. Some of the recent additions are not here—because, I'll state outright, these places won't be around by the time you read this.

Some clubs, too, are just places to duck into and drink, then duck out of again. The major drama of the club scene is to be found in Chapter 8, "Dance and Sweat."

The bar scene changes every day. "To speak is a sin," said the Pet Shop Boys. It's very real in Manhattan bars. The following is an indication of just how wrong the old saying "You can't meet anyone in a bar" *must* be. I mean, look at how many there are!

All bars are open seven days at the described hours unless otherwise noted early in the entry. What may shock you is how incredibly early many of these establishments unlock the door to patrons. It's an odd fact, when you think that in most cities you can't find a decent bagel at eight in the morning!

I visited each bar at least three times—for accuracy's sake.
Drink.

■ chelsea

the break
232 eighth avenue at west 22nd street, 627-0072

The downtown sister of the uptown Works, this smallish bar has a very loyal crowd, a pool table, good-looking bartenders who are always publicly threatening to quit, and a Happy Hour you can depend on: Monday through Saturday 4 to 8 P.M. All drinks are two-for-one—they mean it. On Tuesday from 4 P.M. to 2 A.M., it's a two-for-one *pahty*. And on Thursday Margarita Night, $1 Mexican punch draws cheapo

bars all around town

locals in droves to the most crowded scene in Chelsea. Last summer The Break added a lovely outside area just to annoy the neighbors.

cellblock 28
28 ninth avenue at west 14th street

I add this to the bar chapter because you can actually come to this sex club and pay your ten bucks, have a drink, find your trick and mosey on home. No two-for-one here but it is definitely an adventure. The "Pump!" party is Wednesday night, a day or so away from the "Hot Ash Party," billed as a special time for real men who smoke cigars.

eagle's nest
142 eleventh avenue at west 21st street, 691-8451

An absolute pigsty that puts on a tough atmosphere. The *look* of the Eagle's Nest is what small-town American gay boys think all homo bars in New York must be like. (They're not.) On a positive note, two-for-one exists from 10 to 11 P.M., "with snacks." After two-for-one on Wednesday, they screen a second-run movie. No cover.

mammoth billiards
114 west 26 street
hours for special events vary
special number for lesbian events: karen, 718/857-1793 ♀

Pool halls are everywhere, and though this juice bar doesn't serve liquor, the atmosphere is too much like a bar not to mention it. Mammoth is not totally gentrified, and is not packed with a drunken crowd of rude boys. The lesbian group Gay Women's Athletic Club (718/857-1793) puts on special events here with the blessing of the management. For that, definitely patronize Mammoth. The "Valentine's Day Shoot-Out Party and Tournament" held by GWAC last year provided no liquor and was still a huge hit. If you missed it, you must have been at GWAC's all-lesbian event at Central Park's Wollman

entertain, baby

Rink, which was a hot ice happening. More lesbian events are held at Mammoth too. Ask the management.

rawhide
212 eighth avenue at west 21st street, 242-9332

Another holdover from a long-ago era, Rawhide ("Sir!") represents the time when entering a gay bar meant you had to act tough. (Once a lesbian bar on Sixth Avenue called Network made the girls act the same way.) The bar has on tap a group of people who frequent this place in search of, well, each other. If Norm from *Cheers* fame had been gay, you'd have found him here. One bartender told me, "It's a Western Levi look, but hey, dress as you like."

splash bar
50 west 17th street, 691-0073

On Chelsea's "boardwalk," the street where Chelsea Gym, Video Blitz, and lots of cute guys coexist, this is the bar Brian and Harry from The Pines opened after Brian was booted off Wall Street. The place has one terrific thing going for it: the boys who adorn its brightly painted walls . . . and I suppose the boys who take showers on top of the center bar each night between 10 and midnight. It's also some 162 steps from One More Thing: David Barton Gym, the center of musclehoodness.

If you see Harry or Brian knock on the bar, that means they're telling the bartender to "Smile!" Executive Hour every evening from 5 to 9 means two-for-one drinks and all the résumés you can handle. (Highlights from Broadway musicals instead of disco.)

the spike
120 eleventh avenue at west 19th street, 243-9688

Best leather bar in town and perhaps the only real one. Calling itself the headquarters of the New York leather scene, The Spike still plays more Bruce Hornsby than any other bar I know. Good music; a pool

bars all around town

table and the quickest way to get take-home sex in New York City! There's no two-for-one policy, but you can drink before you get in and have a nonalcoholic grand ole time. During summer it's fun outside this big bar, cruising and talking about Clinton's policies. Lastly, a big leather brunch is served on Sunday.

■ east village

the bar
68 second avenue at east 4th street, 674-9714

Dingy. Dark. Ugly. Beer smell. Strange boys. Loud music. Bartenders with arms folded. Newspapers strewn all over. The best bar around. Here you'll find a long pool table, a Budweiser Long Neck and maybe your type. No freebies, but boys are drinking and picking each other up. To paraphrase someone touring a locker room: "Look: men in various states of undress. What else could you need?"

boy bar
15 st. marks place, 674-7959
closed monday through wednesday

Truly a hateful place. You walk into a tunnelish entrance and the man at the door mutters, "Plenty to choose from," with a smirk. He isn't gay, and you go in anyway. The comfy neighborhood bar this once was is no longer. These days it's just trash, and it really smells like stale beer. Thursday is okay, because an outside promoter brings his Boy Bar Beauties to perform without their clothes on. Saturday night is dancing, two-for-one cocktails and $1 beers from 10 to midnight.

entertain, baby

crowbar
339 east 10th street, 807-9402 (unlisted)
regular hours except monday through wednesday 4 P.M. to 2 A.M. ♀

The back room at CB is quite nice, especially on Thursdays and Saturdays during the "Spunk" evening. Be warned that the bar is smoky, the proprietors often charge an entrance fee even if nobody's inside, and the place is loud! Friday night, "1984" continues to feature music from 1984 but the crowd has been thinning out lately. Call for information on events and staged readings during the week. Drinks start at four bucks a beer! Happy Hour is from 4 P.M. on, and there's a good deejay on tap. No pool. Two things: Women are especially welcome here, and there is a garden outside for cruising, right across the street from the newly refurbished, spacious Tompkins Square Park.

dick's bar
192 second avenue at east 12th street, 475-2071

An aptly named newcomer. Movies on Monday; $2 margaritas and a spinoff of New York's famous "Rock and Roll Fag Bar" Tuesday from 10 P.M. to 4 A.M.; videos and "Disco Dicks" sporadically spinning on Wednesday; Thursday brings $1 schnapps (10 P.M. to 4 A.M.); and Saturday and Sunday, domestic beer for $1.50 till 8 P.M. (Bloody Marys and screwdrivers are always $2). Now the bad news: Nobody comes to this place unless he intends going somewhere else soon after. Goes to show: The best Dicks always have character.

downtown beirut
158 first avenue at east 9th street, 260-4248
monday through saturday 10 A.M. to 4 A.M., sunday noon to 4 A.M.

I love to rock and roll . . . I love a man in uniform . . . I love it when you call me names. It's all at this rock-and-roll bar. A good rowdy crowd, $2 foreign beers, no Coors due to the boycott (see the Glossary for details), and a rollicking jukebox that has every band and song

bars all around town

misspelled. I have been cruised by more men who are with women at Downtown Beirut than anywhere in Manhattan. Need I say more?

gold bar
345 east 9th street, 505-8270 ♀

There are some mixed bars in this area, such as the ultra-trendy Tenth Street Lounge on 10th between First and Second avenues. Yet Gold Bar is my favorite: Years ago, I ran into this place quite by accident. The decor is gold, the place is run by friendly German folk and the floor is raised above a small storage room you can peek down into. Barmaids serve real German Dinkelbokker beer in large German glasses and you can talk to some interesting no-nonsense people who all dress in black. Fraulein is a mini-club set up for lesbians on Wednesday night where women discuss sexuality and politics, and mingle for no specific purpose. There's no cover, drinks are not cheap and *Das es die Kultur*.

tunnel bar
116 first avenue at east 7th street, 777-9232

The kind of place you want to walk into and say, "Okay, let's cut out the crap. Everybody—pair off now!" Smoky, low-key, with men everywhere waiting for the one guy they admire to make the first move. Great strip show on Tuesday night. No drink discounts.

wonder bar
505 east 6th street, 777-9105 ♀

Once upon a time this East Village bar was called the Chameleon. It was a nice size and it had friendly folks. The place showed movies and it was packed with locals who liked to talk. Someone said to me, "When the East Village gets its act together, a smart businessperson will turn this gay." Wah-la! It is now the friendliest bar around, and people are so loyal that there are birthday parties for the patrons. Lots

entertain, baby

of events and lots of women on Tuesday. There is, yes there is, a small back room for instant gratification, as one of Wonder Bar's many ads states. And it's on a very cool street. No two-for-ones. Drinks are pretty cheap and so are the boys.

■ **west village**

boots & saddle
 76 christopher street, 929-9684

An unusual place to spend an afternoon getting drunk, Boots & Saddle is a throwback to the sixties. Manager Rick explained that the bar is an international meeting ground, where guys round each other up from places like Israel, France, Colombia, what used to be Czechoslovakia, Venezuela, and the Caicos Islands. Happy Hour is 6 to 10 P.M. Sunday through Friday. The biggest parties here happen during what they call Leather Pride Week (June's Gay Pride Week). Although a Russian circus bear trainer was spotted at Boots recently, most of the dudes who arrive here decked in leather give this place a dark reputation. The sound system incorporates a bunch of old disco tunes and some new ones scraped together, though the system is touted as "quality laser CD technology by NSM of Germany."

crazy nanny's
 21 seventh avenue south at leroy street, 366-6312
 regular hours except saturday and sunday 3 to 4 A.M. ♀

A truly fun atmosphere, mostly lesbian, with a few gay guys thrown in for added color. There's a giant video screen and dancing every night, making Nanny's one of a few bars that allows people to move their bodies. (Most bar owners do not possess a cabaret license for dancing, so you'll often get stopped for dancing in taverns.) Two-for-one during Happy Hour, early evenings. Nanny's recently introduced women's percussion ensembles on Sunday evening and regular performances of

bars all around town

Middle Eastern belly dancing. Girls, don't confuse that with a Midwestern belly.

d.t.'s fat cat
281 west 12th street, 243-9041 ♀

Monday through Friday 4 to 7 P.M. Two-for-one beer and often a nosh (pizza, Chinese egg rolls, etc.). This place has outlasted the other lesbian hangouts that were strategically closed by the fire department over the years. It's a little less friendly than Nanny's. However, there's a nice piano in the midst of it all. When quizzed, a bartender said she wouldn't want the place to be "thought of as specifically lesbian or anything like that."

dugout
185 christopher street, 242-9113

Tough crowd, more leathery than most. Good for a goof, not for meeting men. "Fabulous Hour" takes place Monday through Friday from 4 to 8 P.M., with everything sold two-for-one. Considering the incredible business this place does on weekends, it's nice to see them give something back. But is *this* where you want to drink, even if they give it away?

the hangout, or j's
679 hudson street at west 13th street, 242-9272
open at 11 P.M. (closed monday)

Hardly a place for discount drinks, it's really a place to jerk off—with or without assistance. If you go here at about midnight, you have a drink, look around, and maybe find a date to bring to Splash. Two notes: One, see Chapter 15, "Where To Go When Everyone's Asleep," for other, similar adventures and more on J's. And two, jazz aficionados

entertain, baby

should know that their bar and club at Ninety-seventh and Broadway is also J's. Call 666-3600 for regular music fests, with $10 cover charges.

✷ henrietta hudson
438 hudson street at barrow street, 924-3347 ♀

This is a small bar that is growing in size and popularity; great juke, lots of video, almost all women. A neighborhood pit stop for *femme* cruising. Happy Hour is from 5 to 7 P.M. Recently, Robert Redford went into the newly enlarged bar and immediately walked out. Seems Redford was filming a movie there and wanted color, but not *that* much color!

hudson bar & books
636 hudson street at charles street, 229-2642

Not a gay bar, but this beautiful place offers British food and drink and atmosphere . . . and books to boot. You can read, you can browse and you can actually meet well-read men and women, straight and gay.

julius
159 west 10th street, 929-9672
monday through friday 8 A.M. to 2 A.M., sunday noon to 4 A.M. ("state law and all")

The most horrific place to ever have a drink in New York City. Julius stays in business because the barstool-warmers are indisputably loyal. (One of the thrills here is watching the cook prepare hamburgers at the grill.) The place should be called GH Downtown, a reference to the Grey Hair Club mentioned in the "East Side" section of this chapter. Two-for-one each day from 4 to 8 P.M. Gruff service. If you hang out at Julius, get to know the bartender. He'll be so happy for the kindness you'll probably get drunk for free.

bars all around town
keller's
384 west street at christopher street, 243-1907

No free drinks. No discount drinks. Pretty much nothing whatsoever. Keller's people were ridiculously rude while explaining the lack of benefits. The former listings writer for *The Advocate* called it "close enough to the piers." Meaning you can go cruise there while you're tanked up. More specifically, the ad for Keller's says, "Here We Are and Here We'll Stay." Rumor has it they mean the crud on the barstools. The crowd is made up of old men.

mike's bar
400 west 14th street, 691-6606 ♀

This is the place to be if you *never* go out: a charming spot where you might want to go for a business conference, though it does not seem conducive to making eyes at another man. The atmosphere is very cold; the crowd follows suit. Women are frequently seen there. Happy Hour is from 2 to 9 P.M.

monster
80 grove street, 924-3558

New York's only three-for-one club: piano bar, drinker bar and loud, sweaty disco for movers and shakers. There's a $5 cover on weekend nights, but often it's worth it. Happy Hour is Monday through Saturday from 4 to 9 P.M., which translates into two-for-one on all drinks. Even premium drinks get reduced in price. The place opens in the early afternoon for those who like to get a good start on those wild and wacky weekends. Or weekdays. There is definitely a certain crowd in here—the jaded bar-crawlers who have and still do it all. Feature: "Ms. Sherry's Madcap Show," the last Tuesday of the month.

entertain, baby

ninth circle
139 west 10th street, 243-9830

A really dingy bar with cheesy-looking bartenders. Downstairs they have a silly-seeming discotheque with a colorful rotating ball. As the legend goes (part one), there have always been a bunch of young hustlers adorning the wall. As the legend continues (part two), this place was a fashionable three-star steak restaurant in the sixties. And, as the legend concludes (part three), Edward Albee allegedly spotted a famous graffito in the bathroom one night ("Who's Afraid of Virginia Woolf?") when he was looking for titles. As for the Ninth Circle bar, circa 1994, the in-house promoters have tried desperately to bring in the new crowd. They do have a nice pool table, though.

pandora's box
70 grove street, 533-1652 ♀

Once known as Duchess, then Duchess II; Pandora's Box is the moniker now. Through it all, the space has always been crammed with a mixture of tough and tender dykes. I suspect they're all into bodies, but I am told that the talk is "more internal." One dollar off drinks from 4 to 7 P.M. Monday through Friday.

pieces
8 christopher street, 929-9291

A brand-new addition to the Christopher Street scene. There's a Happy Hour from 4 P.M. to 8 P.M. and a piano. Darts too. No atmosphere. Too bad Badlands, the classic Christopher bar holdout, didn't hold out long enough. Pieces does have a unique policy of calling out drink specials from the bar: "Now we're doing two-for-one on cloudy beers!" Bottles of domestic are always on special. Now that you've done the drinking, something else has to excite you. Not here, bud.

bars all around town
sneakers
392 west street, 242-9830

A dark place. Leave it at that. Two-for-one is "like from five to eight P.M.," I was told; and they only do it for beer. They are not friendly, but they do offer piña coladas and some *fabulous* blended drinks. They don't seem that excited about patronage, though.

stonewall
53 christopher street, 463-0950

Formerly New Jimmy's. Next door to #51, the original Stonewall Inn, where the riots of 1969 marked the beginning of gay liberation. The trappings of gay life are certainly different in this Stonewall. The police are gone—though there are a few curious holdovers—and owner Jimmy attempts to make the bar festive. But it is tiny, jammed and smoky, and the crowd is not all that friendly. Two-for-one all night on Tuesday and Monday through Friday from 4 to 9 P.M., while on Wednesday there's $1.50 beer. On Friday and Saturday Stonewall does the unusual: hires live deejays to spin danceable tunes. (Other bars have deejays to spin Top 40 and old Madonna *videos*.) Leather night on the second Friday of the month.

The bathrooms are crowded here, though the sign reads "One at a time, guys!"

See Chapter 3, "A Look at Gay Neighborhoods from the Most to the Least," for more on Stonewall the event.

two potato
145 christopher street, 242-9340

one potato
518 hudson street, 691-6260

Here's what the experts have to say about the Potatoes: two old-fashioned watering holes in the Village that are fun and ancient; Two

entertain, baby

Potato can offer a rollicking good time if you don't take decor seriously. It's been here since 1970! One Potato has Jerry Scott on the keyboards Friday and Saturday from 11 P.M. and Sunday from 9 P.M. Scott is the New York pianist who most reminds me of Bill Murray's Catskill entertainer from *Saturday Night Live*. And the Potatoes represent the oldest established gay bar/restaurant in the States. That's quite an accomplishment considering how fickle the gay scene is.

ty's
114 christopher street, 741-9641

I wrote to places like Ty's and said, "Hey, you guys are a mainstay in this business. Tell me something interesting for my guidebook on gay New York." I was shocked when Ty's chose to ignore three requests. They couldn't care less about anyone but the regulars and a few unlucky tourists too lazy to find a more promising bar. Keith, the bartender, is really nice; he tells me all about his monogamous relationship all the time. The bar itself is nothing special, no two-for-one, no air to breathe when you're in there, no decorative wallpaper.

uncle charlie's
56 greenwich avenue, 255-8787

Though the video monitors and sound system have each been updated, something about this bar spells o-l-d; so much so that Uncle Charlie's nearly passed on a few years ago when the aforementioned Splash opened up. But to the place's credit, it's been remodeled a little and the managers have been making an effort to get rid of the stale beer smell. Uncle Chuck's opens at 3 P.M. I like the Thursday-night "Hard Body" competition, for the mere fact that regular patrons show off gym handiwork.

Uncle Charlie's bills itself as "New York's Most Popular Bar . . . in the Heart of Greenwich Village." To which I respond: Who cares about either statement? Movies on Tuesday at 9 P.M. Friday brings dancers not unlike the ones at Splash. Sunday from 5 P.M. Uncle Charlie's offers $1 draft beers and $1.75 domestic bottled beer. Uncannily,

bars all around town

the place did not offer a Happy Hour until they discovered I was listing them . . . Now it's two for one Monday through Friday 5 to 9 P.M., and even hors d'oeuvres to boot.

■ west side

attitudes
30 west 48th street, no phone number
closed monday and frequently on other days

A fun place to go on weekends after you notice how tanked up you are. Go there at 3 A.M. and see what's up. Nothing's free and nothing's discounted. Mostly Attitudinal men, but hot ones.

candle bar
309 amsterdam avenue at west 74th street, 874-9155, 2 P.M. to 4 A.M.

Hard to believe this dingy place still exists. "Come hang out here and let's become best friends," the bartender exclaimed when I came in for a quickie. It's very dark in this old-style bar, which has been in operation since the early seventies. Yet frosty draft beer costs $1 during the week and the crowd is hardly dull. Sunday means it's $1 drafts, and two-for-one on schnapps. The bar starts serving liquor late. Candle Bar often charges a steep cover ($20 to $25) just to enter on the weekends.

cleo's ninth avenue saloon
650 ninth avenue at west 46th street, 307-1503

A fun drinking hole that calls itself a "mixed neighborhood bar." Not a particularly good idea to come here if you're thinking of acting gay; I noted that the bar mistresses do not take kindly to it. Cleo's does penny-rolling parties each month: They ask people to take pennies off the shelf, bring them in and roll ("Everyone, roll!") for God's Love We Deliver, a local AIDS charity that delivers food to homebound

entertain, baby

patients (see Chapter 28, "AIDS Pages"). Cleo's will pick up your pennies for you, which is a damn good offer. No discount drinks, but the friendliest barflies for miles. When you've seen as many bars as I have recently, that's a nice thing. It's the place where *nobody* knows your name.

escuelita
607 eighth avenue at west 41st street, no phone service in building; hours unavailable

Humpy boys and sweaty dancing. Many Latinos and the requisite number of white boys looking for them. No discount drinks at all. But you don't need them here.

hombre
355 west 41st street, 560-9635

Ahem. Best thing I can say is that on Friday night Hombre holds a Big Dick Contest that beats going to your mom's for supper. This bar is pure Port Authority, meaning everyone looks like he just got off a bus. They have bingo on Saturday night—dark bingo—and hot finger foods on Friday and Saturday. Ask for Lou Lou the bartender. Happy Hour is "around four to nine P.M."; to make things confusing, Monday, Tuesday and Wednesday are $10 all-you-can-drink nights. Pure Port Authority also means the men will take you for a sweet ride!

sally's ii at the carter hotel
252 west 43rd street, 944-6000

This place cracks me up. It's in the back of the transient Carter Hotel. All kinds of fun-loving transvestites and their musclebound mates hang out here to watch go-go boys and sometimes an oldies crooner. It's a hoot. Two-for-one? Don't push it.

bars all around town

the works
428 columbus avenue at west 81st street, 799-7365

The guppiest of gay bars. There are some incredible floor shows here —and that's the crowd. Some decent deejays and the best and most original videos shown each night. (One veejay got a bootleg of Jennifer Holiday singing *Dreamgirls*.) A fun atmosphere when it's not too crowded (any weekday evening), but then again, a gay bar on the Upper West Side is sincerely an oxymoron. When you walk up Columbus Avenue, you see many closeted soap actors. The bar is very touristy and offers many discounts: two-for-one Tuesday and spot dollar drafts for twenty minutes at a time, whenever a bartender calls one out. Friday and Saturday, before it gets late, you can find yourself buying $1 margaritas for strangers. You'll often have to wait to get into the ever-popular Beer Blast on Sunday night (6 P.M. to 1 A.M.; $6).

■ **east side**

grey hair club (gh club)
353 east 53rd street, 223-9752

Older crowd, very entertaining. Cheap drinks. Go after you've done it all and want nothing else. Sunday's Beer Blast is from 6 P.M. to 2 A.M. It's like the Pepsi commercials when the old people get a charge from the energy of being around youth. Happy Hour from 4 to 7 P.M. every day they manage to open.

julie's
204 east 58th street, 688-1294 ♀

A very pretty bar that opens late in the afternoon and caters to women who want to have fun with their peers, and that includes peers of all ages networking and "cruising," as women will do. There are no Happy Hour specifics, but specials (cheap margaritas and shots for a buck) occur nearly every day. There is always entertainment of some sort. What's nice is that the management is so laid back that depending on

entertain, baby

how busy it is, Julie's will close whenever they feel it's necessary—or stay open all night long.

rounds
303 east 53rd street, 593-0807

A place to go when you want to *sell* it or *buy* it. No discounts. Then again, the boys might discount themselves.

south dakota, or dakota's
405 third avenue at east 29th street, 684-8376

Dark, dingy and anything but atmospheric. There's a rumor that many folks have met long-term spouses here. Don't make a special trip, though, because while Dakota's advertises itself as a Western bar, it's lying. Cute boys are not really here and there isn't a cowboy in the pokey. Monday through Thursday, the ad continues, it's "Two for one on everything." But men will always be expensive.

star sapphire
400 east 59th street, 688-4710

Chinese, Japanese, Korean, Vietnamese . . . ready for action. (In addition, Cuba, Honduras, Thailand, Tibet, Australia and Europe are represented here. Sort of the UN of boozing it up.) Great dancing, and you don't have to pay anybody for it. Boys have been rumored to sit on your lap while they pour drinks down your gullet. Each night there are special prices proffered on something, whether it's vodka, gin, frozen drinks or domestic beer. It's an odd place, but there's a pool table, game machines and dancing without a cover! No two-for-ones.

bars all around town

townhouse of new york
236 east 58th street, 754-4649

This classy two-tier bar is filled with gentlemen who mingle after hours and throw glances toward each other in a very discreet, nonjudgmental manner. The owner told me he likens the place to an "elegant hideaway," which is New Yorkese for "Upper East Side snobby." Singalongs occur regularly around the ole piano. No two-for-ones, but a very long Happy Hour (5 to 8 P.M.) with reduced prices on most drinks. Top 40 music in the background will not induce the need for Advil. What a place to meet a buddy before the Met, or to go after the Met and meet a new buddy to take the next time . . .

■ brooklyn

hot spot/after 5
5 front street, brooklyn heights, 718/852-0139 ♀

Called Hot Spot, the bar got mocking press coverage. Both names are bad, because people show up *way* after five! The bar is in Brooklyn Heights, which is a pretty groovy place for a gay guy or girl to be, because the residents are pretty hip and the streets have a few very nice boutiques and eateries. Two-for-one drinks Monday through Saturday from 5 to 8 P.M. After 5 advertises "Bar Restaurant Disco Cabaret Show Private Parties" in gay and lesbian magazines. That's an awful lot to do in one spot, which is why the place doesn't excel in a single thing. The cabaret upstairs is a real yawnster, and the piano is off-key. Though the bar was just fine, the dance floor is postage-stamp size and the bartender hadn't heard of a Madras.

entertain, baby

■ **queens**

breadstix
113–24 queens boulevard, forest hills, 718/263-0300

On two visits to Breadstix I truly had fun. The music is good, the videos are up to date and the people love coming here. Monday offers two-for-one on rack drinks from 10 P.M. to 2 A.M.; Tuesday two-for-one on all drinks. Wednesday means two-for-one on beer 10 P.M. to 2 A.M. Thursday is "South of the Border" night for anything even remotely sounding like Mexican. At press time Breadstix had added "Breadstix Exercise Men," an exercise routine on a Soloflex, on several nights. Hot Queens men. "A City Club Without the Trip."

friends tavern
78–11 roosevelt avenue, jackson heights, 718/397-7256

It's dark in there, but the wide-screen television plays nightly network fare and this year's music videos. Multitudes of Latinos are the draw. Extra-friendly bartenders. On Saturday and Sunday afternoon try the delicious barbecued beef on the terrace.

hatfield's
126–10 queens boulevard, kew gardens, 718/261-8484 ♀

A fun, loose place with lots of cute boys; problem is, nobody is especially forthcoming. It appeared that most were on the verge of coming out to their closest friends! There is a Happy Hour (*one* hour) and a liberal dose of drag shows and other quasi-entertainment. Be careful—inhospitable and hardly liberal neighborhood. Lesbian night on Tuesdays and Fridays—always.

You can always end up at one of the following, but at your own bargoing risk. These are very uninteresting to the naked bar-eye, but you might one day be stuck in a neighborhood that you discover to be Queens. Best bets: **magic touch**, 73–12 37th Road, Jackson

bars all around town

Heights, 718/429-8605; **montana saloon,** 48–08 74th Street, Jackson Heights, 718/429-9356 (for the record: a dartboard here!); **naked city,** 56–01 Queens Boulevard, Woodside, 718/899-9031; and **bachelor's tavern,** 81–12 Roosevelt Avenue, Jackson Heights, 718/458-3131.

Keep in mind, barhoppers, that new places for straights, gays, and the "betweens" are popping up everywhere. For two examples, see the **tenth street lounge** in the old gas station on Tenth between 1st and 2nd, and the **twelfth street bar** on 12th and Eighth Avenue in Park Slope, Brooklyn.

Drink up!

chapter eight

dance and sweat (clubgoing)

In other chapters I take a wholesome look at gay and lesbian culture, but it's important to look at clubs with an overtly critical eye. Nightclubs have been an important part of the scene since the early sixties; nobody has thought of anything that new since the days of go-go. So anyone with the gall to open a club had better do it perfectly. In the 1980s clubs peaked. When I list the clubs that were either gay or partially gay and lesbian during the eighties, today's paucity of nightspots seems criminal:

El Morocco, Max's Kansas City, The Continental, The 80's, Chase Park, Tier Three, Mudd Club, Trax, Baja, Peppermint Lounge, The Savoy, The Roxy, The Saint, Bond's, Xenon, Shout, Studio, Five, The Underground, Roseland, Danceteria, The Palace, Le Jardin, Earth's Edge, Zipper's, Beulah Land, Darinka, ABC No Rio, Zulu Lounge, Casey's Dancehall, Alibi, Reggae Lounge, Berlin, The Great American Dance Club, Rage, Island Club, Surf Club, Milk Bar, Nimbus 22, Milky Way, Private Eyes, Johnny Rocket, 40 Worth, Cheyenne Social Club, Zone dk, Lonestar Roadhouse, The Pyramid, Jammin', Nick's Grove, Chevy's, Hotrods, Sonic, Magique, Chippendale, Bedrox, Stringfellow's, Club Paradise, Limelight, The Tunnel, Horatio 113, and The Jungle Jim Club.

Whew.

entertain, baby

So, what's the story today?

Gay people have the four hottest clubs in town. Four. And only two are mentioned above. The Roxy, USA, Limelight and The Sound Factory Bar are the only hot gay places.

A few years ago you would have laughed aloud at the thought of four measly clubs existing for gays. That's the downside. In truth, there are now more than forty places (twelve more counting mainstream clubs that do a gay or lesbian night) where you can party your brains out in a single night. That figure translates to more than ever before. Keep in mind that several of these clubs have benefit nights, where monies collected at the door go to AIDS activism and health, social and other community groups. (For more on giving money, see Chapter 29, "Volunteerism.") This chapter discusses the many places that let charities collect door money, a good way for you to spend your beer allowance.

For this chapter, I've chosen to discuss clubs in categories rather than list them. "The Four" discusses the big ones; "Hot, Hot" is a look at what's still worth wandering into; "Definition of a Standard" mentions five biggies; "The Lukewarm" consists of a few that must be mentioned in a gay and lesbian guidebook; "Extra" is truly unusual because you wouldn't think these places are gay-friendly; and my favorite is the last: "Sunday, the Special Night that Might Be Worth Considering."

Instructions: Go to a club as late as possible. If you go before midnight, expect a dud crowd (except on school nights, when it's feasible to go at about 10:30). Clubs open at 10 P.M. Be the first to arrive, be the first to leave.

Now, take a deep breath—get ready, rev up. Roar . . .

■ the four: limelight, sound factory bar, the roxy, club usa

"It's time to strip down some of the nightlife garbage," says Chip Duckett, granddaddy of the gay club scene and the man who invented one-night-only gay and mixed events. Duckett has more than 30,000 men and women tied to his list of good times in the city. They get the

dance and sweat (clubgoing)

mail—revelers have a seriously fantastic time—and he gets the revenues. It's quite a system.

Though Duckett is more involved in the fight to stop the bigots in Colorado, he's into promoting Friday at the former **mea culpa** (47 West 20th Street, 268-4527, or *fax* to be on a mailing list, 268-5258), which in Latin translates to "through my fault." (Have you ever noticed that gay-run establishments have names that bolster guilt?)

Mea Culpa, now called **res-erection,** has three floors of men, or so the club advertises, and the "ceremonies"—see the list after this paragraph—commence at 11 P.M. each Friday. The location is the old club Limelight, which I'll discuss in detail farther down. This is what Mea advertises:

> Fornicators on the Third Floor
> Voyeurs on the Second
> Acts of Contrition on the Chapel Dance Floor

All that is true.

limelight (47 West 20th Street, 807-7850) is worthwhile for **disco 2000** house parties occurring midweek (also called **queer u** for its propensity to attract college-age boys). It's also good on weekends for a nice, totally acceptable mixed crowd who have no idea where else to go. It's never totally gay, and no one knows why so many are attracted to this place. After all, the Limelight was hot in . . . 1984! Call to get on the party mailing list. Remember, "party" means promotional party in Limelight language, so prepare to shell out $7 for a drink.

For the true queer, Wednesday and Friday are it. Those are the nights when alternatively named Res-erection and **lick it! lounge** parties invite you to "do it up," upstairs in the room outside the library, which is very hot and very sticky.

If you get on the mailing list by calling or filling out a form at the club, they will send you an aptly named Fag Tag, which will gain you discounted admission to these nights; anything at **club usa;** and whatever is happening these days to the club sometimes called **nocturnal** but always known as **tunnel** (Twelfth Avenue and West 27th Street). It is still changing at press time.

One evening the ultimate go-go boy contest was going on during

entertain, baby

Lick It!'s Wednesday 2 A.M. busy period. I saw several of the most ripped men (see the Glossary) I have ever witnessed—and they were proud of their gym work. Advertised as the "horniest, humpiest, hottest men in New York," the evening proved true to its promotion.

On those nights, enter through the side (not the rear) and pay your $12—or shmooze the doorman, who will think you're cute, show off his power, and rush you through the entrance.

Note: On Monday, Limelight often holds **party with a cause,** with dancing from 5 to midnight. You pay $5 suggested admission and they give it to one group on a list of AIDS- and gay-related charities. You decide who gets the moolah; if you give zip, Limelight will donate $1 to that group.

Across from the former Cadillac is the video-inundated dance floor that is **sound factory bar** (12 West 21st Street, 206-7771). This is not to be confused with the Sound Factory house music fest that happens on Saturday and Sunday night early in the morning. (See below.) Some may classify SFB as a terrific evening, but only on Friday is it anything but precocious. Fridays; drinks are two-for-one and there are strippers. Anyone can get on the mailing list, which means you'll receive a card in the mail allowing you free admission. Call the above number and hear the agenda for Sunday—see below—because that's when the *poseurs* (see the Glossary) go out and Friday's friendliness all but disappears.

For weekday excursions, there's **the roxy** (West 18th Street and Tenth Avenue, 645-5156, admission about $17), which used to be a trusty place for having a great time almost every night—and especially on Sunday. But now it's closed on Sunday and the place, which has had more incarnations than Cher, is having problems with its latest look. The giant dance floor and long bar look has faded, and it's so-o loud.

Also, unlike every other club venue in town, the Roxy has a door policy and is picky about whom it allows to enter. It's a little silly, considering the place charges $5 for beer and about $10 for anything harder. The Roxy as club people knew it exists only a few nights each week now, but it's still pretty hot on Saturday night, at a party called **locomotion.** (Roxy is closed Friday.) Admission is $10 to $15, depending on which night you attempt it. Roxy on Tuesday has roller-dancing on the main dance floor that complements regular dancing

dance and sweat (clubgoing)

("Rollerballs," or gay men on wheels) in the Crystal Room, for ten bucks, skate rental extra. I recommend hitting Roxy on Thursday for **disco interruptus,** a big-time dance and performance art party that features hot tunes from the past. The deejay is one of my favorites, Sister Dimension, who used to spin at the Pyramid. On Thursday, LaHoma, late of the now-defunct Palace De Beauté, spins fab sounds in the lounge.

Disco Interruptus is so popular that Roxy has hired a "Door Censor" named Chauncy. Don't like the way that sounds? Spend your money elsewhere and make a statement.

club usa (218 West 47th Street, at Broadway, 869-6103), managed by Peter Gatien of Limelight/Palladium/Tunnel (Nocturnal) fame, is a wonderful idea for a club: the space for those with a tiny attention span. The best bet is on Friday—that is, on the top floor—when gay men hang out together while heteros hang out downstairs. However, on Sunday it's the official home to gay life. At West Forty-seventh and Broadway, Club USA has a room for disco dancers, a room for house music, a rock-and-roll room, a sex room, a video floor for porn-watching, a space for hanging with your friends, outdoor tables for drinking, and in summer and fall, a beautiful roof on the sixth floor where we can watch the stars together. Romance at a nightclub. Wow. Lots of room to get lost—or to lose the people you're with. Sunday at USA is friendly to women and straight people who like to dance. (Friday and much of the week are devoted to heteros, and though the music is hot, the crowd appears to be nasty and definitely not into us fags. Read: unsophisticated.)

One unusual factor on Sunday: Club USA features a long tunnel-like passageway that's so narrow that you have no choice but to be friendly with the person you're squeezing by. It's an automatic attitude adjuster! (See the K-Hole, a gigantic slide from floor four to the ground.) What fun. Costs $15 to get in.

entertain, baby

■ hot, hot: lickety split, pyramid-for-women, boy bar, jackie 60, grand

Roving. That's the name for a party that never settles down. At press time the best one for rave-wishes (a "rave" is a party for house music aficionados; see the Glossary) is titled **lickety split.** Call 281-1703. Eight bucks.

Women: Go to **pyramid** for your first-ever fantastic nightclub experience that is totally run by lesbians. At Pyramid Club on Thursday only, it's called **pure party** and it's $5. Pyramid is at 101 Avenue A, 473-7184. **boy bar** is Thursday night: Boy Bar Beauties and hot men. Costs $7. 15 St. Marks Place, 674-7959. Often a wild party. **jackie 60** is my favorite club experience. No pretensions, just a good $10 time at 432 West 14th Street (no phone number). Bizarre performances, drag shows for the elite, readings. A lot of drama. Good for the soul, I would say. Tuesday only.

As this book went to press, a fantastic party was occurring each Thursday night at **grand,** a new club at 76 East 13th Street (777-0600)—a space that has been occupied by some of the worst nightclubs this reporter has laid eyes on. Drag shows, glitz, a theme, good Larry Tee deejay mixing, and a feast for the eyes—men! What more? How about discount drinks, a first for clubs. Costs $12 and is worthwhile.

■ definition of a standard: meat, clit club, bartsch-events, spectrum, saint-at-large

Saturday is **meat** night. (Meat is a club at 432 West 14th Street, or often at 101 Avenue A; 366-5685.) The event may be held at Pyramind Club. The club has beautiful, mentally alert types who can dance. Mm, they can dance. Admission is $7, beer's $4. See Chapter 15, "Where to Go When Everyone's Asleep," for specific details.

Same space, same channel, same price: Friday is **clit club.** But show up early, because the girls like to go to bed a little sooner! Let me tell you, Julie does a great job of getting ladies of all types to pack the place—and even some who aren't ladies.

bartsch events: Long-legged Suzanne Bartsch, who had a baby recently by gym proprietor David Barton of homosexual-gym

dance and sweat (clubgoing)

fame (go figure), is the wonderwoman who chairs the Love Ball, a giant event that raises a few hundred thousand for AIDS research. She is hostess of the mostess of Palladium's New Year's ball (often held at other night spots; who can tell these days) and also used to do the Copa events before the Copa was closed down by its lazy management and reopened as a "straight" club all the way over near the river on West 57th Street. (Get with the program and *update* if you want to make the grade in the nineties, they thought. *Wrong!*)

Anyway, Bartsch is now knocking them down during monthly soireés at Central Park's tres chic Tavern on the Green, so call Tavern (873-3200), and Grand, where Bartsch often does her thing.

I would get pinched if I didn't bring up **spectrum** (802 64th Street, Bay Ridge, 718/238-8213), located in a fierce Brooklyn neighborhood. This is where Tony Manero (John Travolta) went dancing every night in *Saturday Night Fever*. The spinning disco ball is still there, but Spectrum is out of the realm of the disco queens and is now 100 percent gay. "Hey, Tone!" is heard so often that you'll think you're at an Anthony Convention.

■ **the lukewarm: edelweiss, sugar babies, dimensions, flamingo east, cactus club, the village gate, space, shescape, six bond, palladium**

Nightclubbing in New York is no longer a divided scene. On various nights during the week, gay partyers can check into clubs. Gays and lesbians are welcome, as are nongay partygoers who, in the words of one promoter, "behave."

Though it used to be fun, **edelweiss** is no longer the great transvestite gender-bender wonderhouse it once was. They tried to move it to the famous 20th Street club row, but the place got vandalized *before* it officially opened. Now it's at Eleventh Avenue and 43rd Street—you need to call 629-1021 to find its latest location, I'm told—where Big City often hangs a shingle. If you're on the lookout for a transsexual lover, or you want a good show, this $5 to $10 hangout is your best bet. On Friday and Saturday it's half price for couples. Aw, family values.

entertain, baby

sugar babies (CB's Gallery, 313 Bowery, adjacent to CBGB Punk Club, 477-8427, $4) is an event for boys who are white or Hispanic, not for anyone else. It's the event of the year for Monday-nighters, devised by Sugar Reef restaurant. Other nights, too.

dimensions (Tilt Nightclub, 179 Varick Street, 463-0509, $10) is another attempt by a straight club to go gay. Nice house music.

Salon Wednesday is a hot thing at **flamingo east** (219 Second Avenue, 533-2860), where soul aficionados jam with a great deejay and many of the most inspiring drag queens I've ever met. It's absolutely free. These are the nights you drink, sweat and never regret.

cactus club offers lessons in two-stepping at 327 West 13th Street (631-1079) from 9 P.M. No cover, drinks expensive. Locations change.

At the well-known **village gate** (Thompson and Bleecker streets, 475-5120), which I call The Gate, owner Art D'Lugoff has begun leasing his upstairs room to **girl gate,** a lesbian floating nightclub. He claims the only reason he didn't do so before is because he wasn't asked. "This is a good business deal," he said plainly.

The party planners at **space** (555 West 33rd Street, 947-0400), a gigantic and fairly staid place in the middle of nowhere, have hosted a Friday event right after work called "Jam Session," marketed to men of color. Probably soon to go under.

The passé lesbian event **shescape** takes place at Warsaw (17 West 19th Street), Crane Club (408 Amsterdam Avenue) and Nell's (246 West 14th Street), on alternate Wednesday nights. Call 645-6479. And remember—look sharp. Each week Shescape has a different locale. (And at press time, Warsaw, a small club that failed in its quest to attract men, has Women On Saturdays for $10.)

The low-key downtown venture **six bond** (6 Bond Street, 979-6565) sometimes has "parties for women" on Saturday night.

dance and sweat (clubgoing)
■ extra: a whole bunch

A mess of clubs that will be gone in a matter of months exist now. I can't recommend them because they don't have longevity, but for the adventurous, here goes.

I've included here special dances and parties that didn't fit anywhere else. There are tons of places that qualify as "dives"; for your edification, they include **hatfield's** in Kew Gardens (718/261-8484); **visions** in Woodside (718/846-7131); **excalibur,** a shack behind a football stadium in Hoboken, New Jersey (201/795-1161), and **the box,** a lesbian one-nighter that opens and closes seemingly every week on Grove Street (533-1652). **more men!** (239 Eleventh Avenue, 633-0701) comes via promoters James St. James and Bella Bolski. Often open and often closed. And Thursday nights, the club offers something called "percussion." **tribeca transfer** (148 Chambers Street, 385-7572) is a Kool Komrads' Saturday venture: This club has a habit of staying open until 7 A.M. Not really good if you plan to have a Sunday. **stingray** (641 West 51st Street, 664-8688) is so unclassy no one ever bothers to go. However, for an adventure find this club on the corner of 51st and the West Side Highway. It is *very* Hispanic and only a little gay. **columbia university gay and lesbian dances** (Earl Hall, West 116th Street and Broadway, 629-1989) hosts a dance called "SamE BuT DifferenT" on the third Saturday of each month; admission costs $5. The crowd? A mix of students, wallflowers, pretty boys and sexy gals. Sort of a gay version of your junior prom. Often a very nice youngster-driven crowd. The music is Top 40. *Totally,* man. **the lesbian and gay community services center** (208 West 13th Street, 620-7310) actually holds some of the most incredible dances just for women. Some are for men too, and some mix the two. Usually $8. **night of a thousand gowns** (Roosevelt Hotel, Grand Ballroom, East 45th Street and Madison Avenue, 794-8780) is a $100-ticket event that occurs in mid-March and benefits the L and G Center. It's sponsored by the Imperial Court of New York and hotel rooms are available at good rates. **bedrox!** (316 West 49th Street, 246-8976) is a truly split-personality nightclub. Thus your guess is as good as mine. **sound factory** (530 West 27th Street, 643-0728) is a hellhole of house music and sweaty bodies. Rough, mixed crowd—hard to tell who's of what persuasion. No liquor. And there's an $18 cover charge! No shit.

entertain, baby

better days (316 West 49th Street, 245-8925) is a club set up mostly for men of color; dance to heavy, stomping house music. An add-on is the **new york bondage club** (7280 JAF Station, New York, 10116, locations vary, obviously; 315-0400), a place where people get together to tie each other up—in a friendly fashion, y'know. And **knights wrestling club** (208 West 13th Street, 718/639-5141), has men's and women's training sessions for aficionados of sweating on Saturday, soirees on Sunday.

■ sunday, the special night that might be worth considering

Do us a favor—save Saturday for the bridge and causeway people, and do a Sunday-evening dance-a-thon. Start at **atlantis** (15 John Street, 486-0506, $5), a tea dance (see the Glossary) where the theme is water and includes mermen; go up to the night-to-end-all-nights at **crowbar** (339 East 10th Street, 420-0670, $3), where the theme is "Butch Up!"; head down to Cafe Con Leche at the previously tacky **fuji's tropicana** (Fifth Avenue and East 13th Street, 243-7900, $5), a theme party changing every week, but with a fantastic roof deck; and end up at the often-Sunday-happening **sugar in the raw at sugar reef** (see above Sugar Babies), a bitching good time at 93 Second Avenue (47S-UGAR, $1!). You will then of course be Bump!'d at the above-ballyhooed **usa** (Broadway at West 47th Street, 869-6103) and if that doesn't do it for you, go off to **the playground** at the aforementioned **sound factory bar** (formerly Private Eyes Video Bar, 12 West 21st Street, 206-7770, $8, or free before 10 P.M.), where the boys are sweating even in dead winter. House—butch—a whirling light—no video monitors! . . . And to prove wrong those readers who think I'm *not* a purist, here's the oldest nightclub on earth: the aptly named **monster**, 80 Grove Street at the corner of Stonewall Place. This usually free bastion of New York late-night life charges $10 on weekends and on nights when they know people must come in (Gay Pride Week . . .). It's a disco, it's a piano bar, a cruise bar, a floor wax . . . Call 924-3558 for more specifics. And if you're drunk, the deejay may save your life that night by playing a

dance and sweat (clubgoing)

dance-music craze in the sweltering heat and dim light of the basement. Not a very pretty sight. Open till 4 A.M.

Note: Try as we might to keep this chapter up-to-date, it is recommended that you *call* each place before venturing out. Club promoters are a fickle bunch, you know.

As I'm going to press with this thing: USA announces it's up to its neck in boys with "Four-play" (yes, famous boys too!) on Thursday evenings; Grand says "Fever," with boys and girls on Thursday nights; Crazy Nanny's, the aforementioned lesbian hangout (see the chapter before this) says "Gee!" and dances away Monday nights; and Sugar Babies, talked about ad infinitum in this chapter, goes to CB's Gallery at 313 Bowery for its weekly Monday nights. (CB's was once a punk club, so gather the irony in this!) All else going on will be done with by the time you read this—except for the lesbian happenings on Wednesday nights at Crane Club, 408 Amsterdam Avenue, an often hip bar for all types. Call 645-6479 and get on the list, girl. Oh, another thing: What's with this **kingdom hall**, the name of the place where Jehovah's Witnesses meet, this being a club at 23rd Street and Eleventh Avenue. I pass it driving to the West Side Highway on the way to my parents'. On Wednesday it offers something titled "Reign" and has "men" on the sign. You go figure by calling 388-8711. Tell them to change the venue's name. Thank you.

That's the scoop on dancing. Go and get your Keds out and play.

chapter nine

quiet places for romance

■ teas and bars

the algonquin
59 west 44th street, 840-6800

The hotel that New York's 1920's and 30's literati made famous retains its dowdy and respectable air. It's nonetheless one of the most comfortable and welcoming sites in midtown. The chairs in the lobby are mismatched. Drinks are served.

danal
90 east 10th street, 982-6930

This is a great place for afternoon tea. The menu includes sandwiches, scones, desserts, and tea all prepared on the premises. Tea is prix fixe at $12 and reservations are required. Danal accepts reservations for seatings Wednesday through Saturday between 3:30 and 4:30 P.M. (though, of course, patrons may sit beyond 4:30). Danal also serves Continental breakfast, lunch and dinner. In the winter it's French country bistro food (stews, soups, roasts, etc.) and in the summer it's

entertain, baby

California cuisine (salsas, vegetables, salads, grills). Reservations are also recommended for dinner. Hours are Wednesday through Sunday from 10 A.M. to 10 P.M., Sunday 11 A.M. to 3:30 P.M. for brunch only. Enjoy yourself in the garden when weather permits. No liquor is available but BYOB is allowed.

the omni at berkshire place
21 east 52nd street, 753-5800

Omni sets aside most of its lobby, "The Atrium," as a civilized cocktail lounge where you can enjoy afternoon tea, cocktails, an assortment of sandwiches and pastries and a harpist. Also at the Omni, in the Rendezvous Bar, you'll find cocktails, lunch and more.

the peninsula
700 fifth avenue at 55th street (southwest corner), 247-2200

This was formerly the Gotham, one of midtown's oldest hotels. The new owners have upgraded it from a tourist attraction to an elegant but friendly place for meetings or trysts. A lovely afternoon tea is served daily from 2:30 to 5 P.M. in the grandish Gotham Lounge. The menu consists of finger sandwiches, scones, pastries, cakes and tea or coffee for $20 a person. Alternately, cocktails are served at the Pen-Top Bar, on the roof. During the summer you can enjoy the warmth outdoors, and in the winter you can stay warm inside a greenhouse room. The roof offers a smashing view of Fifth Avenue, particularly of Trump Tower.

rihga royal hotel
151 west 54th street, 307-5000

In the Halcyon Room you'll find an afternoon tea menu featuring a selection of tea sandwiches, scones, cookies, coffee and tea. Very stuffy. Stay here if you are in the mood to impress.

quiet places for romance

top of the sixes
666 fifth avenue at west 53rd street, 757-6662

The penthouse lounge on the thirty-ninth floor has a Happy Hour from 4 to 7 P.M. Monday through Friday.

■ gardens

brooklyn botanic garden
100 washington avenue, brooklyn, 718/622-4433

Here you'll find fifty-two luscious acres including a Japanese hill and pond garden, a rose garden, local flora, the Osborne formal garden, an herb garden and a Shakespeare garden. The grounds are very well maintained and very lovely. There's a conservatory with three pavilions, known for the best bonsai collection in the USA. Join a walking tour at 1 P.M. on Saturday and Sunday, or if you want to learn a little, you might try the special-topic walks and lectures (e.g., see the azaleas and then hear a lecture). The annual Cherry Blossom Festival is wildly popular. Oh, and don't forget to visit the Garden Shop and Terrace Cafe. The garden is just adjacent to the Brooklyn Museum and Prospect Park, and admission is free. Hours: Summer, Tuesday through Friday 8 A.M. to 6 P.M.; Saturday and Sunday 10 A.M. to 6 P.M. October through March, Tuesday through Friday 8 A.M. to 4:30 P.M.; Saturday and Sunday 10 A.M. to 4:30 P.M. To get there, take the 2 or 3 train to the Eastern Parkway Station or hop in your car. The parking lot is attended.

horticultural society of new york
128 west 58th street between sixth and seventh avenues, 757-0915

The Horticultural Society offers a series of classes, lectures and tours of its gardens and nurseries. The society also conducts workshops on topics such as "How to Build a Terrace Garden" or "Cooking with Herbs." In March, the society sponsors the annual New York Flower Show. There is a library which nonmembers may use (but not borrow

entertain, baby

from). And for those interested in shopping, there's a shop selling horticulture-related items like plants, seeds and gardening equipment, and books and greeting cards. The fees for the workshops vary, so call for details and a schedule of events.

new york botanical garden
southern boulevard and east 200th street, bronx, 718/817-8705

Here you can wander through seventeen specialty gardens covering 250 acres. These gardens are host to thematic weekends (Floral Weekend, Perennial Weekend, Day Lilies Day, Harvest Festival, etc.). While you're there, take one of the guided tours offered daily or visit the lovely shop, which features merchandise of horticultural interest like plants, gardening tools and books. For variety the shop also has some jewelry. After wandering stop and dine at one of the restaurants; one is only open in the summer and the other is in an old snuff mill on the banks of the Bronx River. Admission is $3 for adults and $2 for seniors, children and students. Summer hours are Tuesday through Sunday 10 A.M. to 6 P.M.; November through March hours are Tuesday through Sunday 10 A.M. to 4 P.M. Take the D or 4 train to Bedford Park or 200th Street, then walk east for eight blocks; or take the Metro North Harlem Line to the Botanical Garden station.

central park
visitors' info line: 794-6564/65

Besides the many set activities—the zoo, rowing on the lake, Shakespeare in the Park, skating, cruising in the Ramble—there is a huge range of scheduled activities in Central Park, from runs to theater to walking tours to horticultural talks (including one on what's edible on park grounds) to children's activities.

chapter ten

shopping and things to buy

all american boy
131 christopher street, 242-0078

Great place to buy a tank top, maybe some shorts, and definitely check out the local color. I mean boys. For the girls, there are some tchotchkes for your loved ones, too. A very old store for the young at heart. I always seem to find bathing suits here—in the winter.

charles' place
234 mulberry street, 966-7302

Charles Elkaim gave us the costume jewelry rage of the sixties. He sells his exclusive line of costume jewelry from his shop and will also design and make jewelry according to your desire.

entertain, baby

counter spy shop
444 madison avenue at east 51st street, 557-3040

James Bond stocks up here. This shop is filled with protective equipment, shrewd lie and sound detectors, fax interceptors and security gadgets. This is the place to find safes disguised as household items ("Who'd look here?"). Call to make an appointment to see the back room, filled with equipment for "professionals."

eve's garden
119 west 57th street, 757-8651

A sex shop focusing on the special needs of women of all lifestyles. Women and their partners are welcome at all times; men unescorted by a woman may shop between noon and 2 P.M. Eve's Garden is lesbian-owned and -operated. The shop has a large schedule of special events, including readings, video showings and workshops.

future tan
139 east 57th street, 212-tanning

Blazing into a twenty-first century we'll all enjoy, these guys have America's only deluxe wraparound high-speak massage sunbeds as well as the largest plexiglass tanning bed in America. A variety of other stand-up and mega-fast face-tanning devices is available. The introductory price (four tans for $10) is too good to be passed by. Not a care in the world about melanoma among this friendly crowd.

game show
474 sixth avenue at west 12th street, 633-6328

All sorts of games, many of which have a political or sexual angle, like the TV evangelist game, "How to Fleece a Flock."

shopping and things to buy

gay pleasures
   546 hudson street at west 10th street, 255-5756

This is formerly Gay Treasures but now is . . . Pleasures. Who knows why? Anyway, you can get a sex video or a porn book and you'll always be greeted with a smile by the help. Specials at the desk (*Best of Kevin Williams*) and a lot of advice on where the sex clubs are, just for asking. Next door to A Different Light bookstore, a monument of sorts. (See Chapter 18, "Literary New York.")

hammacher schlemmer
   147 east 57th street, 421-9000

"The best, the only, and the unexpected," claims Hammacher Schlemmer. Fancy gadgets and no-pressure browsing. Some of these gadgets include a compleat folding chair or a very cool standing makeup mirror which, the ad states proudly, all the stars use. And then there's a fog-free shower mirror (what, do you mean you *don't* have one?). And toys!!

out of our drawers
   184 seventh avenue at perry street, 929-4473

Specialty underwear and other items such as bolo ties and wild earrings. "Ear Piercing With or Without Pain" is the shop's famous sign.

shades of the village
   33 greenwich avenue across from uncle charlie's pickup joint, 255-7767

Owned by the same woman as Out of Our Drawers, this place sells lots of cheapo and expensive sunglasses and really useless minutiae.

entertain, baby

raymond dragon
200 west 18th street building on 7th avenue, 727-0368

The clothing store of your A-list Fire Island and Universal Grill set. Here's the place to buy slinky T-shirts and trinkets to dress up a gym body. If you haven't got one, see next item, please. Nice-looking help here too. If you're into ALFIUG types.

shocking gray
800/788-4729 for free catalog

A catalog that features pride-related products, trendy, new and hard-to-find merchandise of interest to lesbians and gay men. Same-sex wedding cake toppers and other items you can't find elsewhere. Gay-owned and -operated. The folks at Shocking Gray say they are "a safe place to shop." What, I don't feel safe at Bloomingdale's?

chapter eleven

freebies in new york city

Participation is the key to enjoying New York. "Putting out" is the operative term here.

Sometimes events are advertised as "free" but require a small donation. That could be something to keep the charity or group going or, where liquor is served, a small drink to keep things friendly. But still, New York can be a world of absolutely free living—except when the first of the month comes around—if you know where to find the freebies.

Suspicion abounds: Why are some of these things free? Many societies and cultural organizations receive grants and donations and then have to use the funding to create shows, functions, group events, even art. And you, the lucky and informed, can cash in just by knowing about it.

Best thing to remember: If something on this list strikes your fancy, call the company and demand to be put on its mailing and phoning list. That way the place will get in touch when something is about to happen.

A free poetry reading takes place almost every Wednesday night at **the poetry society,** but call for changing times and locations (254-9628).

entertain, baby

Then there's my favorite activity for those who think they're culturally hip: the dubbed Spanish Film Festivals at **casa de espana,** 314 East 39th Street and other halls (689-4232), which includes films by Buñuel and Almodóvar.

Free cultural activities include a visit to one of Manhattan's high points, literally—**audubon terrace,** at the very steep 155th Street and Broadway, where some five museums (see below) sit near a gorgeous replica of *El Cid Campeador*. It's pretty, it's cultural, and it's a wonderful place to meditate.

Also, see 155th Street's **trinity church cemetery,** near Audubon Terrace, "Graveyard of American Revolutionary Heroes." One of the finest free things to do is get away from television—where you probably watch *Trial By Jury* or *The People's Court*—and go downtown to an actual trial, where it's much more exciting even if you can't change the channel. Call for trial times and exact stations—I mean, locations: 374-8713 for divorce, 374-5880 for regular crimes, and 374-4585 for high-profile blue-collar crimes.

sotheby's (696-7245) is a fine place to see art, because while the auction house asks for bidders, you can just look at what's being offered that day. (Don't sniffle or scratch your forehead, or you'll own the piece.) I see this as the art coming to you, instead of doing it the regular way, walking up to each painting in a museum.

Dance events are free and entertaining at the special **central park formal dances** held each September. Call 380-8126 (and your fairy godmother too). Another Central Park dance event is **summer folk dancing at noontime** (673-3790), along the shore of Turtle Pond.

Free readings by local scribblers of fiction happen at **pomander books** at West 107th Street and West End Avenue (866-1777). Get on the list, for the locals are usually well-known writers. Pomander used to be located along an English landscape at West 94th and 95th streets off Broadway: You can still see Pomander Walk, a lush row of old Tudor-style houses. Breathtaking and free.

Before I forget, see this bit of architecture if you're a buff of the old style: The **king model townhouses** on West 138th Street between Seventh and Eighth avenues are unlikely Georgia-style houses. On **sutton place** at East 58th Street, you can ogle several mossy homes.

freebies in new york city

Catch avant-garde tapings of small films and TV at **p.s. 122** at East Ninth Street and First Avenue (477-5288). Call for details.

Don't miss dropping in at the **whitney museum's equitable branch** at West 51st and Seventh (554-1000) when it holds an evening dance concert, usually once a month.

And watch the **new prospects modern dance shows** at Brooklyn's Prospect Park in the summertime, always featuring strange special guests (718/788-0055). Also at Prospect Park: Every weekend watch the **model mariners' association** on Lull Water with their small miniature outboard motors, decks and sun chairs—their hobby is the tiny craft. Model boaters are also to be found at the Central Park Conservatory Water off East 72nd Street.

free hot dogs on income tax day, courtesy Hebrew National. Go to the General Post Office at Eighth Avenue and West 33rd Street. Free food at Happy Hour at **tiziano,** 165 Eighth Avenue (989-2330), a pretty but relatively pretentious dinner place. At **bamboo bernies,** 2268 Broadway, a crummy-looking, unpretentious bar (a hut) for screamers (see the Glossary), they have Cheese Whiz. Free tea each day in the back room of **spring street natural restaurant,** 62 Spring Street, 966-0290. Coffee? Why, you can get some every summer day at the **colombian tourist office** (140 East 57th Street, 688-0151).

Free events occur regularly at the **park avenue plaza** (East 52nd Street and Park Avenue) during lunch hour. At other indoor atriums too: **citicorp center** (153 East 53rd Street), **galleria atrium** (115 East 58th Street), **harkness pavilion** (West 62nd Street and Broadway), and in the Bronx, at the **new york botanical gardens** (Kazimiroff Boulevard).

Also: See the palms inside and the waterfalls outside the **world financial center,** a fabulous series of buildings that look like giant models of buildings, right off the West Side Highway by the World Trade Center. WFC peers out over the water like a skyscraper in Chicago.

Museums that are free all the time include the four at **audubon terrace,** at West 155th and Broadway, and the ones housing work by students of the **school of visual arts** (679-7350). These makeshift exhibitions go up throughout Chelsea and SoHo, but be sure to stroll by 40 West 17th Street to see a neat sculpture window.

entertain, baby

An almost free museum experience—a dollar donation is considered nice—can be found at **the cloisters** (Fort Tryon Park, West 190th Street overlooking the Hudson, 923-3700) where artistic relics exist amid a replica of ye olde monk days.

The best **free basketball** is at Third Street and Sixth Avenue—the local teams in the Village are fun to watch. But what the heck, why not forgo sports and get a tan?

The best places for free **tanning** are most assuredly large plazas that have unobstructed sun: Sixth Avenue between West 41st and 42nd streets, Fifth Avenue at 59th Street, Second Avenue at East 35th Street, and St. Marks Place and Second Avenue.

You can find free performance art at the **jacques marchais tibetan museum** on Staten Island (718/987-3478). Also, a man named Red Spot performs outside with a slide show Saturday night in the dead of winter. This occurs at Spring Street and Broadway. (No phone number—but of course.)

For free political activities, attend group meetings and lectures given by the **village independent democratic club,** various locations (260-4527). You could always become a leafletter, proselytizing on the latest political candidate's ideas.

Get free housing advice on Tuesday from 6 to 8 P.M. at 280 Broadway from the **lower manhattan foundation for the community of artists.** Good advice on how to obtain and keep apartments.

Free theater is what New York is. **the 52nd street project** (247-3405) gives kids a chance to work with professional actors, directors and writers. The best free show exists at the "best secret in town" (their slogan), downstairs at **westbank cafe,** West 42nd Street and Ninth Avenue (695-6909). It's called "The Free Show At Midnight," which makes them think they came up with the idea of gratis entertainment first and thus means they will usually attempt new ideas. You'd better buy a drink, particularly since the show starts so darn late. There's free theater each lunchtime during the short theatrical season of **quaigh theatre,** 808 Lexington Avenue (223-2547). Bring a bag of food—coffee is served.

freebies in new york city

Many plays at Quaigh are either new ones or ancient ones never premiered in New York. (See Chapter 16, "Theater and Dance, Gay and Otherwise.")

Take advantage of free summer music surrounding the midpark **central park bandshell,** come rain or shine, during the Summerstage series (360-2777). This endangered species is always being threatened with extinction because it doesn't get enough hype! So pretend you already love the series, and support it.

Let's talk free classical events. These occur at the New York Symphony concerts at Carnegie Hall and midtown's **weill recital hall** (581-5933); at **symphony space** up at West 94th Street and Broadway (864-5400), and weekly at the **third street music school settlement** down on West 11th Street (777-3240). Lastly: Probably the best classical experience is the weekday performance at **trinity church** at Wall Street and Broadway, around lunchtime (602-0747).

carnegie mansion is the place to be on Tuesday night in the summertime, when jazz, classical and some chamber music are played in the garden of the **cooper-hewitt museum** at 91st Street and Fifth Avenue (860-6868). This series was one of philanthropist Andrew Carnegie's last willed wishes.

Now that we're on the subject of philanthropic organizations, if you're into public and mostly free readings you must turn yourself on to the **new york public library's** main headquarters, at 42nd Street and Fifth Avenue. Besides the usual exhibits on anything from the history of tobacco to the wildest collection of "original drafts" in several states, you can also inform yourself about ancient couture and the diarists of our nation and learn from such illustrious commentators as Dr. Spock, Judith Malina (cofounder of the Living Theatre) and British filmmaker Michael Powell (*The Red Shoes*). To find out more, stop in the library's spacious lobby. And while you're there, read.

More music for free. **calypso music** is offered daily where the R train meets the 1, 2 and 3, underneath Times Square. It's not free —you need a token to get in—but you'll probably be traveling through there someday. Dance a little!

For free tickets to sit in television studio audiences while the shows are being taped, try **nbc's** tough-ticket line at 664-4444. (NBC's headquarters are West 50th Street and Sixth Avenue.) At

entertain, baby

NBC tickets are available for *Late Night with Conan*, *Saturday Night Live* or its taped rehearsal beforehand, and *Donahue*. Also try the special tix number, 664-3055. **cbs** tapes the syndicated *Joan Rivers* show at its Upper West Side studio, so call 975-5903. Little **geraldo rivera's** midtown screamfest doles out tickets at 265-1283. And tickets to **live with regis and kathy lee,** the morning gab show locally telecast on WABC, can be had by dialing 456-1000. For newsy programs, try the **primetime live** ticket center for ABC's only relevant show, at 580-5169. For **sally jessy raphael,** well . . . she's boring. Warning: You have to sit through several takes on many of these shows, and they won't even let you stand up until the taping is completed.

There is no more live radio, right? Wrong. **wnyc** (633-7600) wants you to be their guests for a series of fun concerts.

chapter twelve

gyms for your body

One of the most necessary inclusions in any book on homo New York: Here are the gyms that welcome gay boys and lesbians all the time. Granted, there are others, but they are not as gay-friendly and will probably sneer if you so much as pat your friend on the back.

better bodies cross-training center
22 west 19th street, 929-6789

Prices: Approximately $290 per year. $8 daily membership. $49 monthly. Extra fees for the aerobics and boxing arena downstairs. Besides the weight-training gym, cross-training machines featuring the only boxing center downtown. Hours: Monday through Friday 6 A.M. to 10:30 P.M., Saturday and Sunday 9:30 A.M. to 8 P.M. Rates are affordable and, for a change, negotiable. An absolute no-frills gym, this. The brand-new Extreme Cardio center upstairs is worth the extra few hundred for a perfect heart rate and pumped-up physique.

entertain, baby

chelsea gym
267 west 17th street, 255-1150

Prices: yearly $499 on sale; usually $600; monthly $80 on sale; usually $100; daily $15. Hours: Monday through Friday 6 A.M. to midnight, Saturday and Sunday 9 A.M. to midnight. Very cruisy, very old-looking gym with nice attendants.

david barton gym
552 sixth avenue at west 15th street, 727-0004

Prices: yearly $659 up front or $59/month for one year with $149 initiation fee; monthly $156; daily $15 but you can't work out from 5 to 9 P.M. Monday through Friday. Hours: Monday through Friday 6 A.M. to midnight, Saturday 9 A.M. to 9 P.M., Sunday 10 A.M. to 11 P.M. Beautiful shower area, attendant, but small amount of weight equipment.

equinox fitness club
342 amsterdam avenue at west 80th street, 721-4200

Prices: yearly $125 initiation + $750 + tax up front; monthly $250 initiation + $75 every month + tax (must commit for at least one year); or pay by month, $175/1 month, $375/3 months; daily $26 guest charge/trial fee or call twenty-four hours ahead to try for free (no true daily option). Hours: Monday through Thursday 6 A.M. to 11 P.M., Friday 6 A.M. to 10 P.M., Saturday and Sunday 8 A.M. to 9 P.M. There are 300 aerobics classes a week, lots of equipment, and Jim Herman, a great salesman who will talk your ear off if you let him. Cross-training center open since 1991.

gyms for your body

equinox fitness club
897 broadway at east 19th street, 780-9300

Opening is scheduled for November, 1994. This new club will cost more and membership prices are set to increase as opening draws closer. So your options are to join as soon as possible, work out and upgrade your membership for an additional $125 (upgrade fee) or hold off your membership and simply pay the price listed above.

powerhouse gym
146 west 23rd street, 807-7255

Prices: yearly $350 (varies), monthly $59, daily $10. Hours: Monday through Friday 5:30 A.M. to 11:30 P.M., Saturday 9 A.M. to 8 P.M., Sunday 9 A.M. to 6 P.M. Powerhouse is an anomaly in that there is a gay crowd and a *very* straight crowd. Go at your own risk and bring your own friends. Powerhouse has a nongay gym at its Wall Street location (88 Fulton Street, 385-2134) with a small pool and a daily rate of $15. Monday through Friday 6 A.M. to 10 P.M., Saturday and Sunday 10 A.M. to 4 P.M.

printing house fitness club
421 hudson street at leroy street, 243-3777

Prices: Yearly prices range from $950 for just aerobics/yoga classes to $1,650 for the works, including racquetball/squash/pool/class privileges and use of all equipment. There's a special membership offered monthly (e.g., a $1,175 membership for use of the racquetball/squash courts). There is no daily or monthly rate; however, yearly memberships can be paid off monthly with payments ranging from $50 to $115. Hours: Monday through Friday 6 A.M. to 11 P.M.; Saturday and Sunday 8 A.M. to 8 P.M. It's a very nicely laid-out gym for the downtown work and live crowd. Spiffy goings-on in the neighborhood famous for its hip corporate buildings, a lot of serious working out, and a heckuva lot of cruising.

times square boxing club
145 west 42nd street, 221-9510

Prices: no yearly fee, $25 a month, $5 a day. Hours: Monday through Friday 11:30 A.M. to 8 P.M.; Saturday 10:30 A.M. to 3 P.M. No Sundays; it's a rest day for boxers. This is my favorite place to watch a sport: the cheapest in town for a training but you have to make sure you really train or you will be laughed out of there. (Not a gym for sissies.) A gym for boxers who consider themselves "elite": **kingsway boxing center**, 300 West 40th Street, 629-6968 (502-4276 for "Kingsway Boxing/Fitness Center).

world gym
404 lafayette street, 260-2534

Prices: yearly $660, monthly $175 ($400/3 months; $500/6 months), daily $15. Hours: Monday through Friday 6 A.M. to 11 P.M., Saturday and Sunday 7 A.M. to 9 P.M. A well-built gym with great equipment kept in shape.

world gym
1926 broadway, 874-0942

Prices: yearly $750, monthly $175 ($450/3 months; $550/6 months), daily $17. Hours: Twenty-four hours weekdays (Opens Monday at 5 A.M., closes Saturday at 10 P.M.), Sunday 8 A.M. to 10 P.M. The twenty-four-hour thing is exceptional. Gym buffs who are in need of a fix, see **johnny lats** at 7 East 17th Street off Fifth Avenue—twenty-four hours all the time and nothing but free weights. Call 366-4426 for details. This World Gym is beautiful but it's also a hectic place because it's the flagship of the chain and it's the one they show to bodybuilders, interested competitors, prospective franchise owners, chain managers, famous people, quasi-celebrities, etc.

chapter thirteen

jazz clubs, cabarets; sit and watch the music

continental divide
25 third avenue at st. marks/east 8th street, 529-6924

This normally straight dive for college-age dudes often stretches to include great jazz artists—recently it had trumpet-player Don Cherry, the ultra-talented stepdad of sexy singer Neneh!

cornelia street
29 cornelia street, 989-9319

A good-food cafe in the West Village that allows for space downstairs where jazz saxophones burst out in song. Nearly every night you can pay a few dollars and see jazz, "new works" (unusual sounds) and "*choros* from Brazil."

entertain, baby

jazz for the homeless
   st. peter's church, east 54th street and lexington avenue, no phone number

While this is indeed esoteric, it is an unsanctimonious hour at the church that features musicians Terry Clark, Roger Kellaway and Robin Eubanks, Saturday at 10:30 p.m.

skylark
   131-34 merrick boulevard, little neck, queens, 718/525-9614

A small place in Queens that is romantic for all types; trios play nicely and the food (quasi-Continental) is good and reasonably priced.

water's edge
   44th drive at the east river, long island city; 718/482-0033

A fabulous small club in the depths of Long Island City that has jazz duos nightly. Water's Edge is fun to get to on the 7 train and it's in a mysterious section of town.

■ other places where you can sit and watch

The following performance spaces do not include places where you can sing and play yourself—those are found in "Piano Bars" below.

adelaide
   492 broome street, 966-3371

Music Tuesday through Saturday night, closed Sunday. Mostly swing and jazz. On Wednesday night, cabaret performance at 9. There's a band from 9 p.m. to 1 a.m., except Wednesday. They play a number of sets. The cover ranges from $5 to $10; $10 to $15 for dinner (Italian menu).

jazz clubs, cabarets; sit and watch the music

the ballroom
253 west 28th street, 244-3005

Cabaret performance at 9 P.M. Tuesday through Saturday, with an additional performance at 11:15 on Friday and Saturday night. Meals are served (Spanish-Continental-tapas). The cover varies from $20 to $35 and there's a two-drink minimum always.

blue note
131 west 3rd street, 475-8592

Jazz performances seven nights a week—often very expensive. Shows are customarily at 9 and 11 P.M., with an occasional 1:30 A.M. show on Friday. (Monday night is scheduled by record companies, called "New Artists' Showcase"; showtimes vary.) On Tuesday and Saturday night a jam session is held after the last show, at 1 A.M.; musicians in the audience play with the band. The music charge is from $25 to $45, and there's a $5 drink minimum. Dinner is served, though the menu is not fascinating in the least.

cafe carlyle
carlyle hotel, 35 east 76th street, 744-1600

Piano and singing by the lounge biggies: Bobby Short, Barbara Cook, Dixie Carter, Eartha Kitt, the Modern Jazz Quartet. Shows begin at 9 P.M. The cafe is closed June through September. The cover is $40 and there is a $10 drink minimum.

caroline's
west 50th street and broadway, 956-0101

Named for the woman who introduced Pee Wee Herman, The Kids in the Hall, and other comedians to New York, this was once the mainstay of downtown. Nowadays the all-star show includes music galore but Caroline has moved the digs to midtown. "Caroline's Comedy

entertain, baby

Club" now has a bit of a touristy feel to it. Still, gay "ranter" Frank Maya appears here, and the crowd, while dull, is attentive. The cover can run about $12.

chez beauvais
852 tenth avenue at west 50th street, 581-6340

Beauvais is intimate, new and a member of the Manhattan Association of Cabarets, meaning it only presents classy performers. MAC, meanwhile, presents a cabaret series in March—Cabaret Month in New York City. Call 206-6681 or 465-2662 and get mailed.

dell's down under
266 west 47th street, 719-4179

Cabaret performances on Friday and Saturday night, and occasionally on weekdays. On the first Tuesday of the month there is a sketch improvisation. The dining room is separate from the cabaret. (No audience-participation stuff.) The cover is $10 and there is an $8 food or drink minimum. It's a restaurant during the day, so call and check; the management is precarious with its planning.

cucina della fontana
368 bleecker street, 242-0636

There are cabaret performances seven evenings a week in the cabaret room (weeknights at 8 P.M. and on Friday and Saturday at 8 and 10). There's a Sunday-afternoon performance as well. It's a good idea to make reservations for the cabaret. You can also have an inexpensive Italian dinner served in the separate dining room. The cover for the cabaret is between $8 and $10 with a two-drink minimum. Beware: They have no piano bar and no patron participation.

jazz clubs, cabarets; sit and watch the music

danny's at the grand sea palace
346 west 46th street, 265-8133

Performances seven nights a week at 9. Sometimes two shows on Friday and Saturday night. The cover varies with performers but is usually $10 plus a $10 drink minimum.

55 bar
55 christopher street, 929-9883

Live music, a band and singers seven nights a week (Sunday through Thursday from 10 P.M. to 2 A.M., Friday and Saturday from 10:30 to 3). There's no cover but there is a two-drink minimum per set.

judy's
49 west 44th street, 764-8930

Cabaret performances every night except Sunday, at 9. Jerry Scott, the pianist, plays from 10 to 2, and patrons are welcome to sing along. Dinner (Italian) is served. The cover ranges from $6 to $15, with a $10 food or drink minimum if you don't dine.

maxim's
680 madison avenue at east 58th street, cabaret reservations 751-5111

Maxim's is posh and expensive and still a place you can't really be yourself at. But the $15 music charge is worth it—you really feel as though you've moved up in the world. "Steve Ross" are the operative words here for a good piano player.

entertain, baby

nadine's
151 bank street, 924-3165

Nadine's restaurant has just taken over the Music Hall at Westbeth and has just begun to book the season, which now includes such wonderful theater pieces as Robert Chesley's *Jerker*. Nadine's offers a wide range of performances and events in this room, including cabaret, performance art, jazz, poetry and theater pieces. Some food available, in addition to a full bar. Get a calendar.

oak room at the algonquin hotel
59 west 44th street, 840-6800

Cabaret performances at 9:30 P.M. Tuesday through Saturday, with an additional show at 11:30 on Friday and Saturday. No patron participation. There's a $25 cover and a $10 minimum.

people's voice cafe
133 west 4th street, at the washington square church parlor lobby, 787-3903

People's Voice is an alternative coffeehouse offering high-quality entertainment. It provides a space for the artistic expression of a wide variety of humanitarian issues and concerns. Open only in the fall and winter months. Not a piano bar or a cabaret, but really neat.

rainbow and stars
30 rockefeller plaza, sixty-fifth floor, 632-5000

This is the cabaret room at the famous Rainbow Room. Cabaret performances are offered Tuesday through Saturday (there's a spectacular view in the cabaret room) at 8:30 and 10:30 P.M. Dinner is served at the 8:30 show and a supper menu is offered at the 10:30 show (the menu is classic Continental). Generally the performances are headline singers, but there are also revues (recently a Rogers and Hammerstein

jazz clubs, cabarets; sit and watch the music

revue, for example). No patron-participation activities. There is a $35 cover for all shows, and no minimum.

russian tea room
150 west 57th street between sixth and seventh avenues, 265-0947

Besides its usual fare—Russian food and atmosphere—the Russian Tea Room offers an evening cabaret series. The Monday-night series is hosted by the Society of Composers and Performers (of Cabaret Performers?). Sunday night is booked by the famous Donald Smith. Soon Sunday night will be dropped, replaced by Tuesday night. The cabaret program runs through the year. Tickets on Monday are $15 with a $10 minimum purchase; on Tuesday, $22.50 with a $10 minimum purchase. A $25 cabaret prix fixe meal is available which includes appetizer, entree, dessert and tea or coffee.

steve mcgraw's
158 west 72nd street, 595-7400

Forever Plaid has been running here forever, a spoof of boys doing fifties doo-wop and making the crowd crazy; shows nightly. Cabaret performances are at 10:30 P.M. Monday through Saturday and at 10 on Sunday. (Sunday and Monday are Broadway Cares benefits.) Dinner is served. Cover $5 to $15. Reservations are a good idea. In addition, there's a piano bar, with a baby grand and a pianist from 9 P.M. nightly. No minimum and no cover in the piano bar.

tatou
151 east 50th street, 753-1144

Dinner is served nightly, accompanied by a jazz ensemble, with dancing after dinner (American cuisine with a French touch). From time to time a cabaret performance is scheduled on Tuesday night. Music begins at 6 P.M. and continues to 11. Jazz every night of the week. Sometimes a cabaret on Tuesday. On Monday night there's "Monday Night

entertain, baby

Live"; auditions are held on Monday from 3 to 5 P.M. No cover with dinner, $10 otherwise, after 9:30 P.M. Warning: Not as chic as when it first opened.

ye olde triple inn
263 west 54th street, 206-6681

This is a lovely club for old-time singers and followers of same.

chapter fourteen

eighty-eight keys (piano bars)

brandy's
235 east 84th street, 650-1944

"Small rustic" place. Waitresses, bartenders and patrons all sing along with the pianist after 9:30 P.M., every night of the week (Broadway, Top 40, rock, blues, standards). There's no cover but there is a two-drink minimum.

don't tell mama
343 west 46th street, 757-0788

Performances seven nights of the week, usually at 7, 8, 9 and 10. "Mixture of things." There's a cover from $5 to $15 and a two-drink minimum. Cash only. There's also a piano bar with a pianist from 9 every night. Patron participation is welcome and there's no cover or minimum in the piano bar. I sent in a questionnaire to this place and the manager scribbled in: "Gays welcome." She was underestimating how huge the gay market is, especially in cabarets. Here is a friendly place that serves drinks, has gay people hanging out in droves—which in midtown is an anomaly—and doesn't charge a cover for people to

entertain, baby

sing with the piano player. (Two shows nightly in the cabaret past the main bar—the cover for that is between $6 and $15.) And though the manager naively forgets, gays and lesbians define this place.

d.t.'s fat cat
281 west 12th street, 243-9041

This is a West Village women's bar. On Friday and Saturday from 9 P.M. to 1:30 A.M. and Sunday from 6 to 10 P.M. there's a piano player/singer. Patrons often sing along. Never a cover, never a minimum. Sometimes the group will order in pizza or Chinese food.

the duplex
61 christopher street, 255-5438

There are performances Monday through Saturday at 8 and 10 P.M. On Friday at 11:30 P.M. there's a Star Search cabaret, in which people sing to a tape or do comedy (sign up in advance or just show up). The cover is from $5 to $12 and there's a two-drink minimum. There's also a piano bar with a pianist from 9 P.M. to 4 A.M. For this there's no cover and no minimum and singing along is welcome.

The Duplex boasts that it's the oldest piano bar in the city, but its recent move from Grove Street to Christopher Street and Seventh Avenue, a heavily populated area, has, in a strange twist of irony, changed it from a gay hangout to a very mainstream place where yuppies get drunk and sing from the rafters. The old space may have been grungy, but hell, it was never tacky. You can still sit, stand or squat and sing along to piano tuners. "Funny Gay Males," an act that often plays weekends, is worth catching. And I should mention that every so often Wicked Trash Productions presents "Bedtime Stories," with the tagline "Ladies with an Attitude." I appreciate their ad: "Laugh Your Fat Tired Lazy Queer Ass Off." With two boys kissing on the poster! Right on, sirs.

eighty-eight keys (piano bars)

eighty-eight's
228 west 10th street, 924-0088

There's a cabaret Sunday through Thursday at 8 and 10:30 P.M. and Friday and Saturday at 8:30 and 11 P.M., and at Sunday brunch as well. The cover ranges from $8 to $15 and there's a two-drink minimum. The brunch cabaret is $2.50 and that includes snacks. Or order meals—prix fixe is $8.88. There's also a piano bar with a pianist from 9 P.M., and patron singalong is welcome. It's a great place to bring your Broadway-attuned parents.

rose's turn
55 grove street, 366-5438

There's a cabaret every night, with performances at 8 and 10. Reservations are required and there's a cover from $3 to $10 plus a two-drink minimum. On Wednesday and Thursday night, Rose's Turn has Open Mike Night at 10. There's also the singalong-friendly Rose's Turn Piano Bar, with a pianist from 9 P.M. to 4 A.M. There's no cover and no minimum in the piano bar.

the townhouse bar
236 east 57th street, 754-4649

Pianist every night, patrons sing along; "belt it out." The theme is show tunes. Pianist from 6 P.M. on weekdays, 9 P.M. on Saturday and 7 P.M. on Sunday. There's no cover and no minimum—hey, it's a gay bar!

chapter fifteen

where to go when everyone's asleep (or, where to sleep when everyone's going)

Note: A lot of gay men will think it's politically yucky that I haven't included women here. But there aren't any sex clubs for women—except for Clit Club (432 West 14th Street, 473-7189), which isn't really a sex club but a cutely named place to pick someone up for coffee. Then again, someone will probably decide to think it's awful that I've described in one chapter all the many places you can go to get your rocks off. (Probably, they would have liked it if I'd devoted *two* chapters to it.) Moralists will say these places are only for certain people; in a poll I took among friends and acquaintances, I discovered that nearly everyone goes to one or two of these so-called sexual outlets during his time in New York.

These are the places where the objective is to get off, or cum. Sex is important to gay men, so there is no way I'd leave it out.

Everything is explained here, except what to do with your dick. (Batteries are indeed optional!)

Note the clubs' slogans—very enlightening. The clubs are also full of it, in that most say they only allow safe sex and most will basically allow anything.

Have a sex-positive time. For the complete story on safer sex, see

entertain, baby

"AIDS Pages," a chapter featured in the back. Not the back *room*—the back of the book!

■ "we meant to be safe . . ."

The fantastic AIDS health organization GMHC (Gay Men's Health Crisis) offers free lessons in controlling sexual situations. You may need to come in for a free lesson. GMHC's slogan is "You are not alone. . . . You are important. . . . Love yourself. . . . Protect your health. . . . We can teach you how." Workshops, called "Keep It Up," are held for good reason: Get questions answered—"How do I make safe sex hot, erotic, varied and exciting?" "What leads to unsafe sex?" "How can I handle unsafe situations better?" "How do I get back on track and stay there?" For information, call the Hotline at 807-6655. See Chapter 28, "AIDS Pages," for a great deal more on GMHC; also see Chapter 29, "Volunteerism."

■ are the clubs regulated?

In a *New York Times* article, Health Commissioner Margaret Hamburg said that the city will inspect sex clubs and site owners who do not enforce safe-sex rules. By doing this, the city has made the places ostensibly legal, as regulated businesses. The inspectors who monitor the sex clubs are looking for three things: closed rooms that allow private and not-observable sex, poor lighting, and the transferral of bodily fluids. The bottom line is, be careful. Practicing safer sex keeps us alive and keeps the sex clubs open. "Sex-positive behavior" is not to be frowned upon.

where to go when everyone's asleep

■ **sex clubs and back rooms**

carter's system
carter lard, 117 storer avenue, new rochelle, ny 10801, 914/576-6945

Carter Lard has a matchmaking service accessed by sending a form to Lard at the above address, or calling him at the number above. Lard says he gets "satisfaction from knowing I've brought a little happiness into the lives of others." *What* happiness he brings, too. Unlike the Prime parties, here he invites variation: Men of color and couples of three or more, singles with or without muscles, and guys who are "hot or hotter than you" are invited to send in a form and find someone who is sexually compatible. All this for no money down!

Examples of questions and answers: *What are you?* Bubble butt, full butt, heavy butt, average butt, below average . . . *What do you want?* Penis width . . . circumcised . . . eye color . . . hair color . . . marital status . . . ethnicity . . . body rating (#1 to #10) . . . *What's especially important—what turns you on?* Thinning hair, workout body, toned, Latin, etc. . . .

cellblock 28
28 ninth avenue at west 13th street, no phone number, but send postcards.

Though the stats are changing, this private club has special events that you need to know about by getting on its mailing list. Open Monday through Wednesday, 8 P.M. to 3 A.M. Special events include New York Bears, New York Strap & Paddle Association, Chest Men of America, Pump! Parties, Hot Ash, and The Renegades. "All safe!" they say.

east side club
227 east 56th street, 753-2222

This bathhouse has the distinction of being open twenty-four hours. (There's a four-hour time limit for you hogs.) Call to discover how you

entertain, baby

get to make it here: by signing a form that swears you'll be safe and buying a "membership card." It's $25 for a year or $10 a month.

82 club
82 east 4th street, no phone number

This is a mysterious place. For some reason, 82 Club is very hush-hush. Here's its history: It was once a gay theater, then did a stint as a nightclub called Woody's, named after its owner, the Stones' Ron Wood; then it became a Japanese after-hours club. When all these concepts merged, it turned into a dance hall and a back area with plenty of nooks and crannies. There are a dozen booths with lockable doors. Some artifacts remain, mostly to titillate the newcomers: maybe a four-foot portrait of Mick Jagger? Sunday through Wednesday midnight to 6 A.M., the cover is $8. Thursday through Saturday midnight to 8 A.M., the cover is $10. East Village crowd—white, young and willing.

he's gotta have it!
135 west 14th street, 677-3599

This gross-looking place is overtly unorganized and worse, it's manipulative: You only get off if you close your eyes and don't look at the person you're with! Hosted by unknowns named Michael and Kenneth, this sex place on the second floor of a grungy building asks for a "$10 donation," and since it calls itself a private place to jerk off, it's legal for anyone to be turned away. Clothing check, relatively cheap drinks, and a Big Dick Contest at midnight. Only on alternate Saturdays, midnight to 5 A.M. Call for more details, including how little clothing to bring. The eclectic crowd leans toward older guys.

where to go when everyone's asleep

j's
675 hudson street at west 13th street, 242-9292

J's is open Tuesday through Friday from 9 P.M. to 4 A.M. and allows you to drink, jerk off or be a real exhibitionist. Not a great crowd. "If you carry your wallet with you, someone will carry it home with them," says a well-lit sign on the wall.

Older crowd, multitudes of staring dour faces, a lot of posturing or posing (see the Glossary). Also known as The Hangout, because that's all everyone seems to do here: Pose, hang out, pull.

meat
432 west 14th street, no phone number

Dark and dingy. The basement staff offers a free T-shirt if you take your clothes off (except for the socks, to make it legal). Meat happens only on Saturday. Friday night is Clit Club for lesbian action. It's not especially interesting, but the techno music and the bodies seemingly in slow motion are an eclectic combination. Fee $7, $5 with invitations found strewn around Chelsea and the Village. The advertised slogan is "Deep & Hard." Assortment of ethnic men.

mount morris baths
1944 madison avenue, at east 125th street, 534-9004

Open "almost twenty-four hours a day," this sleazy bathhouse offers $10 lockers and $15 rooms. Membership is not required. Mostly men of color; however, everyone is welcome.

ny prime's bachelor parties

Exclusive, elitist, ever so much fun, these parties are held every few months at a specified hotel. (It's a great scam; they tell the management a hundred men will be arriving to act a little wild in honor of a friend's upcoming nuptials. In fact, it's all sex in a suite!) Wear very

entertain, baby

little clothing, for you'll have to take it off when you get inside. Enter from 8 to 9 P.M. and then enter at will. Cost is $15 and a portion of all the proceeds goes to charity. Bring your own towels; lube and condoms are supplied.

Of course, you can only go if you're personally invited. And how do you get invited? By going to bars a lot, standing around, looking cute and having someone notice you *often*. Eventually you'll be handed the invitation destined to change your life!

Not.

If this is your cake, call 388-8198 for "Orifice," another private sex party series, or 718/832-3952 for foot fetish parties. Or phone 215/784-7140 for shaving nights (yes, *shaving*). Or, lastly for now, try 908/245-5323 for suburban special nights!

prism sex club
325 west 37th street, 714-2582

The fire department keeps closing this ultimately down-to-earth sex bar. The three-tier playhouse charges for beer ($4) and admission ($15 to $20, though you can get a $5 admish reduction by mentioning *Homo Xtra*). Lots of cute guys, good music, several great-looking bartenders, and private rooms to run into. Very white crowd. Sex, dancing, showers, videos, even conversation. Friday and Saturday 11 P.M. to 9 A.M.; Wednesday and Thursday 9 P.M. to 5 A.M.; Sunday 3 P.M. to 5 A.M. Prism is "a private playground and 'erotic art gallery for men.'" They need this fake title, because "Sex Club" would be uncouth on all those cards strewn around town. This club seems to be reopening all the time along Tenth Avenue in small, seedy places near the river.

where to go when everyone's asleep

spunk at crowbar
339 east 10th street, 420-0670

More sex than on a Christopher Street pier. This is the back room at Crowbar; the bar is incredibly busy on Thursday and Saturday nights. (Crowbar is featured in Chapter 7, "Bars All Around Town.") They call it the "Jack Together Show" and for a good reason. Everything goes at Spunk. While there are sex rooms in bars and discos (e.g., at the Limelight club on Wednesday and Friday night in the Lick It! Lounge), these are bourgeois ways of getting laid. Club sex is boring; dancing *is* foreplay. Move your body on the floor, then leave with whomever you want. There's a time for every purpose under heaven.

Turn, turn, turn.

trouble
540 west 21st street, 601-0792

A private party with "strict discretionary door" that only wants to see well-groomed, in-shape guys (read: men who go to gyms). You may get an invitation in the mail, or someone may hand one to you at a bar. The idea is to go ($10 with membership, $15 if you show at the door) and take off your clothes. You can find out about this in the "Getting Off" section of the weekly magazine *Homo Xtra*. Often you'll find a coupon inside the magazine. Or order the quarterly magazine *Spunk* (not to be confused with Spunk at Crowbar above), which details the sex scene. (Send $1, cash or $6 for five consecutive issues, to Studio Iguana, 450 West 25th Street, Third Floor, New York, NY 10010.) Trouble time is 9:30 P.M.; parties are held on the last Sunday of each month.

Trouble is sponsored by New York Prime, a group you can count on for a good time; the only problem is they tend to invite too many white gym boys and in this case, similarity is key. To find out if you

entertain, baby

"qualify," call. Sometimes Trouble holds parties at 24 First Avenue. Trouble's slogan? "If you catch someone not playing safely, get mad and either tell them to leave or get us to tell them to leave!"

underground
432 east 9th street, no phone number

A "Come Spot," the ad remarks. You need to pay $5 or bring the listing from *Homo Xtra*. No liquor. What is this? A bunch of (mostly) white guys sitting around pulling.

wall street sauna
1 maiden lane, 233-8900

Open Monday through Thursday 11 A.M. to 8 P.M., Friday 11 A.M. to midnight, Saturday noon to midnight, Sunday noon to 8 P.M. Bankers' hours, right? Lockers $9, rooms $15. No time limits on lockers but four hours max in rooms. Membership is not required. Sex pretty much is. Condoms found in each cubicle. While this is a haven for Wall Streeters, tourists converge here.

zone (zone dk)
540 west 21st street, 463-8599

The sex parlor described as "a full dungeon" that portrays men with the best leather outfits, whips, half-harnesses and masks. Videos play all over. Every Saturday night around 4 A.M. it's "Boys Town After Dark"—very sleazy and worth catching. There are other good nights here; you can try a special Society of Spankers gathering on specified Mondays. Call and get recorded information on special and regular events. Open Thursday through Sunday. The hottest crowd in the sex clubs—probably because it's viewed as a special occasion. An alternative to going to Sound Factory late on a late-late Saturday night.

where to go when everyone's asleep
dark rooms

Though they're fatuous, here are the best-known exhibitionist sex cubbyholes and cubicles found in nightclubs and bars. There are more, to be sure, but you have to create those yourselves. These are provided by the establishments: **comeback** (507 West Street at Jane Street) on Saturday night; **limelight** (47 West 20th Street) on Wednesday and Friday night; **club usa** (218 West 47th Street), where there is a spacious room in which to do yourself and friends on the basement level and in **wonder bar** and **crowbar**. I understand the new **tunnel**, called **nocturnal**, has a few dark rooms. For more dark spaces, I recommend shrubbery.

■ movie theaters and the infamous booths for you who can't get enough

movie theaters for quick action

These are places to go to meet other men and do what you wish with them. All of these movie theaters are open twenty-four hours a day, for convenience. Here are the midtown palaces: **adonis** (693 Eighth Avenue, 246-9550); **all male jewel theater** (100 Third Avenue, no phone number); **david cinema** (236 West 54th Street, 974-9362); **eros male cinema** (8th Avenue and West 45th Street, 221-2450, 10 A.M. to 5 A.M.); **king cinema** (356 West 44th Street, 582-8714); **show palace** (670 Eighth Avenue, 391-8820, 10 A.M. to 5 A.M.), with many shows throughout the day, night and early morning. Best of midtown is **the gaiety** (201 West 46th Street), which includes go-go boys and shows at 1:15, 3:30, 6, 8:30 and 10 P.M. There are dancers all night on Friday and Saturday (Madonna was sighted there with "friends").

In the Village: On West Street find **prince theater** (399 West Street at 10th Street, 691-3720); and **west world** (354 West Street at Christopher Street, no phone number), open all night at 6 P.M.

entertain, baby

Lastly: What—you want more? That's enough. Go home to your boyfriend.

booths—a worst-case scenario

Just like heterosexuals since the dawn of the projection booth, we gay people have a few places of our own to drop in a few quarters and whack off. Here are the twenty-four hour emporia: **all male xx video** (14th Street at Third Avenue, no phone number); **bull pen** (21 Ann Street, 267-9760, often closed early mornings); **christopher street bookshop** (500 Hudson Street, no phone number); **les hommes** (217 West 80th Street, no phone number); and **rick neilson's screening room** (210 West 42nd Street, no phone number). I wonder, someone wants his name on a jerk-off booth?

■ sex by phone, by mail—and by street too

adam and eve catalogue
800/334-5474

A complete collection of erotica and related items for "sophisticated" adults. They'll send you a free catalog if you call and ask nicely.

comquest
900/369-0069

A pay-telephone personal ad service. You record a personal message of your own and browse through messages left by other men. Cost is $.69 a minute—what, you were expecting a sane number? This may be the best of its type, because you don't have to stay on the line for*ever*.

where to go when everyone's asleep

fatales video
800/845-4617

Fatales Video is a group of lesbians who produce lesbian erotic videos. (These are the people who bring the world *On Our Backs*; see Chapter 18, "Literary New York.") Fatales' goal is to produce lesbian sexual images that are celebrated and to convey real-life lesbian sex as only lesbians can appreciate and relate to it. Fatales gives voice to the many body types, characters, fantasies and sexual techniques that make up the range of lesbian love.

Since 1985, and trucking. Available at Judith's Room, Eve's Garden, and A Different Light bookstores. Cost $29.95 to $39.95. For rent at some video stores.

the fone book

Found in bars and clubs, this book will give you a listing of the phone sex lines around New York (which charge *big* bucks by the minute) and reviews of dirty videos. I recommend giving each and every one of these a call; I own stock in NYNEX.

home alone
714/697-7833

Call to get connected to a phone line that charges by the month: For $13 you can connect to other sex-positive people who want to talk dirty to you. Through the phone, and by punching in your PIN number, you can select the types you want and even meet people if you're particularly lazy. This is all about phone sex, but you can actually make dates with men on the phone service. The company is called DATE-A-BASE, and it wants to fulfill a variety of needs. For phone-sex selections, **550-prism** is there for hot, dirty sex talk whether the club called Prism is opened or closed.

entertain, baby

phone service information—free!
800/676-guys

For information and updates about phone-sex lines—those you have to pay for—you can call this *f r e e* service. It's like Movie Phone (777-FILM for free film info). Actually, it's just my way of saving my publisher lots of paper and still giving you most of the decent 900 lines. The only one not there is our local line, 550-1000, The Number, which is the chat line on which all my friends (male) have met their guy lovers. That's only fifteen cents for each minute after the forty-five-cent first minute. Also, 222-4665; it's a male-box of sorts. Call it, it's local. Establish a box and a security code and talk away.

Lastly, visit Banana Video at 55 West 38th Street (382-0935), which stocks the male releases you're on the lookout for. Also, lesbian or girl tapes, which should, I guess, be called *kumquats*.

section three

anything arty

By "arty," we don't mean your cousin Arthur. Here is where the theatrical side of all of us comes out—in chapters designed to thrill you in the theater (Bravo!); at the dance (*Merde!*); through gallery outings (stand there with your hands on your chin looking awfully interested); at the cinema and watching television (the only totally American arts); and observing the singing-and-dancing arts specially designed for gays and lesbians (lalala).

The chapters to follow may end up exhausting you—there's a lot to do in these areas. But keep in mind that by reading through every entry, you will find something that is worth the trip. Anything that brightens your spirit is good for you. Like spinach.

chapter sixteen

theater and dance, gay and otherwise

While not suffering in quality, gay theaters and gay and lesbian theater companies have dropped sufficiently in numbers in the nineties. It's hard to say exactly why, but many in the field say it has much to do with the decline in "specialized audiences." Gays and lesbians may support gay-owned stores and artists, but when it comes to theater, well, Neil Simon unfortunately wins out.

But don't despair—gay theater and dance are alive! And so are the multitude of companies, mentioned in this chapter, that are parties to the cause, sponsoring and nurturing gay writers and gay-themed and lesbian-oriented plays and musicals, even supporting the community with benefits and cash.

Here's a listing of some of the best gay theater, and a few main stages that every gay man and lesbian should pay heed to.

anything arty

■ important theater companies for the lesbian and gay on the go

the glines
240 west 44th street, new york, ny 10036, 357-8899

For information about local gay theater happenings, call the one producer (John Glines) who keeps producing when all else fails due to lack of funding. Not all this theater is good, but all of it is gay. Glines presents an array of gay performance pieces, and was responsible for Harvey Fierstein's *Torch Song Trilogy* both off and on Broadway. (Glines also coproduced William M. Hoffman's *As Is*.) However, recently Glines has been presenting too many shows written by John Glines. One show not written by Glines was *Get Used to It: A Gay Musical Revue* by Tom Wilson, performed at the Courtyard Playhouse in March of 1993. Write to The Glines, Forty-Fourth, or call for information on upcoming shows. Important group—but there are many more.

joyce theater
175 eighth avenue at west 19th street, 242-0800

The Joyce stages a terrific range of performances every year. Dance companies that come here range from avant-garde contemporary troupes to international ensembles focusing on traditional dance forms.

manstage
243-9504

This group goes in and out of business with every turn of the economy. Recently, Manstage coproduced *Landscape with Male Figures*, a gay farce about sexual fantasies, with the Glines company. Call for information about a new season.

theater and dance, gay and otherwise

new york city feminist theater
p.o. box 1348, madison square garden station, new york, ny 10159

An organization for women in the theater-related arts. "Promotes feminist ideas and values which contribute a sense of identity, pride and solidarity for women." Informal performances and readings are held from time to time.

p.s. 122
150 first avenue at east 10th street, 477-5288

Founded in 1977 in an old schoolhouse, P.S. 122 is one of the more venerable performance art institutions on the downtown circuit. Stop by or call to get a schedule of performances and gallery shows. If you're not too up on the performance art world, P.S. 122 is a good place to experiment.

queer culture
219-3088

A regular assemblage of gay performers that is in its second run. Hundreds of shows participate at eighteen theaters. The official name for this early-June montage is "Hot! The Annual New York Celebration of Gay Culture." Find out more about it by calling. See Chapter 5, "Special Events Calendar."

ridiculous theatrical company
1 sheridan square, 691-2271

Founded by Charles Ludlam in 1967, Ridiculous now operates under the artistic direction of Everett Quinton. The company stages three performances a year at the Charles Ludlam Theater and performs internationally. Ridiculous is famous for its adaptation of *Camille*.

anything arty

roundabout theater company
west 45th street and broadway, 719-9393

This particularly well-endowed company has a subscription series specifically geared to gay men and lesbians, one or two evenings during each run of the year's regular season. There's a reception after each "special evening's show"; the informal gathering includes wine, soda, Johnnie Walker (the politically correct sponsor) and even some foodstuffs. Some receptions have live music. Five shows or a three-play package. The evenings draw 250 to 400 people.

summerstage
360-2777

Every year the administrative people at Central Park organize a two-month blast of theater and performance art—and music and readings—in the middle of the park. To get the SummerStage schedule, call after June 1.

$3 bill theater
530 west 23rd street, suite 429, new york, ny 10011, 575-0263

Formed in 1988, the $3 Bill Theater is one of the earliest full-time gay theaters in New York. This important group started with an annual series of plays. It got off to a good start—a play about how AIDS affects friendships by Victor Bumbalo called *Adam & the Experts*, and well-staged readings including one of Paula Vogel's *And Baby Makes Seven*, which later played off Broadway—but $3 Bill has since fallen on bad financial times. Call to receive a current calendar.

In the past, $3 Bill has requested scripts and auditioned performers. Productions begun this way have included Tony Boutte's *The Road to Hell* and Madeleine Olnek's *Codependent Lesbian Space Alien Seeks Same*.

theater and dance, gay and otherwise

vortex theater company
206-1764

This group produces contemporary plays by lesbian and gay playwrights and stages five or six performances a year at the Sanford Meisner Theater (see below). The artistic director is Robert Coles. In addition, Vortex sponsors a series of readings of new works and maintains a resident playwrights program. For information and tickets, call. Just call.

wings theater company
154 christopher street, 627-2960

This company produces plays by American playwrights, including a Gay Play Series which runs throughout the year. Wings also offers productions such as musicals about gay and lesbian pride and songfests about gay history. Some of the pieces are stodgy, but it's the thought that counts. Of late, the new play by literary genius Eric Bentley premiered at Wings. Hope is on the way.

york theater company
534-5366

The York Theater Company offers a subscription series to its regular season for lesbians and gay men. Mostly musicals, usually along a Sondheim vein. No summer season.

■ **theater knowledge**

art at st. ann's and the ninth street theater company
718/858-2424

Both of these groups (at the same place) have been known to compose ideas relating to gay culture. Art at St. Ann's is at St. Ann's Church,

anything arty

157 Montague Street in Brooklyn Heights. Remember, Brooklyn is really fun (See A Look at Gay Neighborhoods).

lesbians in the creative arts (lica)
242-0536

Each year LICA presents us with a "Video Cabaret, Video Entertainments by and for the Lesbian Community." To learn about LICA's latest endeavors, call and say, "What's up?"

la mama e.t.c.
74-a east fourth street, 254-6468

This is the oldest off-Broadway space. It proffers a slew of gay-related or AIDS-themed productions in its many spaces. A recent split production of Split Britches and London's Bloolips troupe produced a funny, campy send-up of Tennessee Williams's *A Streetcar Named Desire*. It started at La Mama's Monday-night extravaganza, called The Club at La Mama E.T.C. (Entertainment Theater Complex). This was good, clean, dirty fun and falls in line with many of the outlandish productions found here. Also, *Positive Me*, a musical by Lisa Edelstein that was meant as education about HIV, played here to raves. A positive depiction and one that was sorely needed.

mass transit theater company
740-8589

This is not a gay place but it does deal with related issues in its quest to put on street theater at odd places. Travels frequently.

theater and dance, gay and otherwise

perry street theater
31 perry street, 255-7190, box office 691-2509

Owned and operated by a lesbian, PST is known for producing a variety of lesbian and gay plays. For details, call its owner, Tammis Day, or call the box office. Incidentally, the place was built in the 1850s as a stable and came back as a theater in 1975, where it ran a few good shows. But in 1988, when Day bought Perry Street, she turned it into a home that has since presented one of the longest-running gay plays of the decade: *The Night Larry Kramer Kissed Me*. Not that the decade has gone on that long. Recently, revivals have been the norm.

sanford meisner theater
164 eleventh avenue, between 22nd and 23rd streets, 206-1764

Cute Boys in Their Underpants was just one comedy performance staged at the Meisner. This is a *major* home to off-Broadway gay plays—and important lesbian plays as well. For information and reservations, call and ask to be put on the mailing list. I saw *When Fat Women Ruled the World* and, well, I *still* love the title.

theaterworks: emerging/ experimentaldirections (t.w.e.e.d.)
66 wooster street, 924-0077

As its name suggests, this group offers atypical performances. One show of late was *Pinocchio*, about a boy who is queer and coming of age in an era of AIDS and homophobia.

theatre-at-224-waverly place
564-8038

This is becoming a full-time gay stage house. Recently, *Homosexual Acts* premiered: twelve short plays by seven well-known writers. Call to get a calendar.

anything arty

town hall
123 west 43rd street, 840-2824

Town Hall presents classical and contemporary music and drama throughout the year. A good place to see things, often inexpensively.

women's project
382-2750

Women's theater has come a long way of late, particularly with the new independence of this not-for-lesbians—or at least not specifically—company, which began as an appendage to the American Place Theatre complex of midtown. In the eighties, a rich dowager gave a million or so smackeroos to Women's Project's leader, Julia Miles, and said, "Go forth, women." From then on the company has performed all around town, presenting plays devoted to women's issues. The pledge of the project, which mostly performs at the Apple Corps Theater in Chelsea but has its offices in the Chandler Building in midtown, is "to identify, encourage, develop, and produce women playwrights and to help establish confidence and visibility for women playwrights and directors." Marlane Meyer's play *Etta Jenks* was a touching, comic *and* tragic piece about an unwitting prostitute's down-and-out life.

■ **experimentation**

The best experiment in cheap theater is going to workshops produced regularly by the institutional theater companies. In other words, you can go to their second-string shows—those presumed not ready for prime time—on the cheap. These include **circle repertory** (505-6010); **manhattan theater club** (645-5590); **csc repertory** (677-4210); and the **riverside shakespeare theater** (567-0025). . . . If a theater rents its space to a unique company and you have no idea who it is (The Triplex at 199 Chambers Street, 618-1980, is a good example), don't just wonder whether the theater does that all the time: write to **theater space** and say, "I want to be on your mailing list." . . . One-acts are wonderful because you get to

theater and dance, gay and otherwise

see a fully realized idea in short form. See them during evening-long festivals at midtown locations, including (take a deep breath) **new dramatists** (757-6960); **ensemble studio theater** (247-3405); **manhattan class company** (727-7722); and the much-praised **young playwrights festival** (307-1140), where you see tomorrow's stars of writing today. . . . **festival latino** (598-7155): The New York Shakespeare Festival at the **joseph papp public theater** on Lafayette Street and the **biograph cinema** (at 57th Street and Broadway) hold a festival for Latin theater and cinema each summer. Included are feature films, documentaries, plays and musicals about the Latino/a experience. Little of the gay and lesbian experience is included, but it is art for all kinds. (More on film in Chapter 19.)

■ theater without labels

ny stage & film company (586-5743) produces readings of new plays at spaces throughout the city, free. More freebies like this are discussed in Chapter 11, "Freebies in New York City." **medicine show** (81 East 2nd Street, 254-3566) continues to pore over musicals of the old days and political spiels about today's problematic world. The Gulf war was picked on recently; then it was back to ancient Cole Porter. Call to get on a list that is truly not trendy.

■ ethnic, classic, culturally important theater

True theater buffs should contact the following reputable repertory companies to find out what's new in ethnic, classic and culturally important plays. **the acting company** (564-3510) dotes on the classics, with a twist. **the billie holiday theatre company** (718/636-0918) concentrates on the black experience. **intar** (International Arts Relations, 695-6134) is devoted to Hispanic theater and dance. **jean cocteau repertory** (677-0060) does the classics, and recently a few new plays from the Eastern Bloc, on a tiny stage. **mabou mines** (473-0559) is another floating company, whose sole purpose is strange and unusual theater (stuff no one else would do,

anything arty

such as a female *Lear*). **music-theater performing group/ lenox arts center** (371-9610) combines music, dance and pure theater in an odd assortment of theater pieces based on old stories. **national black theater** (722-3800) does only stage plays by black authors. **negro ensemble company** (575-5860) is an ages-old company of black writers, producers and directors. **new federal theater at the henry street settlement** (598-0400), at 101 years old, is the only complex in the city that promulgates the efforts of a variety of racial minorities. **joseph papp public theater** (598-7100) is an important theater complex, only this one is more for the mainstream arts. **pan asian repertory** (245-2660) is devoted to Oriental/Asian theatrical arts, most presented through modern story lines. **theatre for the new city** (254-1109) is the East Village's oldest avant-garde company, devoting space to new and revered playwrights and the oddest ideas.

■ "more theater worth mentioning"

Gay theater aficionados will want to know about the performers who participate in the *O Solo Mio* festival at **new york theater workshop** each spring at Perry Street Theater (31 Perry Street, 691-2509). **vortex theater company** (164 Eleventh Avenue between West 22nd and 23rd streets, 206-1764) puts on good and mediocre gay theater at the Sanford Meisner Theater; **westbeth theater company** (151 Bank Street, 691-2272) rents its space to several gay companies; the East Village's quite political **rapp** (220 East 4th Street) often inserts gay ideas into its controversial, all-too-hip productions (e.g., *Uncle Vanya* with the uncle as a man of color and slowed down to a crawl); a Brooklyn-based group, **baca downtown** (111 Willoughby Street, downtown Brooklyn, 718/596-2222), often produces gay-themed work at its space; **55 grove street cabaret** (366-5438) presents a few gay performers whose comedy constitutes theater; and lastly, two great organizations on the Lower East Side are **dixon place** (258 Bowery, 219-3088) and a local organization called the **wow cafe** (59 East 4th Street, 460-8067) is a performance

theater and dance, gay and otherwise

artists' showcase and wild Lower East Side institution offering a full schedule of readings and performance art throughout the year. The calendar includes specifically gay and lesbian matter and regular benefits for gay and lesbian organizations. People like Eric Bogosian and Ann Magnuson often show up to hone their craft; a few years ago Joan Rivers came back for a stint to ensure she could make loyal audiences laugh.

■ mainstream theater hints

Here are the more mainstream events and the best of New York's hip theater scene: The **american place theater** (111 West 46th Street, 840-3074) is a regular theater-space-rental house that presents women-oriented theater too, including plays by Joyce Carol Oates and other contemporary females. . . . **forty-second street theater row:** All along the row are a series of theaters showing new and almost-ready-for-prime-time attractions. Tickets can be purchased for between $8 and $22 at Ticket Central (406 West 42nd Street). Visit Ticket Central, pick something interesting on a weekend, and go!

chapter seventeen

galleries and museums for the gay at heart

■ **galleries**

I've listed some interesting galleries around town, but it's certainly not a comprehensive roster. Wander around in the neighborhoods.

artmakers
718/832-1951

An immovable feast of sorts is found in the work of Artmakers, a nonprofit group of muralists who produce surreal pieces, political statements and group and solo inspirations. Artmakers think "underground art" serves a purpose: They want art lovers who will not generally visit galleries to see their work. Muralists don't care where you see their work. See Manhattan examples of Artmakers' work at the Broadway-Lafayette subway station; at 9th Street and Avenue C; and on the wall along West 142nd Street between Amsterdam Avenue and Hamilton Place.

anything arty

bronx river art center and gallery
1087 tremont avenue, bronx, 718/589-5819

Deep in the southeast Bronx, the Bronx River Restoration took a building on the shore of a filthy river in the hope of creating a space for developing art programs. Later, a group of artists working with the local government and stoic residents turned the four-floor space into an artistic diamond in a fairly rough neighborhood. The first floor houses the professional gallery. The upstairs (second and third floors) hosts an artists' studio space program. On the fourth floor is a photography, silk-screen and ceramics center. This floor is also used for teaching classes to children and adults. A special attribute is the sculpture garden, dirty and graffiti-covered, by the river. During the summer, behind the gallery, a fenced area houses complete sculpture shows. (Their doors depict a colorful series of Bronx-born celebrities, by the above-mentioned Artmakers.) Hours for the gallery and community center are Tuesday through Thursday 3 to 6 P.M., and on Saturday for exhibition openings.

ceres gallery
584 broadway at prince street, 226-4725

Founded in 1981, Ceres is the gallery of the New York Feminist Art Institute and presents regular exhibitions of work by women artists. In addition, Ceres offers a comprehensive program of performances (music, performance art, dance, etc.) as well as poetry and literature readings, lectures related to women in the arts and art criticism, and classes and workshops. Ceres maintains a slide library of work by contemporary women artists. Hours are Tuesday through Sunday 11 A.M. to 6 P.M. Go see the gallery or call to find out about women's art.

city hall park sculptures
park row and broadway, no phone number

During some summers, right beyond the steps of City Hall—where Tammany Hall's shifty politics got its start—you will find the best

galleries and museums for the gay at heart

collection of outdoor sculptures in the city. Organized by the New York State Cultural Affairs Division, these art pieces include bird signs that seem oddly out of place. (The division tries to make you aware of non–New York birds by placing signs reading, for example, "New York: Your Host Today Is Cardinal.") Then there's a sculpture of a chain inside a cage, a piece about proud citizens, and one depicting several hands (*Civic Virtue/Civil Rights*). Strange meshes of art and history come together in this important exhibit, and you can see it all on your lunch hour. In the wintertime, it's merely a really nice park.

dia center for the arts
548 west 22nd street, 989-5912, 431-9232

A nonprofit space that develops visual pieces in its galleries on the second, third and fourth floors and on the roof, Dia believes in making atmosphere its focal point. To complement a piece titled *7000 Oaks*, Dia has planted a row of trees in front of the building. After moving from SoHo to Chelsea, the Dia Foundation retained its original commitment to discovering and advancing the work of worthy artists. Dia is well known for having shown Warhol's *Disaster Paintings 1963* in 1986 and in recent years has brought works by Walter DeMaria and other city favorites to light.

The center is open September through June, Thursday through Sunday from 11 A.M. to 6 P.M. Dia also presents modern dance performances every Thursday and Friday, September through June, at its 155 Mercer Street location. For more details about these performances, speak with Joan Duddy, dance program administrator.

■ gay-friendly art galleries

Not a complete listing, but one that can get you *into* NYC art: **jayne baum gallery** (588 Broadway, 219-9854), Tuesday through Saturday 10 A.M. to 6 P.M. . . . **paula cooper gallery** (155 Wooster Street, 674-0766), Tuesday through Saturday 10 A.M. to 6 P.M.; in summer, Monday through Friday 9:30 A.M. to 5 P.M. . . . **fulton gallery** (799 Lexington Avenue, 832-8854), Monday through Friday,

anything arty

10:30 A.M. to 5:30 P.M. . . . **gagosian gallery** (136 Wooster Street, 228-2828), Tuesday through Saturday 10 A.M. to 6 P.M.; in summer, Monday through Friday . . . **galaerie st. etienne** (24 West 57th Street, 245-6734), Tuesday through Saturday 11 A.M. to 5 P.M.; in summer, Tuesday through Friday . . . **hirschl & adler modern** (420 West Broadway, 966-6211), Tuesday through Saturday 10 A.M. to 6 P.M.; in summer, Monday through Friday . . . **barbara toll fine arts** (146 Greene Street, 431-1788), Tuesday through Saturday 10 A.M. to 6 P.M.; in summer, Tuesday through Friday 11 A.M. to 5 P.M. . . . **wooster gardens** (40 Wooster Street, 941-6210), Tuesday through Saturday, 11 A.M. to 6 P.M.; in summer, Tuesday through Friday.

humanities council of new york university
998-2190

NYU sponsors unusual exhibits connected to its humanities program: *Politics and Polemics: French Caricature and the French Revolution* presented cartoons from 1789 to 1799, with modern comparisons. A variety of European painters exhibit at the various houses for foreign languages across the NYU campus. These exhibitions are refreshing to attend, as they usually coincide with an intriguing lecture or other presentation.

Besides European subjects, the Humanities Council commissions poetry and artwork from Africa and Latin America. Call for information and get on the varied mailing lists. Events in the arts and humanities take place in various campus buildings.

international center of photography (icp)
1130 fifth avenue at east 94th street, 860-1777; 1133 avenue of the americas at west 43rd street, 768-4682

Photography at larger art museums tends to consist of "home movie" portraits by the more famous picture takers. Artistic photography found at ICP comes from a wide pool of commercial and abstract artists who offer unique world visions—with risks. This gallery believes in allowing

galleries and museums for the gay at heart

a photographer to make a statement with as many as 100 photos at a time. It also has a room for viewing real home movies or screen bios of photographers.

The midtown space is three times the old Fifth Avenue one's size; there are nearly 5,000 photos in high-tech style. Still, hard-core ICP fans love the Fifth Avenue location because it has a rustic quality like that of a private home. The centers' hours are Tuesday 11 A.M. to 8 P.M., and Wednesday through Sunday 11 A.M. to 6 P.M. The two locations are all over town!

isamu noguchi garden—a gallery
32–37 vernon boulevard, long island city, queens, 718/204-7088 or 718/721-1932

The building has a funny shape because it's situated on a sidewalk curved to make the octagonal structure look natural. Out in Long Island City (near the N train stop), the designer set out to "conserve the artistic environment" by building a theater, a garden, an outdoor lighting scheme, and a fancy setup for unusual pieces that allows an artist's vision to come forth without crowding. The museum of Isamu Noguchi is a rarity that gives visitors enough space to ponder the sculptor's message.

Although it seems improbable that such a beautiful place would sit in the midst of factories and warehouses, Noguchi was truly a pioneer in a neighborhood that soon after became an art circuit. Open Wednesday, Saturday and Sunday from April through November, 11 A.M. to 6 P.M. At 2 there are free gallery tours. On Saturday and Sunday, you can take a shuttle bus from Park Ave and 70th Street for $5 round trip, or travel by the tram to Roosevelt Island. A red bus will pick you up at the tram station and transport you to the museum for $4 round trip.

anything arty

the kitchen center for video, music, dance, performance, film and literature
512 west 19th street, 255-5793

Performance artists say if you watch what the Kitchen does, you'll be ahead of the trends. The first place to house video and performance art has always said its purpose is "to encourage the development of contemporary, high-risk art." The Kitchen has introduced into the mainstream such performers as Eric Bogosian and cult artist Ann Carlson, both of whom started as oddities on the downtown scene. In the eighties, when the Kitchen was based in SoHo, you got assaulted by a vast array of monitors as you entered. Today the Kitchen's skinny Chelsea building is filled with small theaters—a video viewing room, an exhibition space, a 75-seat theater/gallery space with periodic exhibitions and a 200-seat "black box" where one-person shows are performed. Facilities are also available for editing and video transfers. The Kitchen's season runs September through May. Office hours are Monday through Friday 10 A.M. to 5 P.M. Call for a calendar of events or to make an appointment for video viewing.

la mama la galleria
6 east first street, 505-2476

La Mama E.T.C. was the place for avant-garde theater until recently, when it started looking more into moneymaking. Thankfully, the nearby gallery still believes in the outrageous, and if recent exhibits are any indication, that credo is here to stay. *Colours Out!* featured extraordinary hammocks; *Vessels* was one show that really took off with a ship collection. La Mama's additional gallery, **second classe** — a former garage that is a work of art in itself—displays unique and oblique creative pieces.

"As If the Top of My Head Were Taken Off" was the title of a poetry night at La Galleria, which is all that remains of the old guard of the old avant-garde. La Galleria is open September through June, Tuesday through Sunday 1 to 6 P.M. On weekends there are poetry or play readings and a variety of performances.

galleries and museums for the gay at heart

stark gallery
594 broadway, at prince street, 3rd floor, 925-4484

Stark takes a curatorial angle—showing reductive abstraction and conceptual work. No lectures, no events save an annual benefit for changing causes. Open Tuesday through Saturday 10 A.M. to 6 P.M. Stark has been around since 1987.

white columns gallery
154 christopher street, 924-4212

It certainly takes dedication to make it in the art world. The first alternative gallery in New York had to break many taboos to become the hottest place in town. White Columns is a small, highly regarded space with programs that mix political assemblages with picturesque artworks. The gimmick is whiteness: white rooms, white architectural design, white floors and white promotional brochures. The space is ever-changing and it claims to aspire to meaningful works, not to what area artists dub "fun art." The gallery's season lasts from September through May.

■ museums and institutes, etc.

alternative museum
594 broadway at prince street, suite 402; 966-4444

Shows are centered around political issues (domestic violence, history of black cowboys in the American Southwest, anti-Asian violence, etc). The museum seeks to show artists who have been disenfranchised or underrecognized because of their race, gender, ethnicity or ideology. Besides its exhibition schedule, the Alternative Museum hosts panel discussions and lectures and new music and jazz series. Hours are Tuesday through Saturday 11 A.M. to 6 P.M. (Closed mid-August through Labor Day.) Admission is $3, but heck, pay what you can.

anything arty

guggenheim museum
1071 fifth avenue at east 76th street, 423-3500

The Guggenheim has an outstanding permanent collection of modern masterpieces, exhibited in the famous and recently remodeled Frank Lloyd Wright building, as well as special and traveling exhibitions. The Guggenheim is now open every night except Thursday until 8 P.M. The cafe, run by Dean & Deluca, serves until 9. Also, Guggenheim has a new, smaller outpost, open late nights, at the corner of Broadway and Prince Street.

lower east side tenement museum
97 orchard street between delancey and broome, 431-0233

The anything-but-charming Tenement Museum was chartered in 1988, seeking to promote tolerance by teaching the history of the various settlement experiences on the Lower East Side of New York. The museum is housed in a pre–Old Law tenement building, listed on the National Register of Historic Places. The museum shows a few exhibits (e.g., on peddlers, photos of the Lower East Side from the turn of the century, and a scale model of the tenement, with humans demonstrating how people lived there in 1870 and 1915). There's a slide show and a video show. Best time to go is on Sunday, when the museum offers walking tours through the day as well as the slide show. A shop sells books and other materials about the history of the Lower East Side (an excellent place to get materials before starting out on an exploration).

The museum is open Tuesday through Friday 11 A.M. to 4 P.M., Sunday 10 A.M. to 5 P.M. Walking tours on Sunday cost $12, $10 for seniors or students. Admission to the gallery is free during the week but on weekends costs $3.

Rumor has it that by the time this book is in print the *real* museum may have opened; that is to say, the designers will have placed actors in rooms above the ground floor, playing turn-of-the-century families (Irish, German, Jewish, Italian) suffering through their cramped, impoverished daily routine. It's not meant to be fun, but to

galleries and museums for the gay at heart

help you learn some history and cherish New York's rich culture even more.

Closest subway is the F train to the Delancey Street stop.

the new museum
583 broadway at prince street, 219-1355 or 219-1222

This always-new museum is committed to exploring nontraditional ideas and experimental works of art. The exhibition schedule frequently includes shows with a political nature. There's a comprehensive schedule of lectures, films and gallery talks. Hours are Wednesday through Friday and Sunday noon to 6 P.M., Saturday noon to 8. Admission: adults $3.50; seniors, children and students $2.50.

When meandering around SoHo, please note the window at the front of the museum for a floating exhibit of sexually aware art. Sometimes it's quite explicit, such as the Prostitutes of New York/Gran Fury piece on safe sex in 1991 and the fact that the American mainstream is afraid to discuss it. In 1987, the New Museum window made a powerful statement when it featured busts of several world leaders with each one's most prominent statement on the AIDS crisis. Underneath then President Reagan's bust was nothing.

new york transit museum
718/330-3063

Some may badmouth New York's subway system, but it is the world's largest. At the New York Transit Museum you'll learn about the history of this monstrous wonder down under and its relationship to the growth and development of New York. In the summer, the museum offers many activities and tours inside and outside. Inside, there's a series of free workshops for children. Outside, you can explore neighborhoods in the five boroughs while learning about a variety of related topics and issues. Examples are a "Brooklyn at Work" tour series and a bridge and neighborhood tour at either end of the city. In the fall, the museum holds its annual auction of transit stuff from past and present. During the winter, when it's too chilly for exploring, check

anything arty

out the lectures and other events at the museum. The prices for walking tours vary between $10 and $25. The museum's hours are Tuesday through Friday 10 A.M. to 4 P.M. and Saturday and Sunday 11 A.M. to 4 P.M. Admission is $3 for adults and $1 for children and seniors. Part of the museum's charm is its location. It's housed in an old subway station in Brooklyn Heights, at the corner of Boerum Place and Schermerhorn Street. Just walk from the Borough Hall subway stop.

chapter eighteen

literary new york

■ gay bookstores and libraries

a different light
548 hudson street, between perry and charles, 800/343-4002

A Different Light prides itself on its comprehensive selection of books by, for and about gay and lesbian people. Or as they put it: "Everything that covers gays and lesbians and is in print, we carry." The store has 15,000 titles in stock, including more than 500 AIDS/HIV-related titles. Besides books of all sorts, A Different Light carries magazines and newspapers from throughout the United States. Its periodical collection is an excellent resource for people traveling to other parts of the United States who want to read in a local gay rag about cities they may be visiting. A Different Light holds weekly author readings throughout the year, except in July and August.

The store has several bulletin boards as well as racks and racks of flyers about things going on in New York, and prints a monthly calendar of events and a catalog. The store can be reached toll-free! A Different Light has stores in New York, West Hollywood and San Francisco. The NYC store opened in 1984.

anything arty

judith's room
681 washington street, between 10th and charles, 727-7330

Books for women and their friends. This is the only bookstore in the city that relates solely to women. Books, magazines, newspapers. Cards, posters, T-shirts, jewelry. Weekly readings by women authors, several bulletin boards and a table filled with flyers about events and organizations in New York. An excellent place for women to get oriented, get a sense of what is going on in NYC and identify resources. Judith's Room publishes a free newsletter and mails out a monthly calendar of events. Hours: Tuesday through Thursday noon to 8 P.M., Friday and Saturday noon to 9, Sunday noon to 7.

lesbian herstory archives
484 14th street, park slope, brooklyn, 718/768-3953

The Lesbian Herstory Archives has been around since 1976, and was originally in the apartment of the founders (Joan Nestle and Deborah Edel). Their goal was to provide a place where lesbians could preserve their "herstory" and where all lesbian lives would be welcome, regardless of race or class. Now the archives is the largest lesbian archives in the world, operating since mid-1993 in a newly renovated brownstone in Park Slope. This represents the first building owned by a lesbian group. The archives have more than 10,000 volumes, 12,000 photographs, 1,400 periodicals, special collections and files on organizations. It's a great research source and community facility. The archives strive to be inclusive and accessible to all women. Call for events and for hours. The rest, as they say, is herstory.

oscar wilde memorial bookshop
15 christopher street, 255-8097

The world's first gay and lesbian storefront, founded in 1967. The bookshop maintains a comprehensive list of gay and lesbian titles. Excellent bulletin boards and informative staff. Catalog available.

literary new york

pat parker and vito russo center library
lesbian and gay community services center, 208 west 13th street, 505-6246

This is a free public lending library of gay- and lesbian-related books and periodicals which includes more than 5,000 titles and hundreds of periodicals dating to the 1950s. It's a joint project with Publishing Triangle, the group for gay and lesbian authors/editors/etc. Open from 6 to 8 P.M. on Monday and Tuesday and from 1 to 4 P.M. on Saturday.

three lives & company, ltd.
154 west 10th street, 741-2069

You may have seen what the ad refers to as the "sixteen-year-old, old-fashioned, cozy, customer oriented general bookstore" in the movie *Bright Lights, Big City* or as part of a J. Crew ad. This is a lesbian-owned bookstore, and although it's woman-oriented and mostly promotes women authors, the store still remains a general bookstore specializing in art books, garden books, gay literature and, ahem, guides, mystery books and general fiction and nonfiction.

The staffers are well-read and knowledgeable about all the latest general-interest and lesbian- and gay-related books—they have to be to keep their special customers happy. They offer special services to those who ask: special gift wrapping, sending books across the globe or choosing a book that they deem well suited to a customer and sending one per month. They'll even send your mother a book a month at your request (no joke). In general, they're helpful and informative —and active in the community. Three Lives also hosts "Readings and Signings" on Thursday at 8 P.M.—at least half are by gay or lesbian writers. Store hours are usually Monday through Saturday, 11 A.M. to 8 P.M. and Sunday 1 to 7 P.M. Visit or call about events or info on the latest best-sellers.

anything arty

■ other bookstores

new york bound bookshop
50 rockefeller plaza, 245-8503

This bookstore specializes in books about New York—a very important subject to you if you're reading this book. It carries books that cover New York's history, planning, architecture, neighborhoods, immigrant experience, journalism, crime and nightlife. The shop has tons of guidebooks, photographic books, books that are new and out of print. There's a huge collection of New York photographs, turn-of-the-century images and old maps. The shop is in the lobby of the Associated Press building. It's mentioned because anyone reading a guidebook to New York should know there are others—and this is the best place to find all of them. (Not gay, but a bookstore meant for New York–philes to patronize.)

rizzoli book store
454 west broadway at prince street, 674-1616

A fancy bookshop at the epicenter of the SoHo shopping experience, Rizzoli specializes in art and architecture books, many of which Rizzoli publishes. Also, Rizzoli is one of the few nongay shops that features gay writers in its fine reading series. I read there once.

Fine bookstores for everyone else including gays and lesbians are: **murder ink** (2486 Broadway at West 93rd Street, 362-8905) for mystery lovers; **kitchen arts** (1435 Lexington Avenue at East 94th Street, 876-5550) for people who can't stop cooking; **biography** (400 Bleecker Street, 807-8655) for a bio on just about anyone; **s. f. vanni** (30 West 12th Street, 675-6336) for the poop on Italian culture; **a photographer's place** (133 Mercer Street, 431-9358) for photo stuff; **samuel weiser** (132 East 24th Street, 777-6363) for textbooks; and **antiquarian bookshop** (50 Rockefeller Plaza, 757-9395) and **argosy** (116 East 59th Street, 753-4455) for extreme rarities.

literary new york

■ good reads

christopher street

The monthly literary rag by That New Magazine, Inc., publishers of *New York Native* and *Stonewall News*. Publishes fiction, nonfiction, interviews, cartoons, photography and poetry by, for and about lesbians and gay men. Has been in publication for seventeen years. Nationally distributed, with contributors from across the country. $3 per issue. Available at newsstands and bookstores around New York, and at many bookstores around the United States.

chelsea journal
263-a west 19th street

A local giveaway weekly newspaper that regularly addresses gay and lesbian issues and is filled with helpful advertisements about what's going on in Chelsea. Pick it up at coffee shops, restaurants and some stores in the neighborhood. For a free copy, stop by the office.

first hand
310 cedar lane, teaneck, nj 07666

A popular national porn magazine that serves an incredible purpose: Each monthly issue includes a center-section "Survival Kit." This guide will give you AIDS information (well written, informative, with a sense of irony) and the types of facts every gay man needs: divorce laws, domestic laws, wills, gay couple family situations, how to have relationships, what to wear in bars, etc. If you think this sounds trivial, imagine a *Cosmo*-like article for gay men: "How Two Guys Should Argue." A section called "Books: Items from the Gay Book Basket" discusses new books for gay readers, and Ed Hynde's "AIDS Watch" helps us understand the disease of our time.

First Hand is distributed throughout the United States and Canada by Kable News, a mainstream company, assuring that all Americans get a *load* of this.

anything arty

genre out, & metro source

Three magazines that spout politics, lifestyle, fashion for gay men and lesbians. In *Genre*, there is no news or political stuff, only what's important to the personal lives of gay men. *Genre* has regular columns on health and medicine, food and cooking, grooming, and finance. Available by subscription since 1991, it's produced about six times a year (sometimes seven) and is, like *Out*, also available at many newsstands in New York, as well as at the major chain bookstores (B. Dalton, Waldenbooks, Barnes & Noble) nationwide. $3.95 per issue.

Out, at $4.95 per issue, focuses more on national issues and has a helluva lot less New York–based information. It includes a lot more political and topical coverage than *Genre* and the national news magazine for gays and lesbians, *The Advocate* (described in Chapter 1, "Essential Resources"). The arts coverage in *Out* is much more "cultural," as opposed to pop. *Metro source*, a giveaway at local bars, clubs and community centers, is a good source for information, and lets you in on the latest trends.

heresies

Heresies, A Feminist Publication on Art and Politics, is published by a collective of women once or twice a year. Each issue has a theme—media, activism, food, coming of age; there have been lesbian issues in the past. The publication is not targeted exclusively at lesbians, but rather at women and men who are interested in art and writing by and about women, which naturally includes lesbian topics. *Heresies* was founded by artists, writers and curators, who continue to form the core of the collective. It's available at lesbian and gay bookstores in NYC as well as at other independent booksellers. It was recently spotted in the window of Intermale bookshop in Amsterdam—not for women only. Cover price is $8 an issue.

on our backs   800/845-4617

"We celebrate the entire variety of lesbian sexuality and provide a voice that otherwise would not exist today," says the literature. *On*

literary new york

Our Backs is a sexy and sassy journal dedicated to promoting sexual communication and sexual literacy among lesbians. It publishes award-winning fiction, pictorials, columns, reviews and features. *Backs* was created by lesbians in 1984 when an editor of a major magazine realized there was nothing erotic made by and for lesbians; the periodical proudly describes itself as breaking the silence around lesbian sexuality. *Backs* is available monthly in New York at Judith's Room, Eve's Garden, A Different Light, the Oscar Wilde Memorial Bookshop and other independent booksellers, and by subscription. $7 per copy.

out and about
800/929-2268

Begun in September of 1992 and published ten times a year, O & A is the only non-advertiser-biased publication on gay travel—a very important magazine because it has no ax to grind except to help us. Its writers speak especially to the needs of the experienced gay and lesbian traveler. It's one part *Condé Nast Traveler*, one part *Consumer Reports*, one part *Damron's* (the guidebook to gay life if all you do is cruise!).

For instance, *Out and About* will rate Palm Springs guest houses, tell you how Miami Beach ("South Beach," "SoBe") is doing, do a two-part series on international travel precautions for the HIV-positive traveler, or give you the rundown on gay summer resorts such as Saugatuck or California's famed Russian River. The editorial mix represents all travel opportunities for gay men and lesbians, but it is really more for men. (However, there are lesbians on staff and many lesbian freelance writers giving their points of view.)

There's a regular calendar highlighting cruises and where to cruise, tours, special gay-related cultural events and festivals of interest to gay travelers. In each issue there are two or three city briefs—where to stay, where to eat, work out, go out, etc. The editors say it's "not comprehensive but overly selective." Kind of like gay dating. Annual subscriptions are $49. Call and ask for a back issue: "New York Shopping For the Gay Lifestyle." Wow!

anything arty

radical chicks

Radical Chicks is a hip, intelligent and sexy bimonthly by, for and about lesbians and feminists. The *Chicks* publish news stories, lesbian community features, interviews, book reviews, poetry and sports stories. *Radical Chicks* is available at gay and lesbian bookstores and at many newsstands at $2 per issue. Write to them c/o the Lesbian and Gay Community Services Center (208 West 13th Street, New York, NY 10011).

ps for good readers

Found in the unlikely hetero magazine *Men's Fitness* (though is anything unlikely hetero in this world?), a helpful section for people interested in the latest periodical-oriented AIDS info: Called *AIDS Watch*, it is insightful—with research news and safe-sex pointers—and unusual in that it doesn't seem to have an agenda. If you would like to know more about this page, write MF at 21100 Erwin Street, Woodland Hills, CA 91367. You can contribute material. When a non-gay magazine puts this much muscle into AIDS knowledge, it's worth noting.

■ **literary happenings and the like**

in our own write
620-7310

Readings, writing workshops, writers' showcases organized by the L and G Center throughout the year. Call or stop by the center (208 West 13th Street) for a schedule.

literary new york

flat gen poetry series
p.o. box 8355, new york, ny 10116, no phone number

Poet Jody Azzouni runs this annual poetry series. Write to her for more information.

gay and lesbian reading group
213-1813

This group has been exploring gay and lesbian literature together, "without academic jargon," since 1993. Members read an eclectic selection of gay and lesbian writers from all periods. People are welcome to drop in and join or call ahead and see what the group is reading. This is a gay and lesbian offshoot of a suburban New York phenomenon—the weekly women's reading group. What's next? Gay kaffeeklatsches? No, Lesbian est sessions, most certainly. Participants vary in age and background.

metropolitan museum of art lecture series
fifth avenue and 82nd street, 570-3949

In the Grace Rainey Rogers Auditorium at the Met a lecture series is offered twice a year, once in the fall and again in the spring. The lectures focus specifically on either music or art. This is your chance to get it from those who "know," because those lecturing are respected critics, curators, historians, professors and other experts in the field.

Sixteen lectures are offered each season, with one to four talks in each series. Also at the Met are concerts, mostly of chamber music, by well-known New York ensembles. And for the carolers, there is also a Christmas Concert Series. Tickets are available on the day of the lecture at the Met box office, and series tickets are available in advance through the box office or by mail. Ticket prices range from $10 to $25. Call for details or visit the museum for a schedule. And while you're there, catch one of the daily gallery talks or lectures about the current exhibitions.

anything arty

new york public library
fifth avenue at 42nd street, 704-8600

The New York Public Library is a great place to meet people. Period. Though it's mentioned elsewhere in this book, the most outstanding reason to remember the library is the Lecture Bureau at the main location, at 42nd Street. Speakers hired include book authors, journalists, other literati and artists. Often the series brings to the library speakers of particular interest to gays and lesbians. The series has two seasons, fall-winter and winter-spring. Tickets can be purchased in advance by mail, or at the gift shop on the lobby level. Lectures are $6, concerts $7.50. Get a lecture series schedule at the gift shop or by calling the number above. The series is held in the Celeste Bartos Forum (930-0571).

The sixty-five branch libraries, which are administered separately from the main library, have their own series of events. For a schedule, call the branch.

poetry project
second avenue and east 10th street, 674-0910

The Poetry Project at St. Mark's Church sponsors poetry readings throughout the week (Monday nights, "New, Up and Coming Writers"; Wednesday nights, "Established Poets"; Friday "Late Nights" are group readings around a theme.) The Poetry Project hosts a marathon benefit on New Year's Day at which more than 100 performers and poets appear—all day and into the evening. The project also sponsors workshops for poets. Programming runs October through May. You'll be asked for a $5 contribution for all readings. The project publishes a journal, *The World*, and a bimonthly newsletter. You can pick up the newsletter at the church or find listings in The *Village Voice*.

chapter nineteen

film and video—
if you like to watch

anthology film archive
32 second avenue at east 2nd street, 505-5181

Anthology Film Archive has a big collection of independent, avant-garde films from the past, as well as other material related to the history of avant-garde and independent film. In addition, the archive has weekly screenings of independently produced films and videos, mostly on the weekends (to the tune of 400 screenings a year). Every September the archive sponsors "Mix: The Lesbian and Gay Experimental Film Festival," which showcases independent gay and lesbian films and videos each year, around the first week of September. It also has a book service, publishing and hawking books about independent film and video generally as well as about the stuff the archive shows. These are available by mail order through the catalog. The schedule comes out every two months. Screenings cost $6 or $7.

anything arty

downtown community television center
87 lafayette street, 966-4510

DCTV's video screening program—festivals with various themes—includes an annual gay and lesbian video festival. Besides screenings, DCTV offers video production workshops. Editing rooms are available to the public by advance reservation. DCTV maintains a library of tapes by community producers, and publishes a newsletter, *Scanlines*, which you can get at DCTV. At Works in Progress Meetings, every third Wednesday, directors come together to talk about their work.

film at the public
joseph papp public theater 425 lafayette street, 598-7166

A well-plotted selection of good first-run films, political cinema and, often, free shows on weekends about topical events (*Panama Deception*, which won the Oscar in '93, finally opened at the Public when no one else would run it.) Often the Public will take a failed first-run feature that's considered by some to be "art" and run it pre-video. The Public does festivals ("Garbo Talks") and old-fashioned revival-house fare for buffs who can't stand the small screen. A hint about the Public Theater's *film* program: "The more you see, the more you save!" is what will happen once you get the Joseph Papp Public Theater's Filmileage Membership Card. For info about the theater and details on how to join, call.

millennium
66 east 4th street, 673-0090

Millennium, established in 1966, makes 16mm and Super 8 film equipment and video equipment available for anyone to use at very low cost. It also sponsors the Personal Cinema Series, in the fall, winter and spring, during which people come in and coordinate screenings. "Experimental, avant-garde, mostly new works" are shown. Screenings are $6. Millennium also publishes a journal, called *Millennium*, about independent film, and offers film and video workshops.

film and video—if you like to watch

new festival
807-1820

Also known as the New York Lesbian and Gay Film Festival, this is surely one of the most important festivals in the city. The festival is held every year in the first two weeks in June, and has been going on since 1989. In 1993 172 films and videos were shown! The festival shows feature films, short films, and videos by and about gay men and lesbians. In 1993 the festival was at the Cinema Village 12th Street near University Place, but this is not a permanent home. Call the number above, and don't be shy: Find out about gay and lesbian film events any time during the year, for schedules, prices, and advice for a good time!

chapter twenty

the music chapter: sing this list

bargemusic
fulton ferry landing, brooklyn, 718/624-4061

Come hear chamber music performed by outstanding performers on a barge moored in the East River. Winters, too.

brooklyn academy of music
30 lafayette avenue, 718/636-4100

BAM puts on a series of new-wave operatic pieces that start at $15. Such innovative works as Philip Glass's *Einstein on the Beach* and *Hydrogen Jukebox* by Allen Ginsberg have premiered here. It's a good idea to get seats early in the season. Also at BAM is the "What's Going On?" music series, including tributes to soul greats of the past, a festival of gospel music, and even the best look at the musical world of Charlie Parker. For seats starting at $10, call . . . no, fax BAM at 718/857-2021.

anything arty

chamber music society of lincoln center
580-4302

The Chamber Music Society has been in residence at Lincoln Center, Broadway at 66th Street, since 1969. The 1993–94 season, the Chamber's twenty-fifth, runs from October through May and has included twelve programs presented in twenty-four concerts at Alice Tully Hall. The society is also launching a series of all-new-music concerts titled "Music in Our Time." Tickets are available by subscription or at the box office in Lincoln Center.

■ cheapo music events

Are you interested in knowing about some free or cheapo events that happen only seasonally? How about: early-evening recitals on Friday night at the **metropolitan museum** (535-7710) . . . The endangered **symphony space** on upper Broadway, with orchestras, revels, Mozart and Gilbert & Sullivan (864-1414) . . . **washington square on tuesday evenings** in the summertime—visit for a full orchestra and dress casually . . . **village light opera** for $10, the most classical, obscure operas known to man (243-6281) . . . **met opera national council** Audition Winners Concert is a mouthful, sure, but find out who's up and coming (769-7000) by viewing the best open-mouthed youths . . . **merkin concert hall's** Tuesday matinees are at 2 and cost around $7, but only during the school year (362-8719) . . . the **new york philharmonic symphony club** includes, for your $120 membership, musical highlights, a reception and some prestige (875-5700) . . . **great performers at lincoln center** features the greats in their primes (875-5388) . . . **town hall** has the best acoustics for new plays, traditional and classical music and—since I'm running off here—a composers' series titled "New Riffs" that showcases marimba, animal music ("moo," "ruff") and a jazz chamber set (997-1003).

the music chapter: sing this list

jazz babies
979-1065

A social group for lovers of classical jazz who want to get together and share their passion. Jazz Babies go to jazz clubs, swap music and attend other events.

jupiter symphony
122 west 69th street, 799-1259

This is an independent concert series at St. Stephen's Episcopal Church on the Upper West Side. Since the organizers are committed to making concert music accessible, they hold four concerts a year, each concert offered twice, on either a Monday evening or a Tuesday afternoon. The concerts are held in October, December, February and April. Ticket prices range from $6 to $18, or pay what you can.

manhattan school of music
120 claremont avenue, 749-2802

This school features opera throughout the year for a tiny fee. While we're discussing opera—every few Mondays the **mark goodson theater** (2 Columbus Circle, no phone number) presents operatic staged concerts at 12:30 P.M. No bag lunches.

merkin concert hall
129 west 67th street, 362-8719

This place hosts "Music Today" on Tuesday night with some of the sweetest soloists known to mankind. Single tickets are only $12 and up; the strings are beatific.

anything arty

metropolitan opera
769-7000

Summer in the Parks; the rest you can get from the *Cue* section of *New York* magazine.

new york city gay men's chorus
55 christopher street, 924-7770

Performs intermittently at Carnegie Hall and other stops. The chorus also publishes a newsletter called *Chorus Lines Update*.

new york philharmonic
hotline: 875-5709

The Philharmonic at Lincoln Center is one of the pillars of the New York cultural scene. Besides the full schedule of concerts it performs throughout the year, the Philharmonic gives occasional concerts at its original home, Carnegie Hall. And by the way, there's a free summer concert series held in parks throughout the five boroughs on a high-tech portable stage. The programs always begin at 8 P.M., and picnics have become a part of the tradition.

outmusic
533-0598

Outmusic is dedicated to expanding opportunities for gay and lesbian musicians, lyricists and musical performers. The group holds an open-mike night every month at the L and G Center (208 West 13th Street) and organizes other outlets for gay and lesbian musicians.

the music chapter: sing this list

saint andrew music society
921 madison avenue between 73-74 streets, 288-8920

For twenty-five years, the Madison Avenue Presbyterian Church has forgone church-oriented conclusions about having a good time in order to produce chorale recitals that are amazing, and amazingly expensive: For $30 to $499 (for society sponsors), you can see major performances throughout a regular school year (September through June). The concerts are all on Sunday, of course, and start at 4 P.M. When you call, ask for the director of music.

stonewall chorale
608-4504

New York's first gay choir, dedicated to the idea that music can break down barriers between people. Some sixty-five lesbians and gay men sing a more classical-oriented repertoire than other NYC groups.

■ stuff you wouldn't take your grandma to

Concerts at **stonewall** (53 Christopher Street, 463-0950): Some surreal stuff happens at the grungy though fun-filled (as in crowded) bar. I recently caught an actual live singer. **abc no rio** is 156 Rivington Street's answer to a punk club. Call for upcoming events. They have an *answering machine*, unlike many Yew York establishments (imagine!). Call 254-3697 and say, "Hey what's the deal with Amica Bunker and how come they never return Richard Laermer's messages?" Actually, Amica is terrific music with fun improvisation of original songs. And the crowd is wild. Same goes for that neighborhood's **baltyk cafe** (157 East Houston Street, 614-9040). In the East Village, the dives have it. Grandma might like **cafe siné** which offers fantastic *and* okay entertainment for free on Sundays. Drink coffee at **122 st. mark's place** (982-0370). Folksy.

anything arty

world music institute
545-7536

This nonprofit organization—with concert locations citywide—seeks to preserve the diverse musical traditions of the world's cultures, and toward this end presents concerts of traditional and contemporary music from around the world. World Music hosts Caribbean music, Hamaza del Din, Bulgarian and Turkish festivals, shout songs of Georgia (of the former USSR), Yemenite and Iranian songs and Javanese shadow puppets. That's just a small sampling. Concerts happen at such fantastic spaces as Ethnic Folk Arts Center in SoHo and St. Ann's Church in Brooklyn Heights, in addition to the Washington Square Church in the Village (once yearly) and Symphony Space. This is one of the oddity groups that feature anything but hits. Many gays and lesbians swear by such gatherings because the crowd is usually very hip and willing to share the "vibes" with anyone in its midst. Programs run from September through early June. In addition, there are weekend festivals, series on different themes such as gospel, accordion or Caribbean music, and so forth. For information and a copy of the quarterly calendar of events, do call.

section four

social, medical, and political

At this stage the guide takes a more serious tone. After the dessert, in my book, comes some information you will need to get by. Included here are mixed social events, social happenings for both lesbians and gay males, political organizations, religious activities and ideas, education centers and meetings to attend, support areas, anything for people with AIDS or those who support and assist them, and, finally, the ultimate help: a section titled "Volunteerism."

As I mention in Chapter 24, "Political Organizations," anyone can stop watching the Fox Network long enough to learn something new about themselves. I did. All it takes is an organization you like, that likes you too. I joined a group devoted to gay or lesbian computer games. See? Even a nerd can have a good time in New York.

Keep in mind that city gay life can get boring. Here's a look—a long one—at ways to stave off even the scent of boredom.

chapter twenty-one

mixed events and organizations of note

bar association for human rights
459-4873

Through the Lawyers Referral Service for the Lesbian and Gay Community, you can get a full range of legal services by walking in on Tuesday night from 6 to 8 to the Lesbian and Gay Community Services Center (208 West 13th Street).

bi-pac (bisexual political action committee)
459-4784

Political action on issues of importance to the various gay communities—that is, the lesbian, gay and bisexual ones. A monthly meeting and potluck is held at 8 P.M. on the fourth Thursday of the month. No, not at the center—at members' homes. For information, call the New York Area Bisexual Network at the above phone number.

social, medical, and political

bisexual network
459-4784

Sponsors and coordinates a spectrum of activities and groups for bisexuals. Besides the Bisexual Pride Discussion and Support Group, which meets every Sunday at the L and G Community Center (208 West 13th Street), groups and topics include bisexual women of color, "women loving women safe sex," and a "bisexual multi-spirituality circle." Call the hotline to get the rap, times and dates.

bisexual pride discussion group
no phone number

Topical discussions on issues of interest to the bisexual community, followed by an informal dinner at a friendly local restaurant. Every Sunday, 6 P.M. at the L and G Center (208 West 13th Street). Call the New York Area Bisexual Network to get more info.

bisexual dominance and submission group (bids)
459-4784

What they want: you. To share your S&M experiences and fantasies with others in a positive, nonjudgmental atmosphere. Meetings first Sunday of the month at 4:45 P.M. at the L and G Center (208 West 13th Street). Part of the New York Area Bisexual Network (NYABN).

bisexual information and counseling service
874-7937

A professionally staffed nonprofit organization for bisexuals, families, partners and even estranged friends. The service helps its brethren and sistren with psychological and medical problems; it also assists those struggling with their sexuality. Confidentiality is protected by the law.

mixed events and organizations of note

big apple gay lesbian and bisexual association for the deaf
718/399-2662 voice or TTY

It's a new organization set up primarily for social purposes and to bring gays together with the combined goals of networking and increasing support for the hearing impaired. Started by a couple of neat guys who saw a niche that needed to be filled.

bisexual youth
459-4784

An informal social and support group for bisexual kids and youth. Monthly meeting and potluck lunch held at 1 P.M. on the fourth Sunday of the month at a member's home.

broadway cares/equity fights aids
840-0770

This is the organization through which Broadway raises money to support groups fighting the AIDS epidemic and caring for those who are sick. BC/EFA holds charity events year round and can help you raise money for them; the organization produces events throughout the year at Steve McGraw's Theater (158 West 72nd Street): Every Sunday and Monday night (except in August) actors and performers do their stuff. No minimum. Call McGraw's (362-2590) for a schedule. For specifics, call Broadway Cares.

brooklyn's lesbian and gay political club (lambda independent democrats)
718/965-8482

LID endorses and works for candidates in local, state and national elections, lobbies for legislation, and conducts community outreach

social, medical, and political

through street fairs and meetings on special topics. Meetings take place at 336 Ninth Street, Suite 135, Park Slope, Brooklyn.

christopher street financial inc.
80 wall street, new york, ny 10005; 269-0110

The first investment firm for gays and lesbians, Christopher Street Financial has been in business since 1981. The company is registered with the Securities and Exchange Commission as a securities dealer and investor. A full-service investment firm, Christopher Street provides advice, does not require a minimum investment and charges competitive commissions. Christopher Street supports gay and lesbian organizations with investments.

coalition for lesbian and gay rights
627-1398

Located at the L and G Community Center (208 West 13th Street), this coalition of over fifty organizations helps strengthen our community by working on legislative and political issues. Offers free information, referrals, and educational forums on the third Tuesday of each month, for a $3 admission fee.

couples together
662-3080

This organization arranges social activities and provides support for gay men and lesbians who are involved in long-term, committed relationships. They hold monthly rap sessions conducted by peers, as well as a monthly social event. Couples Together is a tribute to gay couples; the organization acts as a Bronx cheer to naysayers who think gay and lesbian couples don't last past the third sex encounter.

mixed events and organizations of note

east end gay organization (eego)
516/324-3699

Located in Bridgehampton, New York, this group claims that it works to unite gay men and lesbians in a concerted fight for total lesbian and gay rights. Actually, it's a networking organization for lesbians and a few gay men located in the Hamptons; EEGO cocktail parties are noted as being fab-u-lous. As for the work they do, goals are continually being set. Its members reportedly helped get the Suffolk County Human Rights Bill passed.

empire state pride agenda
673-5417

With five years' experience behind them, this lobbying group for gay and lesbian issues disperses money to candidates who help homo causes. They organize gay and lesbian voters to put pressure on officials and successfully got good gay people into office in the 1993 School Board elections.

front runners
724-9700

A running club for lesbian and gay athletes of all abilities. Fun runs of one to six miles held every Saturday at 10 A.M. and Wednesday at 7 P.M. in Central Park and every Tuesday at 7 P.M. in Prospect Park. Prospect is the real pretty, well-kept park in Brooklyn.

gay officers action league (goal)
996-8808

Promising name notwithstanding, this is not a dating service. Rather, GOAL is the gay and lesbian police professional association. Social events and support for brethren/sistren.

social, medical, and political

gay and lesbian independent democrats (glid)
727-0008

GLID is Manhattan's progressive gay and lesbian Democratic club. GLID lobbies elected officials, sponsors public forums, conducts voter registration drives, advocates for lesbians and gay men on issues of importance to our community, endorses candidates, and encourages progressive lesbians, gay men and their friends to seek political office. GLID meets on the second Wednesday of the month at 8 P.M. at the L and G Center (208 West 13th Street).

gay & lesbian alliance against defamation (glaad)
80 varick street, suite 3e, new york, ny 10014, 807-1700

GLAAD combats homophobia in the media and elsewhere by promoting visibility of the lesbian and gay community and organizing grassroots response to antigay bigotry.

The PhoneTree is a special arm of GLAAD. It's activated in response to extreme homophobic incidents: You receive a call, dial the hotline for details, and then call the three people on your personal list and tell them to call the hotline. Often you will be asked to write letters too. Within forty-eight hours, the community is alerted and can respond with angry letters and phone calls. GLAAD calls it "A Voice That Says No, You Can't Treat Us Like Second Class Citizens Anymore!", and it's quite effective as a quick-response mechanism. See Chapter 29, "Volunteerism," for more information. For information, and to be part of the GLAAD PhoneTree, well—call.

the green closet
242-0999

This worldwide professional organization of people intrigued by the art and science of horticulture holds meetings and events regularly. Call to tap into what's going on and discover how green their thumbs are.

mixed events and organizations of note

hispanic united gays and lesbians (hugl)
p.o. box 228, canal street station, new york, ny 10013, no phone number

Educational services, political action, counseling and social activities in Spanish and English by and for the Latina/o lesbian and gay community. General meeting at 8 P.M. at the L and G Center (208 West 13th Street).

heritage of pride
691-1774

These are the organizers of the big lesbian and gay pride events such as the march, the rally and the splashy Dance on the Pier, held the last Sunday in June. If you want specifics on the Gay Pride Parade—what, where, when, who is protesting, etc.—call Heritage of Pride. Also call about meetings, held at the L and G Center (208 West 13th Street). Consider volunteering; it's a fine way to socialize, network and do a good deed. See Chapter 29, "Volunteerism," for more.

human rights campaign fund (hrcf)
1012 14th street nw, suite 607, washington, dc, 20005, 202/628-4160

With 80,000 members nationwide, the Washington-based Human Rights Campaign Fund is the country's largest gay and lesbian organization. Focusing on political issues, the fund contributes money to federal political campaigns, lobbies on health care and civil rights issues and mobilizes grassroots activities across the United States. (The fund is coordinating efforts to overturn the ban on lesbian, gay and bisexual servicemen and -women.) Another of the fund's big projects is the "Speak Out" program, through which individuals all over the country are enlisted to write letters to representatives expressing support of legislation important to gays and lesbians. The Human Rights Campaign Fund publishes a quarterly newsletter, *Momentum*, as well as *Capitol Hill Update* and *AIDS Treatment Alert*, and distributes a cable TV

social, medical, and political

show, *Momentum TV*, in fifteen markets. Great cocktail parties often; tickets cost upwards of $1,000.

lavender lamp: national gay and lesbian nurses network
718/933-1158

Lavender Lamp is a social and support group for lesbian and gay male nurses. Besides addressing issues of concern to nurses, the organization undertakes health-related projects in the gay and lesbian community. Lavender Lamp's newsletter is known to support practitioners in the general nursing community, in large part by helping nurses understand the care of PWAs.

lavender light
30a greenwich avenue, box 315, new york, ny 10014, 714-7072

The full name of this group is Lavender Light: The Black and People of All Colors Lesbian and Gay Gospel Choir. Lavender Light puts on gospel concerts throughout the year at various venues.

lesbians and gay men of new brunswick
908/247-0515

The largest gay and lesbian support group in northern New Jersey. The group advertises that it will help with any needs.

men of all colors together new york
330-7678

A multiracial group of gay men working against racism inside and outside the gay community. The group meets every Friday from 7:45 to 11 P.M. at the L and G Center (208 West 13th Street).

mixed events and organizations of note

the center quilt project
620-7310

The L and G Center coordinates New York's contribution to the National Names Project Quilt. Individuals make a quilt in memory of a person whom they have lost in the epidemic, and the quilt is then added to the huge national quilt, currently touring the country. This group of people gather to quilt and to help those who want to make quilts in memory of lovers, friends and family members who have died of AIDS. Sewing machines and materials are available, as well as people who can show you what to sew—the group has even gotten some Amish guys to help with quilting tips. Besides the quilting, the group collects holiday gifts for PWAs, distributing presents to about 10,000 people every year. Time with the quilters is a very touching experience. Call the L and G Center (620-7310) for up-to-date information.

metropolitan tennis group
718/852-8562

Tennis parties, from beginners to tournament level. This is a very special gay and lesbian group. It takes itself very seriously; gays and lesbians feel the same way.

mixed company
679-9379

Mixed Company introduces lesbians and gay men to people of the opposite sex for purposes of marriage, having children, social or business escorts and, they suppose, friendship. Mixed Company seeks particularly to serve the needs of men and women who are in the closet. See the discussion of Mixed Company in Chapter 31, "A Few Personal Favorites . . ."; this organization's existence is a reminder of how unique—okay, silly—this city really is!

social, medical, and political

national gay and lesbian task force (ngltf)
202/332-6483

The Washington-based national grassroots political organization for lesbians and gay men. Membership is important: $30 annually. NGLTF addresses issues such as violence against lesbians and gays, sodomy laws, AIDS and HIV issues, gay rights ordinances, family law and media representation. (See Chapter 29, "Volunteerism.")

national lesbian and gay journalist association
629-2045

NLGJA is a national organization that exists to promote coverage of gay and lesbian topics in the mainstream press and to combat discrimination against lesbians and gay men in media workplaces. There are fourteen NLGJA chapters, of which the NYC chapter is the largest. New York's chapter holds monthly meetings, well attended by journalists and "journalistics," at which are held panel discussions of issues in the news. In 1992, *The New York Times* and *The Wall Street Journal*'s big editors came out to discuss their new, liberal gay standpoints. From September through May, meetings take place on the third Sunday of every month, from June through August on the second Thursday, always at the L and G Center (208 West 13th Street). Call for meeting times and information on other events, such as the big annual convention. NY/NLGJA publishes a newsletter; call to request a copy.

new york advertising and communications network
box 49, 469a hudson street, new york, ny, 517-0390

The largest and busiest metropolitan-area professional group. These people are all in PR, advertising, marketing, etc. They have a busy schedule of events, lectures and workshops, all addressing issues of professional and general interest.

mixed events and organizations of note

new york city gay and lesbian anti-violence project
807-6761

The Anti-Violence Project provides support and counseling for lesbians and gay male victims of battering, combats gay-bashing and counsels victims of all types of violence. The project offers twenty-four-hour telephone counseling and crisis intervention, in-person counseling and support groups, safe houses, info, and community outreach. The Project recently introduced a series of Safety Skills Workshops. All services are confidential and free.

new york ramblers soccer club
724-7992

A gay soccer team. The club holds an annual international tournament, as well as tournaments with other East Coast teams throughout the year. A place for beginners, intermediates and pros, players and coaches. Practice schedule varies.

organization of lesbian and gay architects and designers (olgad)
475-7652

OLGAD is concerned with increasing the visibility of gay men and lesbians in the design community, educating the community at large about our concerns and history, and providing mutual support and networking opportunities. Monthly newsletter. Monthly meetings at the L and G Center (208 West 13th Street) and other events, too.

social, medical, and political

outwatch
 70 greenwich avenue, box 107, new york, ny 10014, 967-7711, extension 3037

These men and women patrol gay neighborhoods at night to combat the increasing incidence of violence against lesbians and gay men in New York City. They also provide security at special events where gay and lesbian groups think there may be violence. Formerly known as the Pink Panthers, the group is nonviolent and trained in self-defense. Meets every two weeks at the L and G Center (208 West 13th Street). (See Chapter 29, "Volunteerism," for how to hitch up.)

queens lesbian and gay pride committee
 718/460-4064

Yes, Virginia, there's a Queens Lesbian and Gay Pride Committee, which organized the first lesbian and gay pride march and celebration in Queens in 1993. This group is the clearinghouse for information on dozens of Queens activities. Since I hail from Queens, this is an important factoid for you to hold on to. (Maybe you've heard the joke: "I'm from Queens. You're from normal parents.") To touch base and learn about the parade, call.

scrabble players club
 425-3289

These dedicated Scrabble-ites meet "like clockwork" every second and fourth Monday from 10 A.M. to 12 noon at the L and G Center (208 West 13th Street). New players, at all skill levels, are always welcome.

senior action in a gay environment (sage)
 741-2247

SAGE provides social services, educational activities and social events for older gay men and lesbians. Events include socials, brunches and

mixed events and organizations of note

trips. Educational seminars address issues of interest to older gay men and lesbians. For more information, call or stop by the SAGE office at the L and G Center (208 West 13th Street) during business hours, or to get involved, stop by during "Drop-In" at the center from 1:30 to 4:30 Monday through Friday. SAGE publishes a newsletter and calendar.

south'ners
p.o. box 1152, old chelsea station, 10011, no phone number

South'ners is a social group of former Southerners living in NY and lovers of Southern culture. The group holds meetings every third Monday of the month at the L and G Center (208 West 13th Street) and regularly dine at Southern-style restaurants in New York.

ticklish society of america
no phone number

This new group, based at the L and G Center (208 West 13th Street), features a marching band who will tickle you on demand. Just wanted to see if you were still there. See the last two chapters for true examples that *seem* like jokes.

we wah and barche ampe
598-0100

We Wah and BarChe Ampe is a group of Native American gay men and lesbians affiliated with the Indian Community House. Call or visit the Community House for a copy of the newsletter and to learn about We Wah and Community House activities. The Community House also maintains a gallery and museum in an adjacent building. The Indian Community House is at 404 Lafayette Street.

chapter twenty-two

where the girls are— social happenings for lesbians

asian lesbians of the east coast/asian pacific lesbian network (aloec east coast)
517-5598

A political, social and supportive network of Asian Pacific lesbians who meet on the first Sunday of the month and have social events on the last Friday.

bronx lesbians united in sisterhood, inc. (blues)
p.o. box 1738, bronx, ny 10451, no phone number; write for activities

BLUeS is a multicultural membership organization dedicated to addressing the social and political needs of the Bronx lesbian community. Visitors are welcome to all activities. BLUeS holds open meetings on the second Tuesday of every month from 6 to 8 P.M. at 1 Fordham Plaza (an office building), Suite 903. Call the hotline to find out what's going on. BLUeS holds a tea dance the third Sunday of every month from 4 to 11 P.M. at the Archway Inn, 2700 Jerome Avenue (corner of Kingsbridge Road); $5, $3 buffet, and there's a deejay and cash bar.

social, medical, and political

butch femme society
388-2736

Butch Femme is a multiracial, multiethnic group of women (with members ranging in age from seventeen to seventy-four) which arranges social activities and educational programs. The group meets on the third Wednesday of every month at 6:30 P.M. at the L and G Center (208 West 13th Street). It holds restaurant gatherings, beach parties, pool nights, dances and other activities throughout the year. All women are welcome. The society also has support groups that address topics of interest to women.

gay women's alternative
universality church, 4 west 76th street, new york, ny 10023, 666-6922

A social and cultural organization offering monthly programs to inform, entertain and inspire gay women. The Alternative provides a warm social atmosphere for women of all ages. Programs first Thursday of every month from October to June, for a $6 fee.

l.s.m.
p.o. box 993, murray hill station, new york, ny 10156, no phone number

A support and information group for lesbians and bisexual women interested in fantasy, role-playing, bondage, discipline, S&M, fetishes, alternative gender identities, costumes and so forth.

riot grrrl
p.o. box 188, cooper square station, new york, ny 10003, 875-7039

A national organization of gay, straight and bisexual women who draw their strength from talking to each other about issues relevant to their lives. Riot Grrrl holds meetings at the Womb Gallery, 500 East 11th Street, at 8:30 P.M. most Mondays.

where the girls are

sex and love addicts anonymous lesbians
(call the l and g community center, 620-7310)

Meets at the L and G Center (208 West 13th Street) on the first and third Wednesday of every month.

social activities for lesbians
741-2610, or call the center

Weekly evenings of fun and board games for women, based at the L and G Center (208 West 13th Street). A fun, stress-free way to meet women. $2 donation requested. What are the options offered? Dial-A-Date in Park Slope. A group march in GMHC's annual AIDS Walk-A-Thon. Brooklyn Pool Night. Gallery talks and Japanese dinners out. Softball Saturdays. A 45–+ group. Manhattan Movie Night. Participation in the Volleyball Tournament at Gay Games '94. Calendar Mailing Party. (Free dance classes!)

women about
p.o. box 280, new york, ny 10010, 642-5257

This is a women's social adventure club with more than 500 members! Outings of between eight and fifteen women include biking, hiking trips and jaunts to museums, sporting events and the theater. Women About publishes a newsletter and calendar. An excellent way for women to get oriented, get a sense of what's going on in NYC and identify resources. Women About publishes a free newsletter and mails out a monthly calendar of events.

chapter twenty-three

where the boys are—
social happenings for
fun gay males

asians and friends—new york

A not-for-profit organization promoting friendships with Asian/Pacific Islander, Asian-American and non-Asian gay men through social, cultural, educational and service activities and programs. P.O. Box 6628, New York City, 10163. The hotline is 674-5064.

gay men in brooklyn

A discussion and consciousness-raising group for gay and bi-sexual men living in Brooklyn. Gay Men in Brooklyn meets on the first Sunday of each month at 2:00 P.M., at the All Souls Universalist Church, 951 Ocean Avenue. Call for more info: 718/390-8894.

gay men of african descent (gmad)

A support group of men of African descent promoting consciousness-raising and the development of this specific arm of the lesbian and gay community. GMAD is inclusive of African, African-American, Ca-

social, medical, and political

ribbean and Hispanic/Latino men of color. Meetings are held weekly on Friday. Call 718/802-0162.

gay men of the bronx

A group of people (sixty active members!) committed to creating a supportive community in the Bronx. Sponsors parties, picnics and fund-raisers. Meetings are held twice a month, business for the first hour and socializing for the subsequent two. Everyone is welcome. Contact these boys to plug in to what's going on and when the next meeting will be held.

gay male s/m activists (gmsma)
department o, 496-a hudson street, suite d-23, new york, ny 10014, 727-9878

Dedicated to safe and responsible sadomasochism since 1981. Open meetings with programs on S&M techniques, lifestyle issues, political and social concerns. Also special events, speakers' bureau, workshops, demos, affinity groups, newsletter, more.

gay circles
242-9165

Gay Circles organizes small groups of men to support one another. Each group is organized with a particular focus and set of participants and meets for eight weeks. Groups are closed once they begin, are led by a facilitator and are structured in a way to make all the participants feel comfortable. Everything is confidential. Gay Circles is an excellent experience for men of all ages, and particularly for men who are interested in meeting other men in a safe, non-cruisey place, and who are interested in learning from one another's experiences. Gay Circles also arranges workshops on specific issues, such as dealing with a breakup, dating and holidays. And organizes social events every year. Get on the mailing list.

where the boys are

radical faeries
   721-5612

Join the delightful faeries in their frolicking exploration of maleness, sexuality, spirituality and intimacy, which more often than not happens in the country. Founded by the granddaddy of the gay liberation movement in the United States, Harry Hays, who can be reached at the above number.

chapter twenty-four

political orgs, professional orgs and business orgs

The following are the most important organizations. I found them after I decided I was watching too much television. I discovered that in a city where men walk arm in arm, there's a group for every liking. For a few seconds it was scary: Not only are we *everywhere*, but we also wear our interests on our sleeves.

After the initial shock, I started wondering: If we have a group that likes to work with clay, one that goes boating, one called the Gay & Lesbian History On Stamps Club, another on natural history, one for Tupperware, another for making gay men and lesbians into couples, what more could there be? I started making a list.

The following groups provide places for gay men and gay women (and bisexuals) to go for political, business and bonding purposes.

act up women's caucus
135 west 29th street, new york, ny 10010, 564-2437

Their work concerns anything to do with the effect of the AIDS crisis on women. Meets every Monday at the Lesbian and Gay Community Services Center (208 West 13th Street) at 7:30 P.M.

social, medical, and political

astrea, or national lesbian action foundation
529-8021

ASTREA funds activities at organizations that address issues of importance to lesbians, ranging from arts to political issues. ASTREA regularly sponsors events, particularly fund-raisers, parties, "arts and leisure auction," and an annual lesbian writers' fund gala, and organizes activism workshops and activist forums. ASTREA publishes a newsletter as well as a list of the organizations it funds. Call to get the newsletter and to find out what's going on at the moment.

dyke action machine
718/965-9591

A direct-action political group for lesbians, fighting oppression and invisibility. DAM organizes actions, media billboard campaigns, zaps, and all-out offensive marching demonstrations. DAM meets at the L and G Center (208 West 13th Street) on the first Sunday of the month, from 6 to 8 P.M.

ecofeminists visions emerging (eve)
402 west 46th street, suite 3w, new york, ny 10036, 315-3107

Ecofeminists believe there is a fundamental connection between the devastation of the earth and violence against women. Ecofeminism brings together feminism, environmentalism and alternative spiritualities. The group calls ecofeminism "a pre-patriarchal analysis of history and the social justice politics of race, class, gender, species and other forms of oppression." Founded in 1991, the group offers a monthly newsletter that takes off from discussions, open to the public, held on the first Monday of each month. Ecofeminists are famous for running around town adding antimisogynist graffiti to ads in poor taste. ("Bad for Women" went up on Eddie Murphy movie posters.) You can attend a "Madison Avenue Graffiti Correcting Party," but I can't tell you when it is, because it's illegal!

political orgs, professional orgs

feminists concerned for better feminist leadership (fcbfl)
p.o. box 1348, madison square station, new york, ny 10159, 362-6962

FCBFL networks with a variety of organizations and professionals, distributes educational materials, and offers publications, information and referrals.

international women's tribune center
777 un plaza, 3rd floor, new york, ny 10012, 687-8633

This center supports the initiatives of women throughout the third world who are actively working to promote more equal participation of women in development plans and policies. The center provides comprehensive information, education and communication support services.

lesbian and gay rights project of the american civil liberties union
944-9800

The Lesbian and Gay Rights Project is a semi-independent component of the ACLU that coordinates and funds the group's work to defend the legal rights of gays and lesbians. "Know your rights and protect them," says the ACLU.

lesbian and gay teachers association
718/626-4699

Through this organization, educators address gay and lesbian issues in the schools. Their involvement ranges from providing support to gay and lesbian teachers, to participating in developing curricula that address gay and lesbian issues, to offering support for gay and lesbian students. All school workers are welcome to the association's meetings, held on the first Monday of the month at the L and G Center.

social, medical, and political

lesbian avengers
twenty-four hour information line: 967-7711, extension 3204

The Avengers are a militant direct-action group who focus on issues vital to the survival and greater visibility of lesbians. Manifesto, video, communiqué. Meetings are held every Tuesday at 8 P.M. at the L and G Center (208 West 13th Street).

lambda independent democrats
336 9th street, #135, brooklyn, ny, 718/361-3322

Lambda, Brooklyn's gay and lesbian political club, is striving to increase the attention paid by Brooklyn's elected representatives to issues that concern the gay and lesbian community. The group has gotten previously uninterested local representatives to attend gay events. Lambda issues a scorecard on Brooklyn politicians, rating them on their support of significant legislation.

lambda legal defense and education fund
995-8585

This is a national group that litigates on behalf of lesbians, gay men and people with AIDS. Membership costs $40 and up and includes a newsletter and special invites. (See Chapter 29, "Volunteerism.")

parents and friends of lesbians and gay men (pflag)
463-0629

PFLAG's slogan is "We love our gay children." The group supports parents and families who are learning about having a gay child or other family member. PFLAG also has a number of educational programs designed to combat bias against homosexuals. Meetings on the fourth Sunday of the month (June meetings are on the third Sunday) at 3 political orgs, professional orgs

P.M. at Community Gallery, 40 East 35th Street. PFLAG has been around since the early seventies. Monthly newsletter.

people for the american way
1460 broadway, 2nd floor, 944-5820

This Washington-based group, begun by Norman Lear of sitcom fame, works to protect constitutional freedoms "in the court of law and the court of public opinion." Its work focuses on safeguarding freedom of expression and fighting censorship, combating racial, cultural and antigay intolerance, protecting abortion rights, and encouraging voter participation.

pony & friends
p.o. box 1331, old chelsea station, new york, ny 10011, 713-5678

A formal organization of advocates of sex workers' rights, dedicated to the decriminalization and deregulation of prostitution. PONY works for an end to street sweeps, entrapment and other forms of police violence and harassment against sex workers, and to overturn existing prostitution laws.

queer nation
260-6156

A direct-action group dedicated to fighting homophobia and invisibility. Queer Nation believes in going after anything and everything that reeks of homophobia. Meets at the L and G Center (208 West 13th Street) on the first and third Thursday of the month.

social, medical, and political

radical women
32 union square east, suite 307, new york, ny 10003, 677-7002

A socialist feminist organization fighting racism, sexism, homophobia and labor exploitation. Holds open meetings, sponsors public forums and works in coalition with community organizations. Publications, referrals.

reproductive freedom project
132 west 43rd street, new york, ny 10036, 944-9800

Formed to protect women's fundamental right to choose whether or not to bear a child, the Project is a part of the American Civil Liberties Union, and is involved in litigation to protect abortion rights. The group publishes a monthly journal and offers limited legal advice; it does not make referrals to clinics.

resource exchange service
122 west 27th street, 10th floor, new york, ny 10010, 741-2955

A women's collective working to confront sexism, racism and classism and to develop an understanding of women's struggles and gains in a global context. Provides published and unpublished accounts and analyses of women's conditions in the developing world. Office open Wednesday only.

stonewall business association
439-1010

"Because the business strengthens the community." The Stonewall Business Association sponsors a range of events and programs during the year that are designed to strengthen the economic development and productivity of gay and lesbian businesspeople. Programs include "Business in the Nineties," "Networking for Success," "Personal Fi-

political orgs, professional orgs

nance," "Out in America—Professional Role Models" and a business fair. Call to join and receive regular info.

wall street project
lesbian & gay community services center, 208 west 13th street, 627-1398

The Wall Street Project's primary objective is to secure equal employment opportunity for lesbians and gay men. The group responds to specific cases of antigay bias and works to implement antidiscrimination clauses at individual firms and among public investors such as pension funds.

women's health action and mobilization (wham)
p.o. box 733, new york, ny 10010, 713-5966

WHAM is a direct-action organization that focuses on women's reproductive rights issues, as well as issues of particular concern to lesbians. WHAM meets Wednesday nights at 7 at the Center of the Rainbow, 147 West 25th Street, 12th Floor.

chapter twenty-five

things spiritual and anything remotely religious

american gay/lesbian atheists, inc.
701 seventh avenue, suite 9w, new york, ny 10036, dial-a-gay-atheist: 718/699-1737

The above phone number is AGA's answer to Dial-A-Prayer. In a nutshell, AGA is a nonprofit educational organization dedicated to preserving separation of church and state and upholding the civil rights of lesbian and gay atheists. Meetings are held on the first Sunday of the month from 1 to 3 P.M. at the Lesbian and Gay Community Services Center (208 West 13th Street).

circle of more light
304-4373

Spiritual support and sharing in a gay and lesbian affirmative group. Takes place on Wednesday at 6:30 P.M. at West-Park Presbyterian Church, 165 West 86th Street. (Program begins at 7:30.)

social, medical, and political

congregation beth simchat torah
57 bethune street, new york, ny 10014, 929-9498

A Reform synagogue for lesbians and gays. Shabbat service Friday at 8:30. Everyone is welcome, dress is informal, tickets are not needed, and services are held on all holidays. The Yom Kippur service is especially touching; the evening's "Sunset Service" is held at the Jacob Javits Center in a room overlooking the Hudson. Events throughout the week include the Feminist Forum, workshops and classes on topics such as coming out to your family and having children. The congregation participates in important community events such as the Gay Pride March (and annual Jewish events such as the Israel Day Parade) and publishes a monthly newsletter and calendar.

dignity big apple
818-1309

A community of lesbian and gay Catholics. Activities include liturgies and socials every Saturday at 8 P.M. at the L and G Center (208 West 13th Street). This group is a splinter of Dignity New York.

dignity brooklyn
718/769-3447

Liturgy in members' homes every third Saturday of the month: an evening service, after which a potluck dinner is served. Call for schedule.

dignity new york
675-2179

This organization offers spiritual support to lesbian and gay Catholics and runs an AIDS ministry. It's a fellowship of lesbian and gay Roman Catholics. The main activity is the eucharistic liturgy and social held

things spiritual and anything remotely religious

on Sunday at 7:30 P.M. at St. John's Episcopal Church, 218 West 11th Street.

integrity/ny
p.o. box 5202, new york, ny 10185, 718/720-3054

Lesbian and gay Episcopalians and friends. Program every Thursday at 7:30 P.M. at St. Luke's Church (Hudson and Christopher streets).

moonfire women's spirituality circle
472-1724

A group of lesbian, bisexual and straight women looking for "inner strength as females," which the goddess provides, and who call on the powers, elementals, goddesses. . . . Holds eight sabbaths on the eight full moons; these nights have so-called new moon rituals.

chapter twenty-six

educate thyself!

brooklyn women's martial arts
718/788-1775

A feminist, antiracist, lesbian-positive school for women. There are continuing classes in tai chi, karate and self-defense, open to women only, and classes in self-defense and karate for children of both sexes. There are also occasional self-defense classes for lesbians and gay men. Classes are priced on a sliding scale. Women who have had prior training may join the karate and tai chi classes in progress.

gender identity
620-7310

Gender identity peer counseling and referrals are available at the L and G Community Services Center (208 West 13th Street). You can find one-on-one peer counseling as well as support groups for people who are addressing issues of transsexuality. (For more on transsexuality, see the Glossary.)

social, medical, and political

hetrick-martin institute
633-8920; tty 633-8926

A place for gay and lesbian youth. Counseling and a drop-in center (Monday through Friday 3 to 6 P.M.). The institute sponsors the public Harvey Milk High School for kids who have trouble completing public school because they are gay. Safer-sex information, referrals and professional education. One of the best things here is the good speakers who influence young gays and lesbians. Funded by state and federal sources, private foundations and individual donors. The institute publishes a funny, fierce and candid comic book for kids called *Tales of the Closet*, as well as the *National Gay and Lesbian Youth Directory*.

meditation class
673-4427

A highly recommended lesbians-only meditation class, offered on a sliding-scale fee, is held each Monday from 7 to 8 P.M. The aim is to learn how to use meditation to resolve relationship and other dilemmas hurting your life. "Meditation and creative visualization are powerful tools," says psychotherapist Joyce Liechenstein. Her expertise in reiki and mariel and as an "omega healer" has helped many women.

multiple personality disorder workshop
979-2979

Deborah Feller, a licensed psychotherapist, leads a support group for women with multiple personality disorders. These twelve-session groups help women with MPD learn more about what it means to be a multiple, develop healthy strategies for coping, and meet and exchange ideas with other MPD women.

educate thyself!

natural gourmet institute for food and health
48 west 21st street, new york, ny 10011, 645-5170

The institute teaches people to understand the relationship between food and health. The institute has an extensive selection of courses that cover a spectrum of issues: healthful cooking, cooking to strengthen the immune system, the sweet tooth, foods of different countries and cultures, and so forth. The institute also presents lectures. On Friday, a dinner prepared by students and instructors is served to anyone who drops by. The cost is $20 per person, and seating is at group tables (groups of six or more can reserve a table). The institute also offers a subscription meal service, allowing subscribers to swing by twice a week and pick up a bag full of healthful prepared food—enough food to last until the next bag is ready. There's a small bookshop in the reception area.

ninth street center
228-5153

Since 1973, this community organization has been demonstrating "that a homosexual lifestyle is a rational, desirable choice for individuals dissatisfied with the rewards of conventional living." Rap groups, peer counseling, more.

self defense academy
787-7161

Classes that teach gay men and lesbians how to defend themselves against violent attacks. Designed and taught by gay men and lesbians.

spirit center: a women's circle for healing
620-7310

Workshops and lecture-demonstrations on creative body and mind and spirit practices that "heal and affirm us as women." First Wednesday

social, medical, and political

of the month at the L and G Center (208 West 13th Street). For $5, the Spirit Center will send a newsletter.

women's studio workshop
p.o. box 489, rosendale, ny 12472, 914/658-9133

Women's Studio Workshop is a multidisciplinary arts organization dedicated to serving the needs of contemporary artists. WSW maintains studios where artists can work on their projects, as well as funding programs. The associated Binnewater Arts Center provides a permanent home for WSW's printmaking, papermaking and photography studios. Lots of activities during the summer.

chapter twenty-seven

lean on them—
support groups

community health project (chp)
675-3559

Provides caring, sensitive and low-cost health care services to the lesbian and gay community. Phone (See Chapter 28, "AIDS Pages.")

gay fathers' forum
979-7541

A support organization for gay fathers, their lovers and others in child-nurturing situations. Monthly meetings include a potluck supper, support groups on varied topics, speakers and socializing. Meetings first Friday of the month at 7 P.M. at the L and G Community Center (208 West 13th Street). Bring a main course for four or pay $5 for food.

social, medical, and political

gay sons, straight fathers

251 central park west, suite 1a, new york, ny 10024, 769-8796

A discussion group of gay men, led by a psychotherapist, which meets monthly to talk about members' feelings about their fathers, about themselves and about their masculine identities as similar or different from those of their fathers. The group has involved a consistent group of participants for a couple of years, but newcomers are welcome. Ari Fridkis, M.S.W., C.S.W., the group organizer and leader, also offers one-day workshops on this and other topics. Write to Fridkis at the above address.

identity house

In twenty years' existence, Identity House has provided drop-in advice, peer counseling, therapy referrals and groups for the lesbian, gay and bisexual community on Sunday, Monday and Tuesday night. People who drop by can talk with a trained volunteer peer counselor and if necessary receive a referral for short-term counseling by an Identity House counselor or an appropriate therapist. Besides drop-in service, Identity House sponsors numerous conferences and rap groups. On Fridays there are the Women's Talk & Listen Rap group from 6:30 to 8:30 P.M. and the Men's Talk & Listen Rap group from 8:30 to 10:30 P.M. Additional rap sessions are held on weekends: women Saturday from 3 to 5 P.M., and men Sunday from 3 to 5. No charge—donations welcome. Identity House sponsors a Men's Conference in the spring and a Women's Conference in the fall. Lectures and panels deal with issues of interest to the gay and lesbian community, usually at the L and G Center (208 West 13th Street). A specialty is coming-out groups; these are largely thought to be the best of their ilk. In existence since 1971, the walk-in referral service is at 39 West 14th Street, Suite 205, 243-8181. Hours are Sunday, Monday and Tuesday 6 to 10 P.M. No appointment.

lean on them—support groups

institute for human identity
118 west 72nd street, new york, ny 10023, 799-9432

The Institute for Human Identity was founded 20 years ago by Bernice Goodman and Dr. Charles Silverstein (coauthor of *Joy of Gay Sex* and author of *Gay Couples*, a fascinating pre-AIDS study of male duos). Both scholars are credited with demanding that the American Psychiatric Association remove the classification of homosexuality as a mental illness. The not-for-profit institute offers affordable counseling for gay men, lesbians and bisexuals. Although the institute does not do crisis counseling, staffers will see people on a short-term basis and make referrals for those in need of crisis counseling. On staff are eighty-five hard-working professionals. Fees are arranged on a sliding scale. The institute is open Monday through Friday 10 A.M. to 9 P.M. and Saturday from 10 A.M. to 5 P.M.

neutral zone drop-in center
162 christopher street, new york, ny 10014, 924-3294

Neutral Zone is a place for gay, lesbian, bisexual and transgender kids to check in and get some peer support, participate in workshops and recreate. The Neutral Zone is open from 4 P.M. to midnight seven days a week.

new york city coalition for women's mental health
320 west 86th street, suite 2b, new york, ny 10024, 787-1766

This organization works to improve the delivery of mental health services to women. It works particularly to improve training in psychology and psychiatry with regard to issues of concern to women, and to ensure that women have a say in shaping mental health treatments for women. The Coalition hosts a number of conferences annually.

social, medical, and political

office of gay and lesbian health concerns
125 worth street, new york, ny 10013, 788-4310

A part of the New York City Department of Health, this agency provides health-related information to the lesbian, gay, bisexual and transgender communities in New York, with a particular focus on AIDS issues. The office maintains an extensive library of materials; it's an excellent resource. In addition, the Professionals Education Project offers educational workshops on AIDS, safe sex, and homophobia to other agencies that work with gay, lesbian, bisexual and transgender constituents.

project return
133 west 21st street, 11th floor, new york, ny 10011; general info 979-8800, direct assistance 463-0629

While they told me not to list it—this is mostly a center for drug rehab—I would like to mention this place as a human services drug rehabilitation center providing outpatient evening programs, a battered women's shelter, parole transition counseling, all kinds of transitional treatment and one special program for gays and lesbians: As funded by Parents and Friends of Lesbians and Gays, this program provides support for those gays on the verge of coming out. Project Return also runs a women's and children's shelter and an AIDS outreach program.

chapter twenty-eight

aids pages

■ the basics

AIDS has taken its toll on the world at large. According to the statisticians from the CDC (Centers for Disease Control and Prevention in Atlanta), some 40 million people on the planet will be infected with the HIV virus, the virus that causes the immune system to break down, by the turn of the century; at press time, around 35 percent of the people with AIDS were gays.

AIDS is transmitted through certain body fluids, specifically blood, semen and vaginal fluids. The most common means of transmission are sexual intercourse, anal and vaginal; sharing of needles among drug users; and transfusions of infected blood. Getting AIDS, or not getting AIDS, has to do with exposure to the HIV virus. People who get AIDS are not limited to any group or any part of the world. Avoiding illness is about avoiding infection by a prevalent virus. Monitoring your behavior is the most important way to do this.

AIDS is an illness in another way: It makes those around people with AIDS (PWAs) act weird. That's why there are so many support groups listed here for both PWAs and the people who live with, love, work with, are friends with, and know PWAs. (In the Chapter 29, "Volunteerism," you'll find organizations that need your help.)

social, medical, and political

AIDS as a chapter in this book was something I thought of from the outset. Many in the gay and lesbian community wanted me to distinguish between information on the gay life and the AIDS life. But really, in this fourteenth year of the epidemic, there is very little separating the two. Most of the AIDS organizations in New York were established and built by gay men and lesbians in response to a crisis that has ravaged our community.

Incorporated in this chapter is information on safer sex, learning about AIDS, activism, taking better care of yourself, living, dying, learning how to cope, and the most recent phenomenon: living guilt-free if you are *not* infected with HIV.

What is safe sex? There is no real safe sex besides masturbation. Even the safety of a deep wet kiss is uncertain. For safety's sake, let's just say that "safer sex" is something that's not entirely safe, but is a great deal better than riskier behaviors.

Basically, there are eleven preventive ways to stay alive; these are guidelines presented by most major health organizations and recommended for use in this book by the New York Physicians for Human Rights, a group that promotes safe activity and studies what that is. This list is not as pithy as the Gay Men's Health Crisis version of the safe-sex rules, but it's thorough:

1. Know your partner, his state of health, his lifestyle and how many different sexual partners he has. If you enjoy being with a partner, see him again. The fewer partners, the less your risks of contracting a disease.
2. Engage in sex in a setting that is conducive to good hygiene. Be certain to wash any part of the body that has contacted the rectal area before it makes contact with the mouth.
3. Shower with your partner as part of foreplay to check for sores, lymph glands, etc., that might not have been noticed.
4. Kiss, cuddle, massage and enjoy mutual masturbation; they have a very low risk of transmitting disease.
5. Avoid exchanging certain body fluids, which has a higher risk of transmitting disease. Swallowing semen, urine or feces increases your risk of contracting a sexually transmitted disease. Oral sex when there are sores or cuts inside the mouth carries a high risk.
6. Know that rimming has an extremely high risk of transmitting

aids pages

disease except in a totally monogamous couple after examination by their health care practitioner.

7. Know that anal intercourse (fucking) causes tiny tears in the anus through which germs from both partners can enter the body. Water-soluble lubricants help reduce friction and tears and should be used even with a condom. Wearing a condom may reduce the spread of disease between partners. (Incidentally, look for condoms that are coated with Nonoxynol-9, a spermicidal that has been known to kill the HIV virus; do not use sheepskin condoms; and look for Mentor, a Minneapolis brand noted for having double strength and being very comfortable.) Women should use dental dams for extra protection against vaginal infections, warts and other diseases. Anal douching (men) and vaginal douching (women) before or after sex increases the risk of acquiring an infection because it removes barriers to infection.
8. Avoid fisting; it's extremely dangerous, except with a glove.
9. Remember that urinating after sex may reduce your risk of acquiring some infections.
10. Reduce or eliminate the use of street drugs, alcohol and marijuana, particularly before having sex with a relative stranger. Studies have shown that these options impair the immune system—and we all know that these things make sex a blur! (When you really want to stay on top of what's going on—stay sober.)
11. Maintain your body's immune system by eating well, exercising and getting a decent amount of rest. Cope with stress by learning relaxation techniques, such as meditation, yoga or tai chi. See your doctor regularly and be honest about what you're doing with your life. This person is your doctor. He or she won't "turn you in." He or she may berate you, but will undoubtedly help.

The following are the most prominent AIDS organizations that can help you or others you might know in a quest for more knowledge about the disease.

social, medical, and political

■ testing: advice, consent, details

If you're thinking of getting "tested" for the HIV virus, be aware that it has been proved that early detection can help you live longer. Testing positive for the HIV virus means you have been "exposed" and not that you are "doomed." Since 1987, the City of New York has advised that anyone at high risk (gay people who are somewhat sexually active are at high risk) be tested for HIV.

You can get free testing, confidentially, at the New York City Health Department Center/Lower Manhattan District Health Clinic in Chelsea (there are others), at 303 Ninth Avenue; phone 239-1700. The clinic will supply you with information about the test, and offer ad hoc counseling to assist you in making the decision and to help you with the news, whether negative or positive. It's illegal for anyone to use this information against you; because nobody knows how defensive the government may get, there is a system of confidentiality widely in place in clinics and doctors' offices around the country. If your doctor suggests placing your name on the vial to be sent to the Board of Health (where tests for HIV go to be analyzed), tell him or her to make it anonymous. You never know.

■ health, service and support groups for people who have aids

aids center of queens county (acqc)
97–45 queens boulevard, suite 1220, queens, ny 10128, 718/869-2500, voice or tty

ACQC was the first AIDS service organization formed to meet the needs of PWAs in the Borough of Queens. ACQC provides important services to people affected by HIV, including counseling, referrals and advocacy, educational programs, numerous support groups, a food program, safer-sex training and a buddy program for people who are sick. Besides the main office in Rego Park, ACQC maintains a satellite office in Jamaica, Queens.

aids pages

aids discrimination project
hotline 800/523-aids, in manhattan 870-8624, tty 870-8999

This division of the New York City Human Rights Commission handles complaints from people who have suffered discrimination in housing, employment and public accommodations. (The Human Rights Commission handles discrimination cases in the areas of sex, race, ethnicity, religion and disability.) Because of the special needs of complainants, the AIDS Discrimination Project is able to fast-track cases, and to achieve prompt results seeks to resolve conflicts through conciliation before taking a case to court.

aids related community services (arcs)
214 central avenue, white plains, ny 10523, 914/345-8888

This group serves Dutchess, Orange, Putnam, Rockland, Sullivan, Ulster and Westchester counties (the suburban counties around New York City), providing AIDS education, client services, crisis intervention, support groups, case management, buddy and hospital visitor programs.

aids resource center
633-2500

The AIDS Resource Center provides nonjudgmental pastoral care and housing to PWAs. The center runs the lovely riverside Bailey House as well as a scattered-site housing program. Clients are referred through the NYC Human Resource Administration.

aids resource center
24 west 30th street, new york, ny 10011, 481-1270

The AIDS Resource Center provides supportive housing for homeless PWAs at Bailey House. This group has provided nonjudgmental pas-

social, medical, and political

toral care for PWAs and loved ones for nearly a decade. Volunteering is essential here.

aids treatment news
800/873-2812

An HIV/AIDS treatment newsletter, begun in 1986, covering experimental and medical treatments. Published twice monthly, in San Francisco. Not available at newsstands; distributed by subscription. Books of back issues are available at gay and lesbian bookstores.

aids treatment resources
268-4196

A bimonthly directory of experimental treatments in New York and New Jersey. ATR sponsors seminars for trial participants and advocates for improvements in the governmental trial system. Call to get ATR's free publication.

b'nai jeshurun
787-7600

Monthly spiritual gatherings and free catered festivals and luncheons for *all* PWAs, their lovers and families. Programs include music and discussion led by rabbis.

body positive
721-1346

Body Positive is a marvelous clearinghouse of information of use to people who are HIV-positive, asymptomatic and interested in preserving their good health. Body Positive organizes support groups, provides referrals and has libraries and seminars. The organization says, "If you or your lover has tested HIV-positive, we offer support groups, semi-

aids pages

nars, public forums, reference library, referrals, and social activities."

A consistently well written monthly national magazine, *Body Positive*, offers a broad range of information, from medical protocols, to ideas about lifestyle adjustments or enhancements, to support resources.

Body Positive has been publishing since 1987. Targeted to people who are HIV-positive and to those affected by HIV—family, friends, partners, etc.—rather than to lesbians and gay men, the magazine is nevertheless sympathetic. The editorial philosophy is that the more information a person has, the more proactive he or she can be about managing the HIV/AIDS situation. *Body Positive* does not make endorsements. The unique focus of this periodical is on people who are HIV-infected and are asymptomatic, for whom there is not a great deal of info about staying healthy. *BP* can be found at lesbian and gay bookstores (A Different Light, the Oscar Wilde Memorial Bookshop); the Lesbian and Gay Community Center (208 West 13th Street); GMHC's offices; the Manhattan Center for Living, and in the Bronx at the Albert Einstein Medical Center. A subscription costs $25.

children's friends for life
p.o. box 991, rockefeller center station, new york, ny 10020, 757-0497

This 100-percent-volunteer organization provides support to children with AIDS and to their caregivers. Children's Friends for Life addresses the basic needs of children, from clothes, transportation and recreation to playmates. Children's Friends also works to coordinate the efforts of various organizations that serve children with AIDS.

community health project (chp)
675-3559

CHP provides caring, sensitive and low-cost health care services to the lesbian and gay community. Besides screening and treatment, CHP provides an inexpensive adolescent health care program, peer counseling and other services. Since 1983, city and state funds have subsidized patient costs. For kids, there is a CHP mobile van that helps them with everything "from zits to asthma." CHP has an "all-woman"

social, medical, and political

clinic too. Meetings at the L and G Community Center (208 West 13th Street).

community prescription service (cps)
800/677-4323

A gay and lesbian, HIV-positive–owned mail-order prescription service. Besides filling drug prescriptions, CPS provides its customers with a stream of information about treatments and medications. A staff pharmacist and other medical professionals are available to answer questions.

community research initiatives (cri)
481-1050

CRI tests experimental drugs and treatments for HIV-related illnesses. The organization holds monthly treatment and research groups for HIV-positive people. In addition, CRI publishes a treatment and research newsletter and holds forums and public health seminars that can be interesting to the layperson uninvolved in the "AIDS world."

gay men's health crisis
hotline 807-6655

GMHC is the oldest AIDS organization in the country.

GMHC is the largest AIDS service organization in the United States. Founded in 1981 by a small group of gay men to address an unknown disease that was striking gay men, GMHC today deploys more than 2,000 volunteers, distributes more than 1.7 million pieces of educational material around the United States, and answers more than 60,000 calls on the hotline annually.

GMHC staff and volunteers provide an array of services and referrals for PWAs: a hot meal program, legal assistance, the buddy program and counseling.

The Communications Department publishes several newsletters,

aids pages

including the widely respected *Treatment Issues*, as well as booklets and brochures that address the spectrum of issues related to AIDS and HIV. The department also publishes excellent safe-sex materials. GMHC materials are available in print and video, in English and Spanish.

GMHC is also a strong advocate at the local, state and federal levels for increased funding for AIDS/HIV services, education and research, and quicker FDA approval of promising AIDS treatments.

The GMHC Dance-A-Thon and Walk-A-Thon are major annual fund-raising drives. To find out more about them, particularly the buddy program, which allows you to do hands-on volunteer work with PWAs, see Chapter 29, "Volunteerism."

Educational Materials: GMHC publishes materials that deal with all aspects of AIDS/HIV, including health, well-living, legal issues, government entitlements and other resources. The best book from these guys is called the "Safer Than Safe" pamphlet, and it gives very serious advice, in a wildly colorful and graphic format, for people who want to be sex-positive and have a safe time at it: "Sex can still be hot, sweet, tender, raunchy or however you like it, *and* totally satisfying. (See Chapter 15, "Where to Go When Everyone's Asleep," for more details on just what that means.) We just need to make it safer. Safer means: No exchange of bodily fluids. Blood, cum, vaginal secretions—fluids we're most concerned with. That's where HIV can be found. Tears and saliva cannot carry enough HIV to be dangerous."

The little book ends with a slogan: "Your biggest sex organ is between your ears, not your legs. Use your imagination, guys. Sex does not have to be genital to be hot."

Good advice from the people who care. And it proves we've come a long way since the first slogan for a condom, circa 1982: "Don't Be Silly. Put a Condom On Your Willy!" (Although my new favorite slogan from the gay-safer-sex-world is "No Condom No Date.")

Education/Workshops: Included are video projects and safe-sex promotion: workshops, posters, condom distribution, T-shirts, publications such as the ones described above, and pre/post-testing counseling. Also, something called workshops for the "Worried Well"—help for those who are indeed HIV-negative but are upset or feeling guilty . . . because they don't understand how.

Direct Services for People with AIDS: These programs include referrals, the popular buddy program and peer counseling. Also, rec-

social, medical, and political

reational activities and a fantastic legal services department for PWAs.

Safe-Sex Workshops: GMHC holds regular safe-sex workshops that address sex and life in the face of HIV. Workshops address staying sexual and staying safe and provide an opportunity for men to learn and share feelings and experiences. Described as "hot" by participants and instructors; I understand that a great deal of so-called networking goes on.

god's love we deliver
868-4800

God's Love We Deliver is a nonsectarian organization that cooks and delivers meals every day to homebound people with AIDS. Meal deliveries are free and consist of two complete meals. Fifteen hundred volunteers keep the meals coming. (For more information, see Chapter 29, "Volunteerism.")

health education aids liaison (heal)
674-hope

Weekly information and support group for people interested in treatments for AIDS which do not compromise the immune system further, including alternative and holistic approaches. Meets Wednesday at 8 P.M. at the L and G Community Center (208 West 13th Street).

housing works
966-0466

Housing Works, Inc., is a community-based, minority-controlled, not-for-profit organization that provides housing, supportive services and advocacy for homeless people living with AIDS and HIV. It's dedicated to serving people whom no one else can or will serve. Housing Works provides safe, supportive housing for more than 400 people with AIDS.

aids pages

The group runs a very ritzy thrift shop at 136 West 18th Street. (See Chapter 29, "Volunteerism.")

legal action center
340-8724

The center offers free legal advice and other legal services to people with HIV-related illnesses. One project that has gotten a lot of press is the HIV/AIDS Training Center and Assistance Project, which provides technical assistance to public and private agencies on legal and policy issues and HIV/AIDS.

lesbian aids project
129 west 20th street, 2nd floor, new york, ny 10011, 337-3531

The Lesbian AIDS Project provides support services for women with AIDS. LAP is one of too few groups that conduct educational programs to address lesbians and HIV/AIDS. LAP provides information, referral services and resources for lesbians living with AIDS. The project produces an excellent quarterly newsletter, *LAP Notes*. Affiliated with GMHC.

manhattan center for living
704 broadway, 3rd floor, new york, ny 10003, 533-3550

Founded by Marianne Williamson of *A Course in Miracles* fame, the Manhattan Center for Living provides support to people confronting life-challenging illness. Services include the Whole Food Project to get healthful food to people who are sick; peer counseling; other counselors; and home companions. The center sponsors an annual HIV Health Day, which includes workshops, lectures, and lots of exchanging of information. A controversial place; some consider many of the lectures and symposia "cultish." Occasional parties at Warsaw benefit the center.

social, medical, and political

national institutes of health open study of new clinical drugs

Strictly confidential studies of new drugs at the following medical centers: Beth Israel, 420-4519; Mount Sinai, 241-8903; and Memorial Sloan Kettering, 639-7163.

northern lights alternatives
255-8554

The primary goal of this group is to improve the quality of life for all people with AIDS and those who are HIV-positive. The monthly AIDS Mastery Workshop helps people cope with the world around them after their diagnosis.

office of gay and lesbian health concerns
125 worth street, room 601, new york, ny 10013, 788-4310

A part of the New York City Department of Health, this agency provides health-related information to the lesbian, gay, bisexual and transgender communities in New York, with a particular focus on AIDS issues. The department has an extensive library of materials, and is an excellent source of information. In addition, the Professionals' Education Project offers educational workshops on AIDS, safe sex, and homophobia to other agencies that work with gay, lesbian, bisexual and transgender constituents.

pet care for hiv+ people (powars)
481-1270

POWARS helps people who are sick care for their pets, at no cost. Contact POWARS at the number above, which is that of the AIDS Resource Center, POWARS's sponsor.

aids pages

pwa coalition
hotline 800/828-3280, office 532-0290

The PWA Coalition is a clearinghouse for information useful to people with AIDS. The hotline is staffed entirely by PWAs. In addition, the coalition publishes two newsletters and holds several conferences every year, all in order to keep men and women living with AIDS educated about treatments, new medicines and other relevant concerns. Sponsors support groups for parents, people of color and siblings, and does outreach in prisons.

upper room aids ministry
207 west 133rd street, new york, ny 10027, 491-9000

The Upper Room AIDS Ministry provides direct physical and spiritual support to homeless people with AIDS. Fostering a "more healthful living that honors the body, mind and spirit," the ministry offers an adult day community center, supportive housing, pastoral care and self-sufficiency training.

■ support groups for friends and lovers of pwas (and others too)

These are the self-help, group help, and money-raising foundations and organizations in the New York area.

broadway cares/equity fights aids
840-0770

This is the organization through which Broadway raises money to support groups that are fighting the AIDS epidemic and caring for the sick. Broadway Cares produces events throughout the year at Steve McGraw's, 158 West 72nd Street: Every Sunday and Monday night (except in August) actors and performers do their numbers and cabaret acts. No minimum. Call McGraw's (595-7400) for a schedule. Every

social, medical, and political

September, a flea market is put together in Shubert Alley, where theatrical memorabilia, autographed playbills, posters and other theatrical stuff are sold. At the end of the day special items are auctioned off, including walk-on roles in current plays and TV shows. It's free. In November, Broadway Cares puts on "Gypsy of the Year"; current Broadway shows send a representative act to the evening. At another popular event, "Broadway Bares," actors from Broadway shows come and strip! (Held at Club USA; see Chapter 8, "Dance and Sweat," for more.) Many theatrical organizations and Broadway and off Broadway also raise money for BC/EFA by passing a hat after a performance and by selling autographed posters.

the center quilt project
lesbian and gay community services center, 620-7310

This group coordinates New York's contribution to the national Names Project Quilt. Individuals make a quilt in memory of a person they have lost in the AIDS epidemic, and the quilt is then added to the huge national quilt, which is touring the country. Admission fees to see the quilt are donated to AIDS research. Making a quilt or helping others complete one is a great way to get involved in the community.

design industries foundation for aids (diffa)

DIFFA raises money to combat AIDS. For more information, see Chapter 29, "Volunteerism." A great charity for those of you who have any interest or involvement in the fashion industry.

fashion accessories industry together for health (faith)
1414 sixth avenue, new york, ny 10019, 355-5049

FAITH is an organization of people involved in the fashion accessories industry who collectively raise money for AIDS research. FAITH sponsors a number of fund-raising events every year.

aids pages

friends in deed
594 broadway, suite 706, new york, ny 10012, 925-9009

"There is an urgent need," says the material rendered by this support agency, which is "dedicated to providing emotional, spiritual and psychological support to all those affected by a life-threatening illness." Also served are the families and caregivers of those who have been diagnosed. Friends in Deed organizes small groups that meet weekly and thereby form a real support family for each member of the group. (According to the group's literature, it has been medically proved that people who participate in support groups live longer and in a better state of health than those who don't.)

■ **political groups for activists**

Here are ways to get involved, on a grassroots and large activist scale.

aids coalition to unleash power (act up)
496-a hudson street, suite g-4, new york, ny 10014, hotline 564-2437

This is the group that radicalized activism in the eighties, has successfully demanded vitally important changes in research and treatment protocols, and has brought public and political attention to the AIDS crisis. The men and women of ACT UP continue to channel their anger into direct action to end the AIDS crisis. In addition to direct actions, ACT UP's Treatment Data and Issues Committee is a clearinghouse of information about treatments. Meetings are held Monday at 7:30 P.M., usually at the Great Hall of Cooper Union, Cooper Square between Astor Place and St. Marks Place.

Organized by pioneering activists frustrated with the initially apolitical response to the AIDS crisis, ACT UP radicalized activism in the gay and lesbian community and changed both public policy and discourse about HIV and AIDS in New York and the United States.

Subgroups address treatment and data issues, AIDS and people of color, AIDS and women, and organizational matters including finance, media publicity and public speaking.

social, medical, and political

act up women's caucus
135 west 29th street, new york, ny 10011, 564-2437

Meets Monday at 7:30 P.M. at the L and G Center (208 West 13th Street). This is a forum for women to help end the AIDS crisis.

hispanic aids forum
886 westchester avenue, bronx, 718/328-4188; 74–09 thirty-seventh avenue, suite 306, jackson heights, queens, 11372, 718/803-2766

The Hispanic AIDS Forum provides both educational and direct services concerning AIDS and HIV issues in the Latino/a community. Case management, counseling and support groups are available. The *Entre Hombres* program is designed to meet the special needs of gay Latinos. All of the staff are bilingual. Services are available in both Queens and the South Bronx.

men of color aids prevention program (oca)
239-1796

Safer-sex and AIDS education information for gay and bisexual men of color. Peer support groups for men of color in all five boroughs.

women and aids resource network (warn)
30 third avenue, #212, brooklyn, ny 11217, 718/596-6007

WARN works to prevent the spread of AIDS among women. The network provides counseling, organizes self-help groups for women and offers referrals, all regarding HIV/AIDS issues. WARN has been at it since 1986.

chapter twenty-nine

volunteerism

Go and get involved... It's the best way to get yourself really *into* the community. Hey, there's too much guilt in your life already without having to feel bad that you're not somehow contributing to the core of our being.

Involvement... In the gay and lesbian world, involvement is usually aligned with romantic commitment or a relationship. In the world of volunteering, it's a whole different ballgame. Here we're talking involvement in an activity that can change your life or in some way make you feel better about yourself. It has nothing to do with cementing a relationship, though giving of yourself often assists those other parts of your life.

As for cruising... Yeah, the best thing about New York is that you can cruise just about anywhere. (I met my 1991 boyfriend at a Knicks game.) So since you feel so good about yourself when you volunteer, you usually light up and look your most attractive. That's the best time to meet someone.

On the subject of pride... "Pride" is a key word for many of the groups that seek volunteers (read below). Pride is something many gay men and lesbians talk about. Here's a way to uplift that pride and show it off to the world. Here's a list of organizations and dedicated groups

social, medical, and political

that provide services, timely help, and encouragement to our brothers and sisters.

So, without further ado . . .

aids resource center (arc)
633-2500

ARC provides housing for people with AIDS and maintains an active volunteer program. Volunteers do everything to keep this organization alive, from office work to teaching classes in photography, cooking, sewing, creative writing, etc., to gardening, escorting clients to appointments and basically being all-around friendly to the clients. ARC also has a buddy program entirely staffed by volunteers. Because ARC is a small organization, volunteer leadership is also welcomed. Volunteers with professional skills can offer time to help with special projects (for example, setting up a public relations campaign).

A monthly volunteer orientation is held to introduce new volunteers to ARC. Call the volunteer coordinator, also a volunteer.

design industries foundation for aids (diffa)
150 west 26th street, suite 602, new york, ny 10001, 727-3100

DIFFA raises money to combat AIDS. Funds are distributed to AIDS/HIV organizations in the categories of care and service, education and advocacy. DIFFA has chapters in fourteen cities in the United States, so if you want to get involved, get in touch in your home city. DIFFA sponsors scores of events in New York every year; call up, get the newsletter, and check out what's going on.

DIFFA uses volunteers to plan and staff its many fund-raising events and to provide general office support. A volunteer-based organization, DIFFA welcomes more hands all the time. In the words of a friend who toils there, "You don't have to be a design queen to help us!" Translation: You don't have to be in the fashion industry to work at DIFFA.

volunteerism

empire state pride agenda
673-5417

This lobbying group for gay and lesbian issues disperses money to candidates who help homo causes. The Pride Agenda organizes gay and lesbian voters to put pressure on officials and successfully got good gay people into office in the 1993 school board elections.

Volunteers staff the phone bank, calling members to alert them about important upcoming pieces of legislation so that they can call or write to their representatives urging their support. Other volunteers work at gay and lesbian events, staffing information tables and passing out fliers to get more people involved in Empire Pride Agenda. Volunteers also do general office work.

To become a volunteer, call and leave your name, phone number and address. Someone will return your call to discuss Pride Agenda's current activities and the type of work you're interested in doing. Then the group will find the most suitable position for you. Pride Agenda's activities are always changing; however, the need for volunteers is constant in the areas of fund-raising, lobbying, elections and administrative work. (During election periods, volunteers may work on the campaign of the candidate endorsed by Pride Agenda.)

Right now there is a drive to get State Senator Ralph Marino to vote for the Civil Rights Bill to include gay and lesbian rights. Empire State Pride Agenda is leading the fight to get gays and lesbians to call Marino (518/455-2800 and 516/922-1811) in order to ensure he votes for us.

gay & lesbian alliance against defamation (glaad)
807-1700

GLAAD combats homophobia in the media and elsewhere by promoting visibility of the lesbian and gay community and organizing grassroots response to antigay bigotry.

GLAAD uses lots of volunteers. Fifty percent of them are media professionals who are working on specific projects, like creating advertisements for a recent subway campaign. Other volunteers do office

social, medical, and political

work or work on committees, which include Visibility Action, Media and Public Relations. GLAAD's bimonthly bulletin and quarterly newsletter are put together by volunteers.

The PhoneTree is a special arm of GLAAD. When the PhoneTree is activated, you receive a call, dial their hotline for details, and then call the three people on your personal list and tell them to call the hotline. Often you will be asked to write letters too. Within 48 hours of an extreme homophobic incident, our community is alerted and can respond with angry letters and phone calls.

GLAAD offers a way to volunteer with an upbeat group and to see improvements in the way gays and lesbians are covered in the media. I have included a GLAAD signup sheet in this chapter. Call GLAAD, and sign up—join the PhoneTree or volunteer to do one of a zillion other things to help keep the homophobes in line.

gay and lesbian switchboard of new york
777-1800

Also called "The Switchboard," this involves rap, referral and just plain facts, man. The Switchboard is staffed entirely by volunteers. Becoming a Switchboard volunteer is a big commitment; it involves an interview with the volunteer committee and a weekend-long training session in peer counseling.

As one Switchboard volunteer noted, the commitment requires independent open-mindedness, since, after all, the task is talking on the phone and not working with other volunteers. On top of that, it requires the ability to be a good listener—most of the people who call have real problems.

Besides working on the Switchboard, volunteers staff the committees that run the organization.

Call the Switchboard and ask the volunteer who answers whatever questions you have. You'll quickly receive an enlightening info packet.

volunteerism

god's love we deliver
865-4800

God's Love We Deliver provides meals to people with AIDS who are homebound or bedridden. Volunteers are used throughout the organization, in food preparation, delivery, office work, data entry, working at benefits or sitting on committees. Committees include Legal Advisory, Financial Planning and the Board.

Volunteering with God's Love We Deliver is a way to become actively involved in helping people with AIDS in a fundamental way—by providing luscious and nutritious food. Volunteers feel they're making a direct and positive contribution to the lives of very sick PWAs.

gay men's health crisis greeting cards program
807-6655

Here's an easy way to support an important institution in the city: You give money to the largest AIDS charity group in town and it mails a seasonal greeting card to whomever you like, mentioning that you've made a contribution to GMHC. Nice way to handle the end of the year card crisis. And a great way to give money to a charity you probably already love.

GMHC has about a million other ways that you can get involved, from the intense work of being a buddy to someone who has AIDS, to working on fund-raising and organizing events. At GMHC, you make an appointment with the volunteer coordinator, go and talk about your interests and skills and then get assigned. *Voilà!*

Still another alternative is to participate in any one of the numerous fund-raising activities mounted by GMHC annually. Of these, the two best known are the Walk-A-Thon and Dance-A-Thon. Walk in May, Dance in late November or early December. During these heartwarming and cruisey events, you either stroll, jog, hop, boogie or hang out with your friends—and often celebrities (okay, Madonna). You collect pledges or donate money and the rest is up to you. It's a mere five kilometers for the walk and a mere five hours for the dance.

social, medical, and political

And for the walk there's a big congratulatory shindig held each year at Palladium to thank you for being part.

heritage of pride
807-7433

These folks are the organizers of the big Lesbian and Gay Pride events such as the March, Rally and the splashy Dance on the Pier, held the last Sunday in June.

The entire organization is volunteers, so anyone who can do anything is encouraged to help. Volunteers are needed to carry out all activities related to the planning, organization and execution of the Lesbian and Gay Pride events and festivals: blowing up balloons, answering phones, selling or ordering merchandise, taking tickets, setting up the sound equipment for the dance, etc. Since everyone is a volunteer, the best way to get involved is to attend one of the meetings held at the L and G Community Center (208 West 13th Street) on every second Monday of the month at 8 P.M.

housing works, inc.
966-0466

Housing Works is a community-based, minority-controlled, not-for-profit organization that provides housing, supportive services and advocacy for homeless people living with AIDS and HIV. Housing Works deploys volunteers throughout the organization, working at its money-making thrift shop, helping with administration and event planning and providing supportive services for clients.

Volunteers with special skills may be of use working with the client population and are welcome to plan continuing programs with the staff.

Housing Works deals with a population of people affected by HIV with whom the larger AIDS organizations are not equipped to deal, and while the work can be difficult, it is also unusually rewarding. To get involved, call the volunteer coordinator.

volunteerism

lambda legal defense and education fund
995-8585

Volunteers contribute to Lambda's work in a variety of ways. Attorneys nationwide can join the Cooperating Attorneys Network and thereby assist by signing briefs, serving as the local attorney on a case, answering questions regarding an area of expertise or accepting referrals. Legal eagles interested in joining the network should write to Lambda.

Paralegal services are occasionally needed; interested paralegals should write. Volunteers who are not legal professionals are also needed. Thursday night is Volunteer Night; people who come work on a variety of office projects.

Says the Volunteer Coordinator, "Liberty must be defended with each generation. Lambda volunteers are footsoldiers for freedom."

lesbian and gay community services center
208 west 13th street, new york, ny 10011, 620-7310

The center needs lots of volunteers: 400 of them work to keep the broad range of programs and services going. Come introduce yourself, get some info and volunteer for committees and projects that need your help. Talk to Trish Kerle, the volunteer director, who was once the volunteer coordinator for Big Brothers/Big Sisters of New York. As the saying goes, "We're *everywhere*." I have included a form in the Introduction that you can fill out and mail to the center, or fax it to 924-2657.

To get involved, drop by the center on the regularly scheduled Volunteer Night, at which you will be able to meet people from different committees and programs who are looking for new volunteers. In addition, eight times a year you can learn as much about the center as I have, at Orientation Nights.

Volunteer opportunities fall into three categories: working on a committee, working on a special project—generally a short-term commitment—or providing support to the professional staff that runs the social service programs. Here's a sample of the thirty-odd committees at the center:

Volunteer members of the Center's International Lesbian and Gay

social, medical, and political

Association run the New York regional chapter of the International Lesbian and Gay Organization, and work on international human rights projects for the world.

Members of the Garden Committee do the gardening of the center courtyard, quite a beautiful site.

Volunteers on the Dance Committee organize, promote and run the center dances—a hoot if you haven't attended (see Chapter 8, "Dance and Sweat.")

In Our Own Write volunteers plan readings and forums of gay and lesbian professional writers and aspiring authors.

Lesbian Movie Night volunteers organize the schedule of movies and videos shown at the monthly (heavily attended) Lesbian Night at the Movies.

The volunteers on the Museum and Archive Committee are trained by the center's well-informed archivist and do archival and cataloging work, and assist in the planning and mounting of exhibitions.

Orientation Committee volunteers organize the monthly orientation night at the center and the center orientation events that go on the road to introduce people in the region to the center.

By the time you read this, a new project will have begun enabling the receptionists at the desk to give out a welcome package to everyone who steps into 208 West 13th Street. There will be information on gay safety issues, health, safer sex, and social activities (some brochures will exist in several languages), supplying you with a primer on gay life in New York, just for stopping by. It's the center's way of ensuring that it serves its purpose: empowerment. For more on the center, see Chapter 1, "Essential Resources."

outwatch
967-7711, extension 3037

These men and women patrol gay neighborhoods at night to combat the increasing violence against lesbians and gay men.

Meetings are held the first Tuesday of the month at 8 P.M. at the L and G Community Center (208 West 13th Street). Although Outwatch is very anxious to get new recruits for their "Pink Panther"-type

volunteerism

outings, no one called back when I left messages. So volunteer, but be forceful.

■ **epilogue**

Volunteers who assisted the successful fight against the Colorado amendment and the military ban had the best of the crop of gay men and lesbians helping out. If the fights are still on upon the publication of this book, contact **new york colorado boycott** at 239-1451, extension NYCB, and the **campaign for military service** at 202/265-6666. Very strong, purposeful groups—and you can help.

section five

oddities and a completely subjective list of things i like

At one point a guidebook author has to have serious fun. When I started hearing amusing stories about things done in spare time, I decided to tribute the many strange ways we busy ourselves in this town.

The following is an accumulation of the most unusual facets of the New York scene. They include everything from odd stores to unusual groups, and a few wondrous ideas thrown into this chapter because I couldn't find another place for them anywhere else. Gay and lesbian living in New York often means living on the edge; here are some ways to enjoy that edge.

If something bothers you in this chapter, skip it. However, you may find yourself engrossed in a specific idea. Call the group or person up and get on the mailing list. Chances are you'll start receiving good mail—offers about special parties, invitation-only sales, or chat about the organization.

A group may share its mailing list—or sell it—to similar organizations. This is a way you'll get mailers from people you *want* to hear from.

Here's to the odd . . .

chapter thirty

odd places, odd people and, of course, odd things

backroom (BCSS, Inc., Box 539, Richmond Hill, New York 11749, 718/849-2225; modem line 718/849-1614) is a big, independent, gay-owned computer network. Chatting with other homos, health and AIDS news, a national resource list, e-mail, weekly gay news and other on-line fun. **synapse** (P.O. Box 0988, Planetarium Station, New York NY 10036, 986-0770) is a lesbian database that's among the best—it's a mere $.50 per minute. Lots of resources and an unpretentious way to network. **sappho's exchange** (P.O. Box 1289, New York NY 10010, 697-3713 modem only) is a very reputable on-line network for lesbians on the go! It's free, too, which makes it one of the best things in life. ($25 annual contribution suggested but only if you're hooked!) Lastly, **compuserve** (800/848-8990), the Ohio-based information services company, has a very popular on-line chat division called Gay Lifestyles for use at a nominal fee. Boys from as far away as Boise use it for hot "phone chat." Call for a free starter kit to use with your machine.

oddities and a completely subjective list

club frottage
491-7228

A multicultural support group for men into frottage. Monthly meetings are held (discreetly) at the L and G Community Services Center (208 West 13th Street).

crystal gardens
21 greenwich avenue, new york, ny 10011, 366-1965

Joyce and Connie, owners of this shop, are reiki masters, hypnotherapists and Flower Remedy practitioners. They sell crystals, minerals, essential oils, flower remedies and the like.

girth & mirth club of new york
p.o. box 10, pelham, ny 10803, 914/699-7735

A social club for heavy gay men and their admirers. Monthly socials held at the L and G Community Center (208 West 13th Street) and bar night Thursday at the Chelsea Transfer bar (131 Eighth Avenue). Monthly *Fat Apple Review* (which makes great reading for skinnies) and bimonthly FAR pen pals. Call Ernie or write him at the above address.

lesbian and gay big apple corps
123 west 44th street, suite 121, new york, ny 10036, 869-2922

The Corps invites you to "get your instrument out of the closet and come play with us." It meets at midtown to perform symphonic, marching band, jazz, Dixieland and rock music. Being in the high school band was never this cruisey.

odd places, odd people and, of course, odd things

military bookman
29 east 93rd street, new york, ny 10128, 348-1280

More than 2,000 titles about military, naval and aviation history, as well as biographies of military giants. The rare-book cases hold treats such as spy journals and naval maneuver manuals. Located at Very butch.

mixed company
332 bleecker street #h24, new york, ny 10014, 679-9379

This organization hooks together gays and lesbians for the purpose of establishing useful relationships with people of the opposite sex. Perhaps a lesbian needs a "beard," meaning a man to show off at a function. Or maybe friendship. Rick, who likes to keep his private life ve-ery private, says he started the group ($20 initiation fee, info kept confidential) as a specialized introductory service with a decidedly politically incorrect method for people to meet, perhaps mate, but mostly use each other happily. A traveling salesman, Rick says he believes firmly in "like" and thinks tricking out (see the Glossary) is the only way to be happy. He would like to go national but figures the demographics in New York are best suited for the profile of gay-man-seeks-lesbian. What does he really want out of life? A happy relationship with a kid, a lesbian collaborator and a lot of sex on the side. Write him.

program solutions
140 euclid avenue, hackensack, nj 07601, 201/646-0243

Customized computer programming services and other high-tech business services specially marketed for gay men and lesbians. Why use one of the million companies in Manhattan when you can send your queer dollars to Hackensack?

chapter thirty-one

a few personal favorites that i get to put in because i'm the author (nyah, nyah, nyah)

big apple bowling league
718/204-2133

This four-year-old group is a source of entertainment for many gay men and lesbians, and a source of exercise for those who don't get out. Meets Wednesday at 8:30 P.M. at Bowlmor Lanes, 110 University Place. As a friend put it, "It's a great place to find a husband."

carapan for massage
5 west 16th street, new york, ny 10011, 633-6220

Fully clothed, you sit in a chair with your head and chest resting against a firm cushion and get an expert massage in twenty minutes. And this only costs $25. The expert kneads your neck, shoulder, back, arms and hands. Then you stagger out into New York, blissfully limp. Book in advance by calling ahead. Like the ads say . . .

oddities and a completely subjective list

clocktower
108 leonard street, new york, ny 10013, 233-2096

This contemporary museum and art gallery is okay—a little pretentious—but the best attraction is an accidental extra. After spending time looking at the abstract art here, you can climb several winding staircases and end up facing an actual clock high atop the tower, some fourteen stories up. If that doesn't sound like fun, imagine watching the giant structure tick-tock, then peering into the mechanics as you hear far-off sounds below. Look down at City Hall and enjoy the cloudy view. Then check out sculptures and message paintings downstairs. Hours are Wednesday through Saturday noon to 6 P.M.; closed July and August.

lee schy: street art

Though the ones on the street are fading, a young artist has produced strewn-on-street stories of his family life by photocopying photos and inscribing little messages on them. Titles such as "Exhilarated Family Independence" and "Extended Family Fable" can be found on walls of old buildings and fences and the like, in Chelsea, the East Village and SoHo—with inscriptions that are at times bizarre and touching. These raw works are called "Lee's."

the shop
105 east 9th street, new york, ny 10003, 674-8963

This place sells deep house vinyl, underground music, acid jazz, trans rave and rap. It's an excellent store with some of the best ads. What's more, it carries both records and CDs. Store hours are Monday through Saturday 1 to 9 P.M., Sunday 1 to 6.

glossary:
endearing terms and otherwise

In an effort to be more than helpful, I've included a glossary of words and terms that you may or may not find in the hippest available dictionary. These are terms I've used in the book, although some may have been left out in editing. If you're looking for specific examples of their usage, don't bother. Best to read this as entertainment—and to prove that our language is specific.

These definitions are my views and it's not necessary for everyone to agree with me.

ac/dc   Flips back and forth, a bisexual man or woman. Often derogatory.
act up clone   That guy who can't stop talking about his activist group and wears combat boots, dog tags and close-cropped hair.
after-hours club   A place that's open when most bars are closed; usually illegal (liquor is not supposed to be sold after 5 A.M. in New York City but is).
back room   A place to go to have sex in a bar or club.
barhopping   The art of going to bars one after another; usually entails having a hangover the next day.
basket   The bulge in his pants—look at the fly.

glossary

body fluids   Generally, the body fluids that carry significant quantities of the HIV virus: semen, vaginal fluids and blood.

bondage   Being tied up and whipped; S&M practice.

bottom   The receptive partner.

bubble butt   A nicely shaped, rounded ass.

bull dyke   A woman who is tough and butch and maybe scary.

butch   A tough-acting guy or a masculine woman, or a man or woman in a toughie outfit.

a butch number   Someone who is about to be "chosen" because he's tough. A sexual look that's often pulled off.

cash bar   You pay for the drinks.

chicken   Very young trade, very young meat, very young boy who could get you into trouble.

christopher street   The place in the Village most associated with gaydom.

clone   Typical Queer, and not the Absolut Vodka Version! The seventies: mustache; tight jeans; longish hair, if any; some kind of bandanna in pocket; cigarettes; plaid shirt. The nineties: ACT UP or similar statement button; moussed hair and one earring; tight jeans and probably a leather jacket.

cock ring   A ring made of leather or metal and placed around the base of the cock to make orgasm more intense.

colorado boycott   A boycott of Colorado for not having the foresight to stop the passage of the amendment to its state civil rights laws allowing discrimination against homosexuals. Since found to be unconstitutional, but people are being cautious.

companion   Lover, boyfriend, friend, girlfriend, partner, significant other, *I'm with Stupid.*

the community   Who we are.

community spirit   The essence of our collective souls.

coors boycott   A boycott of Adolph Coors, an antigay businessperson who never seems to learn a lesson. If you buy a Coors or Coors Light beer you are making a statement: The Coors family directs the profits to extremist right-wing causes. (Until recently, the same boycotters targeted Philip Morris, whose cigarette firm helped reelect Jesse Helms. The boycott ended when Philip Morris gave tons of money to several AIDS organizations in an effort to "make up.")

glossary

cover (no cover) What they do (or don't) charge at the door.

cross-dresser Someone who dresses like the sex he or she isn't.

cross-training Cardiovascular workouts that get the heart beating. Very good for you, unlike weight training, which is very good for your looks and inner strength.

cruise bar A place that sells liquor and allows you to look for a man or woman to have sex with.

cruising Looking for sex. I mean *really* looking.

daddy Some men call their lover this if that person is someone they look up to. Quite literally.

dental dam A plastic sheet to cover the vagina, an essential component of safe sex for women.

dildo Something long and cylindrical to put inside.

direct action Something people do when they want the world to change, such as when ACT UP fights City Hall with a march or an indiscreet sit-in.

discretionary door The gallish idea that a bouncer can say "No" to you at the door of a club for no real reason except that he doesn't like your look.

domestic partnership This new law on the books in New York which patronizingly states that a couple who are not heterosexual are married in respect to insurance, hospital visiting hours, and leases (which are already legally sharable by lovers in New York City law)

drag queen A man who dresses up like a woman and performs (where the phrase "Sing it, girl" comes from; also "drag king.")

dreamboat An effusive phrase describing a man or woman who has that look. Mm, that look.

earring on the right ear The way to wear "I'm a homosexual" on your body—for men only. A gay guy who wears an earring on the left ear is saying he believes in classified advertising only.

fabulous A truly overused term; means absolutely nothing.

faggot Horrible way of describing one of us.

fag hag A woman who seems to adore gay men.

femme A gal or guy who is pretty into being a *lady*.

fetish My favorite sexual thing: when you can't get enough of something—like feet, or whips, or using globs of Cool Whip!

glossary

fisting Sticking your hand up someone's anus (be sure to wear a surgical glove).

flamer An effeminate man (homophobic term).

friend The person you can call at 3 A.M. to ask the meaning of life. A confidante.

friend of dorothy Blatant gay man and lesbian "code word."

fuck buddy The person you go to bed with regularly who is *not* your lover.

gbm A gay black man.

get laid Have sex, most usually means fucking.

girlfriend The person who is the dating partner of a woman (the lesbian definition).

go-go boy A man who dances with little or no clothing on.

going down Blow job, head, dick-sucking, etc.

golden showers Urinating on someone in a sex act; unclean.

greek active Someone who likes to fuck—and that's it, okay?

guppie A gay urban professional—"very BMW scene."

gwm A gay white man.

the gym Where gay men and lesbians hang out after work, pre-bars.

happy hour The time between 5 and 9 P.M. to drink.

harness (Half-harness too.) What to wear to a leather party, a leather bar or a leather night out, or during S&M play. Best to wear to The Saint's Black Party in March.

head Oral sex. (But people said you know this.)

hiv Human immunodeficiency virus, the virus known to cause AIDS, which is not a disease but an immunodeficiency breakdown that causes diseases.

home boys Men or boys "from the hood."

homophobia The act of hating a homosexual for some inane reason; a social disease that is curable.

hotline A place to call for immediate help.

hung Big dick. It's always so debatable, what precisely a big dick is. How big is *big*? (Eight inches, I'm *sure*.)

hunk See *Stud*.

jam session A band or group or singer that performs, usually in a format that requires no rehearsal.

glossary

jimmy cap   Condom (slang).

karaoke   A ridiculous electronic singalong.

leather bar   A place where lots of people dress in leather. And drink. Very often, if you tickle a leather man he'll get all poufy.

lipstick lesbian   A fancy lesbian. Look for a purse. Femme.

mary   A term of address first popular among gay men born before 1960 and now enjoying a resurgence.

milquetoast   A big sissy or an inanely passive person.

misogynist   Someone who hates women and is usually proud of the fact.

miss thing   A weird, old-fashioned term for your friends—boys say that to other boys about other boys. Unnecessary term, *Mary*!

mixed   Lesbians and gay men together; sometimes means l & g's and straight people at the same club, party or gathering.

no host bar   You have to pay for drinks at an event or reception.

outing   A picnic. No, actually it's when someone is publicly noted for being homosexual (when he or she has been telling people otherwise). Made famous by Michelangelo Signorile a few years back (*Outweek*).

partner   A lover, companion or significant other. Some people say such terms as "partner" and "significant other" are wimpy misnomers. I prefer *"that guy."*

passes   Get them at gay venues or from club promoters; they usually offer a discount on the cover charge at a club. Drinks can still wipe you out!

passing   Pretending to be straight.

pc   Politically correct.

people of color   African-Americans; Latinos and Latinas; Asians.

performance art   One person getting onstage and doing his or her dramatization (i.e., Eric Bogosian, Whoopi Goldberg before she became famous and boring).

phone sex   Getting on, getting off, hanging up, cleaning the phone. A few are listed in the book. Find listings in the back pages of almost any male homosexual magazine. You can call to your heart's content but before you know it, you will have run up quite a phone bill. The ads that say "15 cents a minute" are for

glossary

the second minute; often the first is $1.95. (New York Telephone will allow one month's worth of mistakes to be wiped from your bill if at first you don't succeed . . .).

piano bar A place to go to get yourself singing again; you stand by the piano and sing musical showstoppers.

the piers Off Christopher Street, West-Side-beachfront places to go for quick sex. Once very popular all year round, now just in the summer. Rumor has it they're all being closed off permanently.

posing Standing (e.g., in a bar) doing nothing but doing it quite well. Often-used description of a man or woman who does this well: *poseur*. (See Chapter 7, "Bars All Around Town," and then see Uncle Charlie's as exemplary.)

positive HIV-positive.

poofter An effeminate man. Not a nice word, I think.

pride What any self-loving gay man or lesbian has about his or her sexuality. "Pride is a deeper love," the song goes.

pwa Persons/person with AIDS; politically correct term.

queen A person who is effeminate or dramatic. "Drama queen." Some say anybody who is obviously gay is a queen. I disagree. Still offensive uses include "rice queen," meaning he's into Japanese men. "Theater queen" implies he's into musicals. (There's the British Queen, a royal Miss Thing, *her*.)

queer A once-derogatory word for a gay person or lesbian, now a pretty cool word used by many to mean militant gay. Controversial, this.

ramble A place in Central Park for group or individual sex. I saw a famous Broadway musical star (British, big in a Lloyd Webber piece) there once. He was having a very good time. Me? Just looking for fauna.

rap group A support group to talk about common issues. And, if you really must know, then Run DMC too!

rave A party with house music, drugs, boys, girls. Much of it is straight, all of it is fast and frenzied. Locations are "secret."

ripped A muscular man whose veins pop out. Can be captivating, can be disgusting if there are too many.

role-playing What adventurous people do in bed. One is the top, another is the bottom. One plays the "room service boy" while the other plays the trick from hell . . . Can add spice to an

glossary

otherwise unexciting sex life. You get the idea; if you don't, try it. Could save your marriage (don't I know it).

safe or safer sex Sex that is less risky in terms of HIV and STD infection.

saint, the A disco in the seventies; today it's "at large."

scene A sex scene is a place arranged for sex; making a scene is something people do when they want to cause an unpleasant moment; an event/scene is a large gathering; making the scene means you showed up, you were noticed.

screamer One who is loud and often obnoxious; heard a fun definition of this as one who makes others laugh.

sex addict A person who cannot get enough of a good thing. Yes, we're all like that sometimes.

sex-positive Feeling or being positive about sex, AIDS epidemic and homophobia notwithstanding.

sex toys *Objets de sex.*

significant other Another version of lover (see Lover, Companion, Boyfriend, Girlfriend).

size queen (opposite of being a "liar") A gay man who desires big penises.

slave Someone who will willingly do anything for another; a sex definition for the passive.

stds Sexually transmitted diseases such as herpes, AIDS, chlamydia, gonorrhea, etc.

stonewall Where the Riots took place in '69 that were the genesis of the gay liberation movement in the United States. (See Chapter 3, "A Look at Gay Neighborhoods. . . .")

straight-acting, straight-looking "Nobody Knows I'm Gay."

stud A man who is either large or terrific-looking. In the case of Billy Baldwin, fuckable.

sugar daddy Someone willing to pay the bills.

swish Someone who is lispy, gay-acting, effeminate; often a derogatory word, unless you like it.

tea dance Usually held on Sundays. This is a way to let people know that Sundays are good times to come to bars. Started by bar owners in the seventies when business sucked on a Sunday. It's the usual drink-and-make scene, though, so don't look for finger sandwiches.

glossary

tea room A rest room or rest stop where men have sex with each other. No leaf readings!

top The penetrator in intercourse.

trade A guy who is "straight," wants a blow job, never puts out; or, a working class, one-time sex partner. Big-time homonym.

training What people in gyms do. Requires no manual.

trick A sex partner. Usually means one night and rarely even cab fare after that night.

trick-out What you do when you cheat on your friend.

two-drink minimum What horrible places make you pay when they want your money more than your regular patronage. (Pay only when there's *good* entertainment at stake.)

two-stepping A really nice country-western dance.

transsexual Someone who was once one sex, is now another.

transvestite Someone who wears women's clothing when he is a man. (I understand it's not the same word for a woman who does it in men's clothing.) Not necessarily a gay man, this person.

wam Waiter, actor, model. Something a lot of *new* New Yorkers do when they get here. Not to be confused with WHAM, the organization devoted to women's concerns with AIDS. Not to be confused with the group Wham!, which George Michael was in before he became a Freddie Mercury clone.

zap An action that groups like ACT UP and Queer Nation invented, pursue and condone: Everyone incessantly calls, visits and faxes someone who did something bad to gays and lesbians (bad by their standards) and lets that person know it was a no-no.

acknowledgments

I'd like to thank the lesbian community and the gay community for their assistance in this venture.

Thank you's to John Ware and Matthew Carnicelli for allowing this book to occur. Also to a variety of friends and family who coped with me during deadline periods: Jonathan Herzog, Doug Loewe, Mary Boone, Suki M. John, Ilene Diamond, Laurence Lerman, Natalie A. Ungar, David Morgenstern, Ellen Cooper, Michelle Picher, M. Victoria Robbins, Rona Carr, Clifton Stone, Lou and Gloria Laermer. I don't know how many times I can thank Rachel Kranz . . . here I go again! Special thank you to Steve Bradley.

But, mostly, thank you to the three people who helped me put this thing together: *Eric Lee*, Eric Flynn, Thea Sternbach. (These three put up with a lot from me.) Thank you to Fred Morris.

The establishments that helped the most need to be thanked for never hanging up on me: Lesbian and Gay Community Services Center, ACT UP, Gay Men's Health Crisis (GMHC), and the Gay & Lesbian Alliance Against Defamation (GLAAD). And 411, expensively.

And lastly, a sincere thank you to Columbia, which gave me the time I needed to write a book I believed was important enough to keep asking for more time. Time is irretrievable, kids.

index

ABC No Rio, 169
Abortion rights, 200
Acting Company, 137
Act Up hotline, 31
Adam and Eve Catalogue, 124
Adelaide, 104
Adonis, 123
Adult Children of Alcoholics Hotline, 31–32
Advertising, 182
Advocate, 11–12
AIDS, 3, 4, 13, 215–30
   basics, 215–17
   Catholic ministry, 204
   charities, 76
   counseling and support groups, 6, 214
   Dance-A-Thon, 235
   education, 19, 216
   Quilt, 181, 228
   testing, 218
   and theater, 134
   Walk-A-Thon, 189, 235–36
AIDS Center of Queens County (ACQC), 218
AIDS Coalition to Unleash Power (ACT UP), 19, 31, 229
   Women's Caucus, 195, 230
AIDS Discrimination Project, 219
   hotline, 31
AIDS in Focus (radio show), 17
AIDS Mastery Workshop, 226
AIDS Related Community Services (ARCS), 219

index

AIDS Resource Center (ARC), 219, 232
AIDS Treatment Alert, 179
AIDS Treatment News, 220
AIDS Treatment Resources (ATR), 220
AIDS Watch, 158
Albee, Edward, 62
Albert Einstein Medical Center, 221
Alcoholics Anonymous Hotline, 31–32
Algonquin, 85
  Oak Room, 108
All American Boy, 89
All Male Jewel Theater, 123
All Male XX Video, 124
Alternative Latina (radio show), 17
Alternative Museum, 147
American Civil Liberties Union (ACLU)
  Lesbian and Gay Rights Project, 197
  Reproductive Freedom Project, 200
American Gay/Lesbian Atheists (AGA), 203
American Place Theater, 139
American Psychiatric Association, 213
Anthology Film Archive, 161
Antiquarian Bookshop, 154
Apple Corps Theater, 136
Architects, 183
Argosy, 154
Art
  auction, 94
  galleries and museums, 131–32, 141–50, 248
  lectures, 159–60

  at St. Ann's, 133–34
Arthur's Tavern, 39
Artmakers, 141
Artists organization, 210
Asian Lesbians of the East Coast/ Asian Pacific Lesbian Network (ALOEC East Coast), 187
Asians, 138, 187, 191
Asians and Friends—New York, 191
ASTREA, or National Lesbian Action Foundation, 196
Athletics and athletes, 36, 37, 53, 82, 96, 177, 181, 247
  gyms, 99–102
Atlantis, 82
Attitudes, 65
Audubon Terrace, 94, 95
Azzouni, Jody, 159

Baca Downtown, 138
Bachelor's Tavern, 71
Backroom (BCSS, Inc.), 243
Bailey House, 219
Ballroom, 105
Baltyk Cafe, 169
Bamboo Bernies, 95
Bar, 55
Bar Association for Human Rights, 173
Barbara Toll Fine Arts, 144
Bargemusic, 165
Bars, 2, 51–71
  Brooklyn, 70
  Chelsea, 53–55
  Downtown, 69
  East Side, 67–69
  East Village, 55–58
  history of, 51
  Queens, 70–71

index

piano, 111–13
romantic, 85–87
West Side, 65–67
West Village, 26, 58–65
Barton, David, 78. *See also* David Barton Gym
Bartsch Events, 78–79
Basketball, free, 96
Bathhouse, 117–18, 119
Battering, 183
Battery Travel Associates, 23
Bedrox!, 81
Bentley, Eric, 133
Beowulf, 169
Better Bodies Gym, 99
Better Days, 82
Big Apple Bowling League, 247
Big Apple Gay Lesbian and Bisexual Association for the Deaf, 175
Billie Holiday Theatre Company, 137
Binnewater Arts Center, 210
Biograph Cinema, 137
Biography, 154
Bi-Pac (Bisexual Political Action Committee), 173
Bisexual Dominance and Submission Group (BIDS), 174
Bisexual Information and Counseling Service, 174
Bisexual Network, 173, 174
Bisexual Pride Discussion and Support Group, 174
Bisexual Youth, 175
Bi-Ways New York, 29
Blacks, 137, 138, 180, 191–92
Black Sheep, 47
Blue Note, 105
B'nai Jeshurun, 220

Body Positive, 220–21
Body Positive (newsletter), 221
Bogosian, Eric, 139, 146
Bolski, Bella, 81
Bookstores and libraries, 19, 151–54, 221, 245
Booths, 124
Boots and Saddle, 58
Boutte, Tony, 132
Bowling, 247
Box, The, 81
Boy Bar, 55, 78
Bradley's, 39
Brandy's, 111
Breadstix, 70
Break, 51, 53
Bridgehampton, NY, 177
"Broadway Bares," 228
Broadway Cares/Equity Fights AIDS, 175, 227–28
Bronx
AIDS support, 221, 230
social clubs, 187, 192
Bronx Lesbians United in Sisterhood, Inc. (BLUeS), 187
Bronx River Art Center and Gallery, 142
Brooklyn
bars, 69
dance shows, 95
political clubs, 198
social clubs, 191
Brooklyn Academy of Music (BAM), 165
Brooklyn Bed and Breakfast, 21
Brooklyn Botanical Garden, 87
Brooklyn's Lesbian and Gay Political Club (Lambda Independent Democracts), 175–76, 198

index

Brooklyn Women's Martial Arts, 207
Bull Pen, 124
Bumbalo, Victor, 132
Burke, John (Sybil Bruncheon), 15
Burns, Richard, 6, 18
Business organizations, 195, 200–1
Butch Femme Society, 188

Cabarets, 103–10, 112–13
Cable TV, 14–16, 179–80
Cactus Club, 80
Cafe Bustelo, 137
Cafe Carlyle, 105
Cafe Siné, 169
Cafe Luxembourg, 47
Calypso music, 97
Campaign for Military Service, 239
Candied Camera (TV show), 15
Candle Bar, 65
Capitol Hill Update, 179
Carapan for Massage, 247
Carlos I, 39
Carlson, Ann, 146
Carnegie Hall, 97
Carnegie Mansion concerts, 97
Caroline's, 105–6
Carter's System, 117
Casa de Espana, 94
Catholic organizations, 204–5
CBS tickets, 98
Cellblock 28, 53, 117
CenterBridge, 19
Center of the Rainbow, 201
Center Quilt Project, 181, 228
Centers for Disease Control and Prevention (CDC), 215
Center Voice, 19
Central Park, 88
  Bandshell, 97
  Conservatory Water, 95
  folk dancing, 94
  formal dances, 94
Ceres Gallery, 142
Chamber Music Society of Lincoln Center, 166
Charles' Place, 89
Chelsea, 4, 25
  bars, 53–55
Chelsea Gym, 100
Chelsea Journal, 155
Chelsea Pine Inn, 21
Chez Beauvais, 106
Children's Friends for Life, 221
Chorus Lines Update, 168
Christopher Street, 25, 26, 62
Christopher Street, 155
Christopher Street Bookshop, 124
Christopher Street Financial Inc., 176
Christopher Street Liberation Day Committee, 3
Circle of More Light, 203
Circle Repertory, 136
Citicorp Center, 95
City Hall Park Sculptures, 142–43
Civil Rights Bill, 4
Clam House, 51
Classic Theater, 137
Cleo's Ninth Avenue Saloon, 65–66
Clinton, Bill, 3
Clit Club, 78, 115
Clocktower, 248
Cloisters, 96
Club Frottage, 244
Clubs
  dancing and nightclubs, 73–83
  jazz and cabaret, 103–10
  sex, 115–23
Club USA, 75, 77, 83, 123, 228

index

Coalition for Gay and Lesbian Rights, 18, 176
Coles, Robert, 133
Colombian Tourist Office, 95
Colonial House Inn, 22
Colorado boycott, 75, 239
Columbia University Gay and Lesbian Dances, 81
Comeback, 123
Coming out support groups, 214
Community Health Project (CHP), 18, 211
  AIDS support, 221
Community Prescription Service (CPS), 222
Community Research Initiatives (CRI), 222
CompuServe, 243
Computer
  networks and bulletin boards, 243
  programming, 245
Comquest, 124
Condoms, 217, 223
Congregation Beth Simchat Torah, 204
Continental Divide, 103
Cooperating Attorneys Network, 237
Cooper-Hewitt Museum concerts, 97
Cooper Square Theater, 134
Corduroy Club, 51
Cornelia Street, 103
Council on Equality for Homosexuals, 3
Counseling, 207, 209
  phone, 233
  for PWAs, 223–24
Counter Spy Shop, 90
Couples Together, 176

Crazy Nanny's, 58–59
Crowbar, 56, 82, 123
  Squirt Farm backroom, 121
Crystal Gardens, 244
CSC Repertory, 136
Cucina Della Fontana, 106
Curry, Scott, 80

Danal, 85–86
Dance on the Pier, 179, 236
Dance performances, 130, 145–46
  free, 95, 96
Dancing, 74–83, 238
  free events, 94
Danny's at the Grand Sea Palace, 107
Dark rooms, 123
DATE-A-BASE, 125
Daughters of Bilitis, 3
David Barton Gym, 54, 100
David Cinema, 123
Day, Tammis, 135
Dell's Down Under, 106
Democratic clubs, 96, 175–76, 178, 198
Dental dams, 217
Designers, 183, 228
Design Industries Foundation for AIDS (DIFFA), 228, 230
Dia Center for the Arts, 143
Dial-A-Date, 189
Dial for Gay Places, 29
Dick's Bar, 56
Different Light, 151
Different Light Bookstore, A, 23, 91, 151, 221
Dignity
  Big Apple, 204
  Brooklyn, 204
  New York, 204–5
Dimensions, 80

index

Disco 2000, 75
Disco Interruptus, 77
Dixon Place, 138
Does Your Mother Know, 75
Donahue (TV show), 98
Don't Tell Mama, 111–12
Downey, Morton, Jr., 16
Downtown Beirut, 56–57
Downtown Community Television Center (DCTV), 161–62
Drool Inn, 51
Drugs
 and AIDS, 217, 226
 hotline, 32
 rehabilitation, 19, 214
D.T.'s Fat Cat, 59, 112
Duberman, Martin, 3
Duchess, 51, 62
Duckett, Chip, 74–75
Dugout, 59
Duplex, 112
Dyke Action Machine (DAM), 196

Eagle's Nest, 53
East End Gay Organization (EEGO), 177
Eastern Athletic Club, 28
East Side, 27
 bars, 67–70
East Side Club, 117–18
East Village, 4, 26, 138–39
 bars, 55–58
Ecofeminists Visions Emerging (EVE), 196
Edelweiss, 79
Education, 207–10, 214
 AIDS/HIV, 223–24, 226, 230
Education in a Disabled Gay Environment (EDGE), 32

82 Club, 118
Eighty-eight's, 113
Elkaim, Charles, 89
Empire State Pride Agenda, 177, 233
Ensemble Studio Theater, 137
Entertainment, 41–126
Entre Hombres program, 230
Episcopalians, 205
Equinox Fitness Club, 101
Eros Male Cinema, 123
Escuelita, 66
Ethnic Folk Arts Center, 170
Ethnic Theater, 137–38
Eve's Garden, 90
Excalibur, 81

Faderman, Lillian, 51
Fashion Accessories Industry Together for Health (FAITH), 228
Fashion industry, 228, 232
Fatales Video, 125
Fat Apple Review, 244
Fathers, 211–12
Fat Tuesday's, 39
Feinstein, Diane, 37
Feller, Deborah, 208
Feminists Concerned for Better Feminist Leadership (FCBFL), 197
Feminist groups, 131, 197, 200
Festival Latino, 137
Fierstein, Harvey, 130
55 Bar, 39, 107
55 Grove Street Cabaret, 138
52nd Street Project, 96
Film and video, 36, 94–95, 125, 126, 137, 161–63

index

Film at the Public, 162
Firehouse bar, 51
First Hand, 155
550-prism, 125
Flamingo East, 80
Flat Gen Poetry Series, 159
Flower Pot, 51
Fone Book, 125
Food
  cooking instruction, 209
  free, 95
Food Bar, 43
Forever Plaid, 109
44 at the Royalton, 48
Forty-second Street Theater Row, 139
Freebies, 93–98, 137
Free hot dogs on income tax day, 95
Fridkis, Ari, 212
Friends in Deed, 229
Friends Tavern, 70–71
Front Runners, 177
Frottage support, 244
Fuji's Tropicana, 83
Fulton Gallery, 143–44
Future Tan, 90

Gagosian Gallery, 144
Gaiety, 123
Galaerie St. Etienne, 144
Galleria Atrium, 95
Galleries, 141–47
Game Show, 90
Gardening, 238
Garden Party, 19
Gardens, 87–88
Gatien, Peter, 77
Gay Activists Alliance (GAA), 3
Gay & Lesbian Alliance against Defamation (GLAAD), 19, 178, 233–34
  Phone Tree, 178, 233
Gay and Lesbian Independent Democrats (GLID), 178
Gay and Lesbian Reading Group, 159
Gay and Lesbian Switchboard of New York, 30, 233
Gay and Lesbian Visitors Center of New York (GLVC), 12–13
Gay Cable Network (GCN), 15
Gay Circles, 192
Gay Couples (Silverstein), 213
Gay Entertainment Network (GEN), 14
Gay Fathers Forum, 211
Gay Games 1994, 3, 37, 188
Gay Liberation Front (GLF), 3
Gay Liberation Monument, 27
Gay Male S/M Activists (GMSMA), 192
Gay Men in Brooklyn, 191
Gay Men of African Descent (GMAD), 191–92
Gay Men of the Bronx, 192
Gay Men's Health Crisis (GMHC), 222–24
  Dance-A-Thon, 223, 235–36
  Greeting Cards Program, 235–36
  hotline, 32, 116
  safe sex workshops, 116
  Walk-A-Thon, 223, 235–36
Gay Officers Action League (GOAL), 177
Gay Pleasures, 91
Gay Pride Month, 17
Gay Pride Parade, 179, 204, 236
  See also Pride Party
Gay Roommate Service, 22

index

Gay Show, The (radio show), 16–17
Gay Sons, Straight Fathers, 212
Gay USA (TV show), 15
Gay Women's Alternative, 188
Gay Women's Athletic Club, 53
Gender Identity, 207
Genre, 156
Geraldo Rivera (TV show), 98
Girl Gate, 80
Girth & Mirth Club of New York, 244
Glines, 130
God's Love We Deliver, 65, 224, 235
Gold Bar, 57
Goodman, Bernice, 213
Grand, 78
Grand Army Plaza's Farmer's Market, 28
Great Performers at Lincoln Center, 166
Green Closet, 178
Greenwich House, 39
Greenwich Village Jazz Festival, 39
Grey Hair Club (GH Club), 67
Guggenheim Museum, 148
Gus' Place, 43–44
Gyms, 99–102

Hamburg, Margaret, 116
Hammacher Schlemmer, 91
Hamptons, 177
Hangout, or J's, 59–60
Hanjar Bar, 52
Haring, Keith, 19
Harkness Pavilion, 95
Harvey Milk High School, 18–19, 208
Hatfield's, 71, 81

Hays, Harry, 193
Health care, 211, 221
Health Education AIDS Liaison (HEAL), 224
Hebrew National, 95
Help lines, 29–31
Henrietta Hudson, 60
Heresies, A Feminist Publication on Art and Politics, 156
Heritage of Pride, 38, 179, 236
Herman, Jim, 100
He's Gotta Have It!, 118
Heterodoxy, 51
Hetrick-Martin Institute, 19, 208
Hirschl & Adler Modern, 144
Hispanic AIDS Forum, 230
Hispanics. *See* Latina/os
Hispanic United Gays and Lesbians (HUGL), 179
HIV/AIDS Training Center and Assistance Project, 225
HIV Health Day, 225
HIV virus, 215, 223, 224
  testing, 218
Hoffman, William M., 130
Holidays on Skis, 36
Hombre, 66
Home Alone, 125
Homeless people, 227, 236
Homophile Youth Movement (HYMN), 3
Homo Xtra, 12, 121
Horticultural Society of New York, 87–88
Horticulture organization, 178
Hot Feet bar, 51
Hot lines, 31–33
Hot Spot/After 5, 70

index

Housing
  advice, free, 96
  lodging, 21–22
  for PWAs, 219–20, 224, 227, 232, 236
  roommates, 22
Housing Works, Inc., 224–25, 236
Hudson club, 69
Hudson Bar & Books, 60
Humanities Council of New York University, 144
Human Rights Campaign Fund (HRCF), 179–80
Humm, Andy, 16

Identity House, 212
IGTA Today, 23
Incentra Village House, 22
Indian Community House, 185
Indochine, 48
Info lines, 29–33
In Our Own Write, 158, 238
Institute for Human Identity, 213
Intar, 137
Integrity/NY, 205
International Center of Photography, 144–45
International Gay Ski Week, 36
International Gay Travel Association (IGTA), 23
International Lesbian and Gay Association, 19, 237–38
International Women's Tribune Center, 197
In the Dungeon (TV show), 15
In The Life (TV show), 17
Investment advice, 176
Isamu Noguchi Garden, 145
Israel Day Parade, 204
IV Substance Abuse AIDS Information Hotline, 32

Jackie 60, 78
Jacques Marchais Tibetan Museum, 96
Jayne Baum Gallery, 143
Jazz Babies, 167
Jazz clubs and cabarets, 103–110
Jazz for the Homeless, 104
Jean Cocteau Repertory, 137
Jewel Theater, 123
Jewish organizations, 204, 220
Joan Rivers (TV show), 98
Johnny Lats, 102
Jo's bar, 51
Joseph Papp Public Theater, 137, 138, 162
Journalists, 182
Joyce Theater, 130
Joy of Gay Sex (Silverstein), 213
J's, 119
Judith's Room, 152
Judy's, 107
Julie's, 67–68
Julio Rivera Lesbian & Gay AntiViolence Coalition of Queens, 28
Julius, 60
Jupiter Symphony, 167

Kahiki Lounge, 46
Keller's, 61
Kerle, Trish, 237
King Cinema, 123
King Model Townhouses, 94
Kitchen Arts, 154
Kitchen Center for Video, Music, Dance, Performance, Film and Literature, 146
Knights Wrestling Club, 82

index

LaHoma, 77
La Mama E.T.C., 134
  La Galleria, 146
Lambda Independent Democrats (LID), 175–76, 198
Lambda Legal Defense and Education Fund, 198, 237
LAP Notes, 225
Lard, Carter, 117
Late Night with Conan (TV show), 98
Latina/os, 17, 66, 70, 81, 137, 138, 179, 192, 230
  also Hispanics
Lavender Lamp: National Gay and Lesbian Nurses Network, 180
Lavender Light: The Black and People of All Colors Lesbian and Gay Gospel Choir, 180
Lavender Women (radio show), 17
Lawyers Referral Service for the Lesbian and Gay Community, 173
Lear, Norman, 199
Legal Action Center, 225
Legal organizations and help, 173, 198, 225, 237
Lesbian AIDS Project (LAP), 225
Lesbian and Gay Big Apple Corps, 244
Lesbian & Gay Community Services Center, 4, 6, 18–19, 81, 173, 174, 176, 179, 221, 222
  dances, 81
  International Association, 237–38
  volunteer data form, 20
  volunteering for, 237–38
Lesbian and Gay Men of New Brunswick, 180
Lesbian and Gay Pride events and festivals, 236. *See also* Gay Pride Parade; Pride Party
Lesbian and Gay Rights Project of the American Civil Liberties Union, 197
Lesbian and Gay Teachers Association, 197
Lesbian Avengers, 198
Lesbian Herstory Archives, 152
Lesbian Movie Night, 238
Lesbian Referral Hotline, 30
Lesbians, 6
  online services, 243
  social happenings for, 187–89
Lesbians in the Creative Arts (LICA), 134
Lesbian Switchboard, 18, 31
Les Hommes, 124
Lickety Split, 78
Lick It! Lounge, 75–76
Liechenstein, Joyce, 208
Limelight, 75, 123
Lincoln Center, 166
Lion's Head Bar, 27
List, The, 12–13
Literary interests. *See* Bookstores and libraries; Readings and lectures
Literary New York, 151–60
Live With Regis and Kathy Lee (TV show), 98
Locomotion, 76
Lodging, 21–22
Long Island, 14, 17
Love Ball, 79
Lower East Side Tenement Museum, 148–49
Lower Manhattan Foundation for the Community of Artists, 96
L.S.M., 188

index

Ludlam, Charles, 131
Luma, 48

Mabou Mines, 137–38
MacDougal Street Strip clubs, 51
Magazines and newspapers, 11–14, 155–58
Magic Touch, 71
Magnuson, Ann, 139
Mail order, 124
Malina, Judith, 97
Mammoth Billiards, 53–54
Manatus, 44
Manhattan Association of Cabarets, 106
Manhattan Center for Living, 221, 225
Manhattan Class Company, 137
Manhattan Punch Line, 137
Manhattan School of Music, 167
Manhattan Theater Club, 136
Manstage, 130
Marino, Ralph, 233
Marion's/The Kahiki Lounge, 46
Mark Goodson Theater, 167
Martial arts, 207
Massage, 247
Mass Transit Theater Company, 134
Mattachine group, 3
Maxim's, 107
Mayor's Office for the Lesbian and Gay Community hotline, 32
Mea Culpa, 75
Meals for PWAs, 224, 225
Meat, 78, 119
Medical
    clinics, 218, 221–22
    counseling, 174
    See also AIDS; HIV
Medicine Show, 137

Meditation Class, 208
Men & Film (TV show), 15
Men of All Colors Together New York, 180
Men of Color AIDS Prevention Program (OCA), 230
Men's Conference, 212
Men's Fitness, 158
Men's Talk & Listen Rap group, 212
Merkin Concert Hall, 166, 167
Met Opera National Council, 166
Metropolitan Community Church/NY, 18
Metropolitan Museum of Art
    concerts, 159, 166
    Lecture Series, 159
Metropolitan Opera, 168
Metropolitan Tennis Group, 181
Metro Xtra, 12
Mike's Bar, 61
Military, 239
Military Bookman, 245
Millennium, 162
Mixed Company, 181, 245
Mixed events, 173–85
Model Mariners' Association, 95
Momentum, 179
Momentum TV (TV show), 180
Monster, 61, 83
Montana Saloon, 71
Moonfire Women's Spirituality Circle, 205
More Men!, 81
Mount Morris Baths, 119
Movie Phone, 126
Movie theaters, 123
Multicultural/multiracial groups, 180, 187, 188. See also Asians; Blacks; Latina/os

index

Multiple Personality Disorder Workshop, 208
Murder Ink, 154
Museums, 19, 147–50
  free, 95–96
Music
  events and concerts, 136, 146, 159–60, 165–70
  free events, 97, 98
  groups, 244
  records and CDs, 248
  See also Cabarets; Jazz clubs; Piano bars
Music-Theater Performing Group/Lenox Arts Center, 138

Nadine's, 108
Naked City, 71
Names Project Quilt, 228
National Black Theater, 138
National Gay and Lesbian Task Force (NGLTF), 182
National Gay and Lesbian Youth Directory, 208
National Institutes of Health Open Study of New Clinical Drugs, 226
National Lesbian and Gay Journalist Association (NLGJA), 182
National Museum and Archive of Lesbian and Gay History, 19
Native Americans, 185
Natural Gourmet Institute for Food and Health, 209
NBC TV tickets, 97–98
Negro Ensemble Company, 138
Neighborhoods, 25–28
Network bar, 51
Neutral Zone Drop-In Center, 213
  hotline, 32
New Brunswick, NJ, 180
New Dramatists, 137
New Federal Theater at the Henry Street Settlement, 138
New Festival (New York Gay and Lesbian Film Festival), 36, 163
New Museum, 149
New Prospects modern dance shows, 95
Newsletters, 18, 19, 174, 182, 220, 227, 233
New York Advertising and Communications Network, 182
New York Area Bisexual Network (NYABN), 174
New York Bondage Club, 82
New York Botanical Garden, 88, 95
New York Bound Bookshop, 154
New York City
  Department of Health, 214
  Human Resource Administration, 219
  Human Rights Commission, 219
  Lower Manhattan District Health Clinic, 218
  School Board elections, 177
New York City Coalition for Women's Mental Health, 213
New York City Feminist Theater, 131
New York City Gay and Lesbian Anti-Violence Project, 18, 183
  Rape Intervention Hotline, 33
New York City Gay Men's Chorus, 169
New York Colorado Boycott, 239
New York Daily News, 4
New York Improvisation Game Show, 96

index

New York Native, 13
New York Philharmonic, 168
　Symphony Club, 166
NY Prime, 117, 121
　Bachelor Parties, 119–20
New York Public Library, 97, 160
New York Ramblers Soccer Club, 183
New York Shakespeare Festival, 137
NY Stage & Film Company, 137
New York Theater Workshop, 138
New York Times, The, 5, 116, 182
New York Transit Museum, 149–50
Next, 13
Nick and Eddie's, 46
Night of a Thousand Gowns, 36, 81
Ninth Circle, 62
Ninth Street Center, 209
Ninth Street Theater Company, 133
Nocturnal, 123
Northern Lights Alternatives, 226
Nurses, 180

Oak Room at the Algonquin Hotel, 108
Odeon, 48
Office of Gay and Lesbian Health Concerns, 214, 226
Olnek, Madeleine, 132
Omni at Berkshire Place, 86
One Potato, 46, 63–64
122 St. Mark's Place, 169
On Our Backs, 125, 156–57
On the Wilde Side, 14
Opera, 167, 168

Organization of Lesbian and Gay Architects and Designers (OLGAD), 183
Orientation on the Road, 19
Oscar Wilde Memorial Bookshop, 14, 152
O Solo Mio festival, 138
Out, 156
Out and About, 23, 157
Out in the Nineties (radio show), 16–17
OutLooks (radio show), 16
Outmusic, 168
Out of Our Drawers, 91
Outwatch, 37, 184, 238–39

Pan Asian Repertory, 138
Pandora's Box, 62
Paralegals, 237
Parents and Friends of Lesbians and Gay Men (PFLAG), 198–99, 214
Paresis Hall, 51
Paris Commune, 46
Park Avenue Plaza, 95
Park Slope, 28
Park Slope Activities for Lesbians, 28, 31
Party Talk Inside and Out: Documentary (TV show), 14
Party Talk (TV show), 14
Party With a Cause, 76
Pat Parker and Vito Russo Center Library, 19, 153
Paula Cooper Gallery, 143
Paul & Joe's, 51
PBS, 17
Peninsula, 86
People for the American Way, 199

index

People of color, 137–38, 180, 191–92, 230. *See also* specific groups
People's Voice Cafe, 108
People With AIDS (PWAs), 6, 171, 181, 215
  friends and lovers of, support groups, 227–30
  health, service and support groups, 33, 218–27, 235–36
  housing, 224, 232
  meals, 224
  peer counseling and buddy program, 223, 232, 235
  pet care, 226
People With AIDS Coalition hotline, 33
Performance art, 96, 146
Perry Street Theater, 135, 138
Personal ads, 124
Pet Care for HIV + People (POWARS), 226
Phone Tree, 178, 233
Photographer's Place, 154
Piano bars, 111–13
Pieces, 62
Pink Panthers (*later* Outwatch), 37, 184
Playground, 83
Plazas, 96
Poetry Project, 160
Poetry Society, 94
Police association, 177
Political organizations, 3, 171, 173–85, 195–201
  AIDS, 229–30
  free activities, 96
  volunteering for, 233–39
Pomander Books, 94
Pony & Friends, 199

Positive Connection (radio show), 17
Positively 104 Street, 44
Powell, Michael, 97
Powerhouse Gym, 101
Prescription service, 222
Pride Party, 38
Pridetime Productions, 23
Primetime Live (TV show), 98
Prince Theater, 123
Printing House Fitness Club, 101
Prism Sex Club, 120, 125
Professional organizations, 195–201
Professionals' Education Project, 214, 226
Program Solutions, 245
Project Connect, 19
Project Return, 214
Project X, 14
Prospect Park, Brooklyn, 95
Prostitute groups, 199
Provence, 49
PS For Good Read, 158
P.S. 122, 95, 131
Psychological counseling and support, 174, 207, 208, 211–14
Public relations professionals, 182
Pure Party, 78
PWA Coalition, 227
Pyramid, 78

Quaigh Theatre, 96–97
Queens, 28, 230
  AIDS support, 218
  bars, 28, 70–71
Queens Lesbian and Gay Pride Committee, 184
Queer Culture, 37, 131

index

Queer Nation, 2, 18, 199
Queer U, 75

Radical Chicks, 158
Radical Faeries, 193
Radical Women, 200
Radio, 14–19
  live events, 98
Rainbow and Stars, 108–9
RAPP, 138
Rawhide, 54
Raymond Dragon, 92
Readings and lectures, 93, 94, 97, 131, 132, 133, 137, 151–52, 153, 154, 158–60
Religious organizations, 203–5, 209–10
Reproductive Freedom Project of the ACLU, 200
Res-erection, 75
Resource Exchange Service, 200
Restaurants, 43–49
Rick Neilson's Screening Room, 124
Ridiculous Theatrical Company, 131
Rihga Royal Hotel, 86
Rimming, 216
Riot Grrrl, 188
Rivera, Geraldo, 98
Rivera, Julio, 28
Rivers, Joan, 139
Riverside Shakespeare Theater, 136
Rizzoli Book Store, 154
Rocking Horse Mexican Cafe, 44
Roettele A.G., 49
Rompiendo Silencio (radio show), 17
Roommates, 22
Roost, 28
Rose's Turn, 113

Roundabout Theater Company, 132
Rounds, 68
Roxy, 76
Royalty Bookshop, 154
RSVP Gay Cruises, 23
Running club, 177
Russian Tea Room, 109

Safer sex, 115–16
  basics, 216–17
  education, 214, 216, 222–23, 230
  workshops, 223–24
"Safer Than Safe" (pamphlet), 223
Safe-Sex Workshops, 224
Safety Skills Workshops, 183
Saint Andrew Music Society, 169
St. Ann's Church, 170
  Art at, 133–34
Saint-at-Large Parties, 35
Saint club, 35
St. James, James, 81
St. John's Episcopal Church, 205
Sally Jessy Raphael (TV show), 98
Sally's II at the Carter Hotel, 66
Samaritans Suicide phone, 30
Samuel Weiser, 154
S&M, 174, 188, 192
Sanford Meisner Theater, 133, 135, 138
Sappho's Exchange, 243
Sappho's Isle, 14
Saturday Night Live (TV show), 98
Sazerac House Bar and Grill, 45
School of Visual Arts, 95
Schy, Lee, 248
Scott, Jerry, 64
Scrabble Players Club, 184
Second Classe, 146
Security organizations, 184

273

Segal, George, 27
Self Defense Academy, 209
Senior Action in a Gay Environment (SAGE), 18, 184–85
Sex
  booths, 124
  clubs and back rooms, 91, 115–26
  movie theaters, 123
  by phone and mail, 124–26
  regulation of, 116
Sex and Love Addicts Anonymous Lesbians, 189
Sex workers' rights group, 199
S. F. Vanni, 154
Shades of the Village, 91
Shescape, 80
Shocking Gray, 92
Shop, The, 248
Shopping, 89–92, 244, 248
Show Palace, 123
Silverstein, Dr. Charles, 213
Sister Dimension, 77
Six Bond, 80
Skiing, 36
Skylark, 104
Slide bar, 51
Sneakers, 63
Soccer teams, 183
Social Activities for Lesbians, 189
Social clubs, 244–45
Social happenings
  for gay males, 191–93
  for lesbians, 187–89
Social service and political organizations, 18–19, 171, 173–239
Society of Composers and Performers, 109
Sotheby's, 94
Sound Factory, 81
Sound Factory Bar, 76, 83

South Dakota (Dakota's), 68
South'ners, 185
"Spa Agog", 28
Space, 80
Spanish Film Festivals, 94
"Speak Out" program, 179
Special events calendar, 35–39
Spectrum, 79
Spencer, Craig, 69
Spike, 54–55
Spirit Center: A Women's Circle for Healing, 209–10
Splash, 51, 54
Spring Street Natural Restaurant, 95
Spunk, 14–15, 121
Spunk at Crowbar, 121
Stark Gallery, 147
Star Sapphire, 68
Steamboat Jazz Cruise, 39
Steve McGraw's Theater, 175, 227–28
  cabaret, 109
Stingray, 81
Stonewall (bar), 63
  concerts at, 169
Stonewall (Duberman), 3
Stonewall Business Association, 200–01
Stonewall Chorale, 169
Stonewall History Project, 38
Stonewall Inn, 26, 27, 63
Stonewall News, 15
Stonewall Place, 4, 26
Stonewall Place (TV show), 15
Stonewall Riots, 3, 169
  commemoration, 38
Stonewall 25, 19
Stonewall 25—June 26-27, 1994, 38

index

Street Transvestites Action Revolutionaries, 3
Suburban counties AIDS support, 219
Suffolk County Human Rights Bill, 177
Sugar Babies, 80
Sugar in the Raw at Sugar Reef, 83
Suicide hotline, 30
Summer Folk Dancing at Noontime, 94
SummerStage, 97, 132
Support groups, 211–14, 244
  for friends of PWAs, 227–29
  for PWAs, 220–27
Sutton Place, 94
Sweet Basil Jazz Club, 39
Symphony Space, 97, 166, 170
Synaps, 243

Tales of the Closet, 208
Tanning, 90
  free, 96
Tatou, 109–10
Tavern on the Green, 79
Teachers' organizations, 197
Tea rooms, 85–87
Telephone
  help and info lines, 29–33, 125–26
  Phone Tree, GLAAD, 178, 233
  sex, 124–26
Television
  stations and shows, 14–18
  tickets, 97–98
Tennis, 181
Tequila Sunset, 113
Theater, 129–39
  free, 96–98
  workshops, 136–37

Theater Space, 136–37
Theaterworks: Emerging/Experimental Directions (T.W.E.E.D.), 135
Theatre-at-224-Waverly Place, 135
Theatre for the New City, 138
Third Street Music School Settlement, 97
This Way Out (radio show), 16
$3 Bill Theater, 37, 132
Three Lives & Company, Ltd., 153
Ticket Central, 139
Ticklish Society of America, 185
Time Cafe, 45
Times Square Boxing Club, 102
Time with the Quilters, 181
Tiziano, 95
Top of the Sixes, 87
Town Hall, 136, 166
Townhouse Bar, 113
Townhouse of New York, 69
Transsexuality, 207
Travel arrangements, 23
Traveling Gay Performances Company, 138
Travolta, John, 79
Treatment Issues, 223
Trials, 94
Tribeca Transfer, 81
Trinity Church
  cemetery, 94
  free concerts, 97
Trouble, 121–22
Tunnel Bar, 57, 123
Tunnel/Nocturnal, 75, 123
Two Potato, 63
Ty's, 64

Uncle Charlie's, 2, 51, 64–65
Underground, 122
Universal Grill, 43, 45, 46–47

index

Universal Harmony, 45
Upper Room AIDS Ministry, 227
USA, 83

Video and film, 125, 134, 146, 161–63
Village Corner, 39
Village Gate, 39, 80
Village Independent Democratic Club, 96
Village Light Opera, 166
Village Vanguard, 39
Violence prevention and victim support, 28, 183, 184, 209, 238–39
Visiones, 39
Visions, 81
Vogel, Paula, 132
Volleyball Tournament, 189
Volunteer Data Form, 20
Volunteerism, 6, 171, 220, 222–25, 231–39
Vortex Theater Company, 133, 138

Wall Street Journal, The, 182
Wall Street Project, 201
Wall Street Sauna, 122
Warsaw, 80
Washington Square Church, 170
Washington Square on Tuesday Evenings, 166
Water's Edge, 104
WBAI (radio station), 16–17
Weill Recital Hall, 97
Westbank Cafe, 96
Westbeth Theater Company, 138
West-Park Presbyterian Church, 203
West Side, 27
 bars, 27, 65–67

West Village, 26–27
 bars, 58–65
West World, 123
We Wah and BarChe Ampe, 185
White Columns Gallery, 147
Whitney Museum's Equitable Branch dance concert, 95
Whole Food Project, 225
Wicked Trash Productions, 112
Williamson, Marianne, 225
Wilson, Tom, 130
Wings Theater Company, 133
WNET (TV station), 17
WNYC (TV station), 17
Wollman Rink, 53
Womb Gallery, 188
Women About, 189
Women and AIDS Resource Network (WARN), 230
Women's Conference, 212
Women's Health Action and Mobilization (WHAM), 201
Women's Project, 136
Women's Studio Workshop (WSW), 210
Women's Talk & Listen Rap Group, 212
Wonder Bar, 57–58, 123
Wooster Gardens, 144
Works, 67
World, The, 160
World Financial Center, 95
World Gym, 102
World Music Institute, 170
Wow Cafe, 138–39
WQXR (radio station), 98
Writers, 238
WUSB/Stony Brook (radio station), 17

index

Yampolsky, Michael, 23
Ye Olde Triple Inn, 110
York Theater Company, 133
Young Playwrights Festival, 137

Youth Enrichment Services (YES), 19
Youth organizations, 208

Zone (Zone DK), 122